The Legends of King Arthur : Book 3

LANCELOT OF THE LAKE

By Ben Gillman

For Grandma

and the Gillmans from the Garden

Where many a tall tale got started while picking strawberries

FOREWORD

"Lancelot tried to have a Word. His Word was valuable to him not only because he was good, but also because he was bad. It is the bad people who need to have principles to restrain them."

The Ill-Made Knight

Book Three of *"The Once and Future King"*

By T.H. White

TABLE OF CONTENTS

FOREWORD 4

PROLOGUE - A History of Knights................................7

CHAPTER 1 - The Return to the Lakes........................24

CHAPTER 2 - Lancelot's Greatest Challenge 30

CHAPTER 3 - The Dream 40

CHAPTER 4 - Back to the Beginning 50

CHAPTER 5 - A Welcome from Wildelions 61

CHAPTER 6 - Waterfalls and Hot Springs...................69

CHAPTER 7 - Corbenic Castle 77

CHAPTER 8 - Plucking Wild Roses 90

CHAPTER 9 - The Troublesome Troll 103

CHAPTER 10 - A King's Request 114

CHAPTER 11 - Of Onerous Ogres...............................120

CHAPTER 12 - Moonlight in the Garden....................130

CHAPTER 13 - The Lady and the Boy 137

CHAPTER 14 - Grappling with Goblins......................149

CHAPTER 15 - Galahad's Greatest Challenge 160

CHAPTER 16 - With Wretched Wildelions..................165

CHAPTER 17 - Elaine's Desire....................................176

CHAPTER 18 - Victory and Failure 182

CHAPTER 19 - No Way Out 189

CHAPTER 20 - The Fire Descends 197

CHAPTER 21 - Dark Places and Terrible Choices 210

CHAPTER 22 - The Conditions for Escape 221

CHAPTER 23 - Nimue Is Right Again 227

CHAPTER 24 - Taming the White Dragon 236

CHAPTER 25 - From the Bottom of the Lake 242

CHAPTER 26 - The Battle for Avalon.......................252

CHAPTER 27 - Elaine's Greatest Challenge 272

EPILOGUE - The Fate of the Dragon 282

THE LEGENDS OF KING ARTHUR.........................284

PROLOGUE
A History of Knights

From the moment Lancelot learned to read, he only wanted to read about one thing:

Knights.

When he was four years old, Lancelot's favorite knight was Sir Elyian the Shiny. Elyian was strong and handsome and brave, but his most well-known attribute was that of his suit of armor, which he insisted on keeping at a state of glimmering perfection. It should be noted that, in those days, it was common for knights to stick an appropriate adjective after their name. There was Sir William the Hungry, known for his appetite and also for his inability to spell the country of his birth. Additionally, there was Sir Tommery the Smelly, who had an amazing knack for tracking his foes if he knew precisely what they had eaten for breakfast that morning. He also smelled bad. In Sir Elyian the Shiny's case, since the most notable characteristic for him was his sparkling armor, it only made sense that his own name should become synonymous with it. And as his fame grew, so too did the shininess of his armor increase to match it.

Sir Elyian rescued a village from marauders. His armor twinkled.

He snatched a fair damsel out of a pit of quicksand. His armor shimmered.

He slew a rampaging dragon. His armor gleamed like the sun.

Eventually, it got to the point where Elyian could be spotted from miles away simply due to the extraordinary sheen on his flawless metal suit. Men and women who wished to catch a glimpse of him were forced to look away so as not to scorch their eyes. Kings and lords had to develop specially tinted pieces of glass to place on their faces when they met with Sir Elyian.

And villains were able to spy on him from great distances.

One sad day, a band of rival swordsmen watched as Sir Elyian took a shortcut through a rocky ravine on his way to celebrate the opening of a new castle. Following the glare from his armor, the swordsmen carefully followed Sir Elyian's movements as he rode beneath a steep cliff. Shielding their eyes from the brilliance of the armor, the villainous swordsman sent a boulder careening down the slope. It sparked a rock slide, and mounds of earth showered down into the ravine. Under normal circumstances, Sir Elyian could've easily avoided the falling debris; after all, he was a famous and capable knight. However, by this point his armor had grown so impressive that even he found himself blinded by it on regular occasions. That was the case on that unfortunate day, and it proved to be the end of Sir Elyian and his beautiful glimmering armor. A stray beam of sunshine refracted off of Sir Elyian's breastplate, which roasted both of his corneas momentarily. It was a moment too long, and the rocks battered down upon him, crushing Elyian to death and tarnishing his armor to the point of dullness.

When Lancelot turned nine, his interests fell onto knights who were known for more than just their bravery and strength. He was learning that there was a lot that went into becoming a legend. Muscles and good teeth were important, there was no doubt; however, Lancelot came to appreciate that brains were equally crucial.

And so, his favorite knight became Sir Wyrral the Wise.

Once again, historical context should be given to explain that at that time it was all the rage to match one's name with an attribute starting with the same letter. And so it was that some of the most notable knights of the age were Sir Turquine the Terrible, Sir Hamish the Humiliating and Sir Quinn the Quick, who was actually quite slow but he couldn't think of many other attributes starting with "Q" for him to choose from, and he wasn't able to label himself as "quiet" due to his unfortunate bouts with flatulence.

Sir Wyrral the Wise was a fitting name for he was renowned for his devastating intellect. While other knights relied solely upon their skills in battle, Wyrral was just as deft with an argument, a debate, or a strongly worded letter-writing campaign. His opponents often conceded to his powers of persuasion without the need to draw weapons, and more than once, a rival knight had thrown himself into the sea or swung himself from a tree based solely on Wyrral's reasoned argument that it would save them both a lot of time and energy.

He dazzled foreign kings, not with his blade, but with displays of oratory.

He wrote petitions to create nesting sanctuaries for harpy hatchlings.

He even unraveled the riddle of the zebra and determined definitively whether it was black with white stripes, or white with black stripes, although sadly his discovery has been lost for centuries.

Nevertheless, there are always certain instances when words simply aren't sufficient. A stampede of rampaging rhinocephants, for example. Arguing with a band of drunk, illiterate Vikings was another. Or facing off against a deaf person. The problem was that it was impossible to convince Sir Wyrral the Wise of that reality. He simply refused to believe that there was any situation where his intellect and arguments weren't more effective than the use of a sword or spear. As time went on, Sir Wyrral practiced with his weapons less and less until his combat skills had depleted to nil.

In the end, it was his soft spot for activism and his disinterest in the sword that was Sir Wyrral the Wise's undoing. One unfortunate evening, when Wyrral sat down to write a dissertation on the perfection of the phrase *"the pen is mightier than the sword"* using himself as an example, he received news about a pod of stubborn mermaids who refused to acknowledge that the moon exerted influence on the tides. The mermaids insisted that the rise and fall of the shores was due to the fluttering of their luscious eyelashes while blowing kisses to passing sailors. Sir Wyrral the Wise could not let this confusion stand. He dashed to the nearest harbor, chartered a ship, found the pod of salty seawomen, and demanded an audience. Not ones to be persuaded, however, the mermaids quickly seized Wyrral and dragged him beneath the water. His perfectly reasoned arguments and ironclad logic were no good down there. And he hadn't bothered to bring so much as a dagger. So that was the watery end of Sir Wyrral the Wise.

By the time Lancelot turned eleven, he made a life-altering choice.

He decided, once and for all, that he was going to become a knight himself.

At first this only led to more reading. Lancelot pored through any book or scrap of parchment he could find that made any mention of knights. The simple reason for this was that Lancelot was looking for a mentor. This was easier said than done. Lancelot had no noble blood to fall back on, and the small village he grew up in wasn't exactly teeming with champions. Nonetheless, he was determined to find a knight that would take him under his wing. Lancelot researched Sir Leodegrance, but while the dashing nobleman was a perfect specimen of knighthood in his youth, he had recently been made a minor king and had a young daughter who took up all of his time at present. Lancelot tracked the current station of Sir Aggravaine, but there was something about that hulking behemoth that didn't strike Lancelot as quite right. Lancelot turned his attentions to Sir Gawain, but the grizzled warrior's far-flung adventures took him all over the world and it was anybody's guess where he might be found.

Finally, after nearly a year of studying, Lancelot settled on the Copper Knight.

All that was left to do was for Lancelot to track him down.

This was a tricky task for two reasons. One, no one knew what the Copper Knight's true name was anymore; as his fame and reputation had grown, the man had discarded his identity and fully embraced his most notable attribute: his suit of copper armor. To give some brief context, it was now very fashionable and mysterious for a knight to drop their name and just go by an adjective or noun. There was the Star Knight, who liked the play on words. There was the Cutting Board Knight, who used his shield to serve cheese and cold cuts to his opponents before he slaughtered them. There was even the Tree Knight, who was very tall and had a habit of barking when he fought, although most of his fans never got the pun.

The second problem for Lancelot, and the one that would prove even more difficult to solve, was that while Lancelot searched for the Copper Knight, the Copper Knight was intently searching for the Lakes of Avalon.

To understand why, however, it's essential to go back to the days of a young boy who had an uncommon gift with a sword. Though he came from humble beginnings in a small village where he couldn't have hoped for any formal training, this boy simply understood steel in a way that shocked even grown men who had spent their lives studying swordcraft. Very quickly, this boy showed brilliant displays of his skills, and in return, his grateful audiences would shower him in copper coins. Within a few years, the boy's skill with a sword was unparalleled for miles, and as a result, he had been positively deluged with copper coins. As he grew a bit older, the teenaged boy decided that it was time to test his abilities against greater opponents.

He needed to enter a tournament.

The problem was that he couldn't hope to enter without a proper suit of armor. And simple copper coins would never add up to enough for him to buy anything made of steel. Nonetheless, the copper coins became his means for creating a suit of armor all his own. After agreeing to help a local blacksmith to teach a lesson to a cocky rival, the blacksmith took the piles of the young man's copper coins, melted them down and used them to forge a beautiful suit of red-tinted armor. With that, the young man set off for his tournament, feeling wonderfully elated at the future ahead of him.

The crowds were not so impressed:

"*Red* armor?!"

"He'll get himself *killed* with that suit!"

"I know, I wouldn't trust a *copper codpiece!*"

When the young man first presented himself, the crowd's reaction was riotous. They laughed and snorted and squealed with derision. The notion of a suit of copper was ridiculous. It was ludicrous. It would never work. As everyone knew, copper was a soft metal and could never provide adequate protection for the beating that came with any tournament.

But the young man shrugged off their criticisms.

Because none of them had seen him wield a sword.

In record time, he dispatched the other champions and not a challenger was able to land a blow upon his beautiful armor. The stunned crowd quickly changed their tune:

"What remarkable *red* armor!"

"I always knew that boy was *something special!*"

"I'll buy five *copper codpieces* this very day!"

In no time at all, the young man with his copper armor became an absolute sensation. He travelled amongst the larger villages and towns and competed in every tournament he could find. Just as easily as the first, he won each tournament that followed. People were showering him with gold and silver coins now, and he could've bought ten suits of proper armor, but he was no longer interested. The copper armor was his trademark and his good luck charm, and he proudly wore it as he competed in a melee at one of the outer kingdoms for which the prize was the honor of a proper knighthood.

Of course, he won.

And thus, the Copper Knight was officially dubbed.

Everywhere he went, the Copper Knight was a celebrity. Men and women travelled for days to see him compete and to marvel at his beautiful red-hued armor. By this time, people had stopped asking his true name, and he stopped giving it. Not only that, but as his name disappeared, so too did his face. He went weeks without peeling off his armor. He would wear it to breakfast. He would wear it to bed. He would have even worn it into the bath, if he could; instead, he just chose to bathe less and less often. He had become the Copper Knight and he needed no other title as he basked in the glory of it.

Unfortunately, copper doesn't keep its sheen forever.

As the years crept by, the armor started to green ever so slightly around the edges. Not long after that, the joints began to dull and change colors too. And slowly but surely, the crowds began to mock him once more:

"Oy! I thought your red armor was supposed to be, you know, *red*?!"

"*Nothing* to see here…"

"I hope that discoloration doesn't creep onto your cod — *oh, you get the picture!*"

As a fully grown man, and a knight besides, the Copper Knight could no longer shrug off the criticisms. He tracked down the people who dared to heckle him and he made them pay. He wailed on his hecklers. He trounced his critics. He pummeled his disbelievers. Quickly, he developed a reputation for cruelty and poor sportsmanship, and then his invitations to tournaments began to dry up. The other knights banded together, since none of them could handle him alone, and they sought to run him out of town. Most embarrassing of all, however, was that the other knights were now able to defeat him. The Copper Knight, who had once been unbeatable, even against a dozen men, was thoroughly disgraced, beaten, and sent on his way.

Yet the Copper Knight knew what went wrong, and the discolored green streaks that littered his once beautiful armor told the whole story. His aging muscles had gone just as soft as the weak bits of his copper armor. His knees and back creaked along with the joints of his suit. He had once been beautiful and flawless, and he resolved that he would be that way once more.

His salvation lay in Avalon.

The mystical lakes of Avalon were a place unlike any other throughout the land. It was a realm of peace and healing, filled with crystal clear waters that could restore perfection to any flaw. However, their whereabouts were one of the most closely guarded secrets throughout all of history. It was rumored that the magic of Avalon made it so that no one could find it if they had not already been there. So the Copper Knight set about finding someone who had already been there. He used all of his guile and cunning to manipulate and cajole anyone who had any information. He threatened druid clans who had been rumored to take pilgrimages there. He roughed up scribes and historians so that they would provide any clues. He bullied cartographers and stole their collections of maps as he searched for that mysterious lost land. And finally the Copper Knight found it.

As he approached the beautiful grotto, the Copper Knight barely took notice of the serenity with which the soft clouds floated overhead through perfectly blue skies. He failed to appreciate the wonderful softness of the thick green grass beneath his boots. He didn't even pause to breathe in the scent of the flowering trees or to appreciate the coolness of the breeze over the waters of the lake.

He also didn't notice Nimue, the stout little Lady of the Lake, who was bound to protect the sanctuary. Whether or not the knight glanced in her direction, though, Nimue had no intention of letting some joker in clunky red armor ruin it.

"Hey, hey, hey! And just what do you think you're doing there?!" shouted Nimue, throwing herself in the path of the Copper Knight as he approached the edge of the lake.

She was a short woman, and only came up to the Copper Knight's navel, but she was broad and she spread her pudgy arms wide to make it clear that he wasn't taking another step closer to her precious well-spring.

"Stand aside, woman!" demanded the Copper Knight, although by this time his armor had become so cumbersome that his words were muffled, and what actually came out was, "Mmmm mmmmm, mmmmm!"

"Umm… Didn't really catch that," said Nimue. "Wanna try me again?"

"I said, stand aside!" he repeated. But once again, it just sounded like, "M mmmm, mmmmm mmmmm!"

"Yeah… No… Still not getting it…"

In frustration, the Copper Knight finally struggled with his rusted visor and managed to wedge it open far enough that his voice was intelligible.

"I said, stand aside, woman! I seek to claim these waters and their healing powers for my glory!" he stated plainly. Actually, about every fifth word was still muffled and unintelligible, but Nimue got the idea.

"Oh, no you are not," she said, thrusting a stubby, slightly webbed finger in the Copper Knight's face so that he was sure to see it even through his damaged visor. "You don't understand how these waters work. You can't just take a dip in them whenever you like. These lakes will—"

"These lakes will ensure my strength and greatness forever!" said the Copper Knight. "They are the key to my renewed beauty and my strength. They're my ticket back to greatness! Now, stand aside."

And with that, the Copper Knight roughly shoved Nimue out of the way. Little or not, however, Nimue intended to put up a fight. She charged back at him and threw all of her considerable bulk behind it. He stumbled and his aging armor groaned, but the Copper Knight couldn't be deterred. The two of them began to shove and wrestle with the ultimate prize, the lake's waters, just feet away.

"You really don't want to do that, friend," grunted Nimue as she dug her bare feet into the soft earth and pushed with all her might. "These waters are a reward, not a privilege. You've got to work for them. You've got to be worthy."

"I am worthy!" insisted the Copper Knight, although his visor had slipped down again and all that came out was, "M mm mmmmmm!"

Try as Nimue might, the Copper Knight was larger, stronger, and, well, a knight, and he finally managed to grab her under the arms, twist and toss her aside. She fell to the ground with a thud and rolled slightly away. Once more, the Copper Knight wrenched his visor open.

"You'll see, the Copper Knight will rise again!" he said. "Young and strong and better than ever! And my legend will grow until all know the name of —"

Bang!

Just as the Copper Knight was about to step into the lake, a rock bounced off of his helmet. Momentarily stunned, the Copper Knight looked around for the source of it, but his vision, much like his voice, was very impaired by the old rusty helmet.

Bang! Bing! Clunk!

Three more rocks ricocheted off the helmet, and finally the Copper Knight roared in frustration, "What is the meaning of this?! Show yourself! Who are you?!"

And a lean black-haired boy of only twelve but with the demeanor of a much older, much more confident man stepped out from behind a nearby tree.

"The name's Lancelot," said the boy. "And I think the lady told you to stop. But you didn't listen to her. So I'm going to make you stop."

Lancelot had been searching for the Copper Knight for nearly a year at this point. Lancelot had finally found him. And in less than a minute, Lancelot was going to fight him.

With a grumble of frustration, the Copper Knight drew his sword and charged at Lancelot.

"I'll teach you some manners, boy!" said the Copper Knight, but with his visor down again all that came out was, "M'mm mmmm mmm mmmm mmmmmm, mmm!"

Lancelot couldn't have understood a word of it, and he didn't care. He was welcoming his first real battle. True, Lancelot only had a handful of stones to defend himself, but he was determined that they would be enough. With expert aim, he flung them at the Copper Knight's helmet and succeeded in denting it even further than it had been before. The knight's vision became even more obstructed than usual, so when he swung his sword, it was clumsy and only too easy for Lancelot to dart out of the way. From close range, Lancelot beamed the Copper Knight's helmet once more with a perfectly aimed stone. This one caused the knight's helmet to spin ever so slightly, which blocked his vision entirely. Stumbling and disoriented, the Copper Knight didn't stand a chance. Lancelot let loose a relentless onslaught of stones that hammered the Copper Knight's soft armor. All the while, Lancelot easily leapt, bounded and avoided the Copper Knight's clumsy, blinded slashes. Finally, after scooping up a rock the size of his fist from amongst the roots of a nearby tree, Lancelot wound up and let fly his final blow. It connected with a resounding rattle and left an impressive dent in the side of the knight's helmet. The Copper Knight staggered, collapsed, and moved no more.

Looking down on the crumpled form of the once great knight, Lancelot shrugged and said, "Look, you shouldn't be ashamed. You couldn't have expected to run into someone like me. You couldn't have expected to run into the mighty Lancelot!"

The sound of soft clapping shook Lancelot from his cloud of pride, and he turned to see that Nimue had gotten back to her feet, and was now waddling toward him on her short little legs.

"Whoa... Well, my, my, oh my..." she said as she looked Lancelot up and down. "That was unexpected."

"Eh, no big deal."

"No big deal? You do know who that was, don't you?"

"Of course," said Lancelot as if it were the most obvious thing in the world: "the fearsome Copper Knight. He's been winning tournaments and terrorizing village folk for well over a decade."

"And that didn't scare you?"

"Scare me?! I wanted to study with him. Lots of people say he's the greatest knight in the world! Or at least he was. I don't think many people will say that about him anymore."

"You're not a normal boy, are you?"

Lancelot shook his head as he looked down on the heap of knight crumbled at his feet. "I'm sorry to say but the more I learned about him, the more I learned that he wasn't such a nice guy. It became obvious to me that I shouldn't study with him. Instead I should..."

21

And here Lancelot mimicked throwing a stone. Then he mimicked a loud cracking noise. And to finish it all off for good measure, he mimicked a spectacular crashing sound like a mighty oak tree snapping and falling with a mighty thud. Then Lancelot pantomimed the Copper Knight going down hard.

"...Take him out."

Nimue cocked an eyebrow and said, "You weren't afraid he might, you know, kill you?"

"Hmm…" said Lancelot as paused to consider it. Then he replied honestly, "You know, it never actually crossed my mind."

With that, the boy shrugged and turned to walk away.

"Well, I suppose I'll be on my way. I guess I'll need to find a different mentor…"

But young Lancelot had barely taken a half-dozen steps when Nimue shouted at him, "Wait! Where are you going?"

"To the next challenge. The next battle. The next adventure."

"But you're just a boy. You have no idea what's really ahead of you. Trust me, you don't want to head down that path."

"What path?"

"The one the Copper Knight got lost on years ago. Do you really want to end up like this?"

And then Nimue peeled the helmet off of the still unstirring Copper Knight. For the first time, Lancelot laid eyes on the man who had been under the copper for so long. His skin was pale and splotchy red. His hair was sparse and looked like it had fallen out in uneven clumps. And there was a large bloody wound on the side of his battered skull.

"I hate to break it to you, kid," said Nimue as she tossed the helmet aside. "But if you follow the road you're on, ahead of you is only pain, death, and destruction."

Lancelot gazed down at the body on the ground and it finally hit him with a jolt that he wasn't looking at the first knight that he had beaten—he was looking at the first man that he had killed.

Reading the somber expression on Lancelot's face, Nimue said, "Stay here. You helped me. I can help you. Maybe you can find some peace."

But Lancelot wrenched his gaze away from the crumbled form of the Copper Knight. He closed his eyes and shook his head, as if to dispel the image and the thoughts that had just flooded his mind. He met Nimue's eyes and flashed her the kind of broad grin that only a young boy who feels like he can take over the world can muster.

"I'm terribly sorry, but I'm afraid I must refuse your most generous offer, my good lady," he said as he gave Nimue a flashy bow. Then he turned and strode away, only pausing long enough to call over his shoulder, "I'm off to become the greatest knight in all the world!"

And that's exactly what he would become.

~ ~ ~

CHAPTER 1

The Return to the Lakes

Seventeen years passed and the Lakes of Avalon stayed the same.

The beautiful crystalline waters continued to glimmer peacefully beneath bright sunshine and clear blue skies. Soft cool breezes never failed to whisper along through fields of lush green grass. Tall healthy fruit trees of every color and variety grew long, full branches that strained under the weight of bows filled with apples, pears and nectarines.

But when Lancelot finally returned, he was quite changed.

The once bright-faced boy of twelve had long since disappeared beneath a blanket of scars that touched nearly every inch of his body. His soft youthful body had grown lean and hard with the years and the many battles. A myriad of wrinkles had slowly crept in along the edges of his eyes, and sparse gray hairs had snuck in amongst his once thick black hair.

And his right arm was missing from just below the elbow.

Nonetheless, Lancelot's eyes twinkled softly as he approached the magical grotto that had marked the beginning of his career as a knight. When he arrived as a boy, Lancelot hadn't taken the time to admire the trees and the clouds and the waters. Now, he feasted upon the beauty of the place as he approached. Lancelot quickly found Nimue still standing guard and also looking as if she hadn't aged a day. When Lancelot was a boy, there were many things about the world that he still didn't know, and he hadn't given Nimue much thought. Over the years, however, he had encountered all manner of man, beast, and creature, and as he looked over Nimue's generously soft bulk and clumped waxy hair, he realized that she must be part-mermaid. Yet despite her unusual shape, Nimue maintained a surprising grace, and as Lancelot approached her, she delicately balanced upon one foot with her arms outstretched in front of her, all the while keeping her eyes closed and her mind apparently calm and clear.

As Lancelot's feet crunched upon the soft grass, however, Nimue opened an eye, and with a quick sweeping glance she took in his beaten tired countenance and remarked:

"So… how'd things turn out for you?"

Lancelot shot her a bemused smirk.

Less than an hour later, Lancelot and Nimue walked side-by-side through the orchards of Avalon. The branches overhead were filled with shiny green leaves and plump juicy fruits that hung low and plentiful. As they walked, Lancelot plucked a peach and bit into it with relish, the plentiful juices flowing messily down his chin.

"Somehow I always had a feeling you'd come stumbling in here again," said Nimue.

"This place was too beautiful to only visit once," Lancelot said as he sucked some of the extra juice out of his peach. "It kind of sticks with you."

"You know, I did tell you, you could've stayed here."

As they continued through the orchard, they passed a small grove filled with a dozen or so simple grave markers. With a slight lurch in his stomach, Lancelot read the name "THE COPPER KNIGHT." Lancelot quickly looked away, and reminded himself that there were now many graveyards spread throughout the land that bore the names of men he had killed.

"It seems like you did just fine here without me," remarked Lancelot.

"Oh, them?" said Nimue with a remorseful shake of her head. "There have always been those who seek the waters of Avalon for their own evil purposes. I'm happy to say, I've always been able to show them a thing or two."

"You've got a few tricks up your sleeve, do you, Nimue?"

"Me? Oh yes, I'm a regular all-powerful enchantress. Master of the elements and queen over the skies and the earth," she stated as she pointed a stubby, somewhat webbed finger at the clouds and caused them to swirl and slightly darken.

"Remind me never to make you angry," said Lancelot as he casually began sucking the last bits of pulp off of his peach pit.

With a wave of her hand, the clouds overhead dispersed, and Nimue sighed, "Unfortunately, my powers aren't much good beyond helping this orchard to flourish. If you need a soft shower for the oranges, or a bit of frost for the apple blossoms, then I'm your woman. Past that, I've got to use these," she said as she held up her small but menacing hands.

"I have no idea what it must be like to live by the fist," said Lancelot with a twinkle of irony.

"I'll bet you don't, big guy. Nonetheless, I'm sure I could've used your help around here over the years. And, I think, you might've been able to use my help too."

"I think we both did just fine on our own," said Lancelot as he casually tossed aside the peach pit, then tugged a golden apple from another tree and hungrily began to devour it.

"Not bad, huh?" Nimue said as she watched Lancelot eating the apple in a few ravenous bites. "Probably a little better than how you've been living lately."

"Eh... Life hasn't been so bad out there."

"Fair enough. I didn't mean to imply you haven't done perfectly well for yourself. I apologize," she said as she put out her hand to shake. "Put it there."

Reflexively, Lancelot's right arm twitched to shake Nimue's outstretched hand, but of course, Lancelot no longer had a right hand to shake with. Instead, he just shot Nimue a stern glance that clearly said, "*Really? You're going to going to pull a trick like that?!*"

"I'm not here to heal my arm," he said coolly. "I'm here to heal everything else."

Nimue smirked and nodded.

The two of them had finally looped back to the lake's edge. Lancelot stepped toward it, bent and reached out his left hand. He was about to dip his fingers into the pool when:

"Whoa, whoa, whoa!" Nimue shouted. "Hold on there, little pony!"

Nimue slapped Lancelot's wrist, and he jerked his hand away from the water's surface.

"What'd you think you are? Some kind of a madman, just looking and touching whatever you want?" she asked. "Didn't I just tell you that's a good way to get yourself a nice soft bed beneath the grass? You can't just dive right in there."

"Sorry, it's just…" said Lancelot, blushing a little. "It's just so shiny."

"It'll turn your head. That's for sure. And that's why it's drawn men and women to its shores for times untold. But you have to be ready. And you, boy, you are not ready." Nimue surveyed him with a tough stare, then continued, "You seek the Lakes of Avalon that you once sought to protect. And after all that you've been through, I can't blame you. You think they can make you whole again."

"Can they?" asked Lancelot.

"Oh, absolutely!" said Nimue. "Without a doubt. I'm surprised you even have to ask."

"Excellent!" said Lancelot. "Then let's get started."

"It's not going to be easy, Sir Impatient Pants. You see, while the waters can heal the body, if the soul isn't prepared, they will tear you apart."

"Then let's get started," he repeated without a hint of fear in his voice.

"You really think you're up for this?"

Lancelot puffed out his chest, and said in his most boastful tone, "Do you think I'm afraid? I've served as a knight in some of the greatest kingdoms in the land. I've rescued damsels from the most dire of circumstances. I've slain beasts too terrible to be named. I've journeyed through realms that struck terror in the hearts of the bravest of men. I've even ridden a dragon and—"

"Oh yes, the dragon! I heard about that!" cut in Nimue, who had been looking a little bored at the rest of Lancelot's long-winded list. "So, tell me something then: if you rode on a dragon and all that impressive heroic stuff, why did you walk all the way here? Couldn't you just hitch a lift here on that White Dragon of yours?"

Lancelot winced slightly and seemed to be ignoring the question with some irritation.

"As I was saying..." he continued through gritted teeth. "I've overcome obstacles that would make any man cower in fear. I can take anything you throw at me."

Nimue just shrugged.

"Evil kings. Marauding armies. Rampaging dragons. Pffft! The challenges you face here will be nothing like anything you've ever struggled through before."

~ ~ ~

CHAPTER 2

Lancelot's Greatest Challenge

As Nimue led Lancelot into a wide, beautiful meadow, he felt his pulse quicken and his breathing deepen. He was preparing for battle. Over the years, before he faced any danger, he had learned the importance of taking full control over his faculties. He tensed his muscles while at the same time staying light and flexible on his toes. He sharpened his eyes as he took stock of his surroundings. He heightened his focus and stilled his mind. Whatever struggle Nimue had in store for him, Lancelot was certain that he was ready to face it.

He was very wrong.

Nimue took Lancelot into the quiet center of the open green plain. He looked to the nearby hills for an ambush. The grass danced ever so slightly in a gentle breeze. Lancelot sniffed the air for any scent of predators. The bright sun shone down and gave just the right amount of warmth to be comfortable yet invigorating. Lancelot squinted for any sign of an approaching army. But there were none to be found. In the middle of the meadow, Nimue simply pointed to a particularly soft-looking bit of earth and said:

"Sit."

"Ah yes…" said Lancelot warily. "Will I be waiting for some beast from the depths of the underworld to come bounding over the distant hills?"

"Just sit, Lancelot."

"You mean I should do some crunches first? Engage my stomach, legs and back? In order to warm myself up for the dangers ahead?"

"Down on the ground. Let's go."

"Oh, I know; I'll be taking on a battalion of flesh-eating field mice, shall I?"

"WOULD YOU JUST SIT ALREADY?!"

"All right, all right!" said Lancelot, jolting at Nimue's sudden outburst. "And then what?"

"Don't you worry about that. You haven't even sat down yet."

"Yes, I know. But that's a simple enough request. I assure you, I've already wrapped my brain around that part. So, tell me, once I've done it, what can I expect to be doing next?"

"Are you going to sit or am I going to have to make you sit?!"

"I will sit! And then what happens?"

"And then you'll be sitting."

With an offbeat frown, Lancelot finally sat down in the middle of the peaceful meadow.

"How long will I be sitting?" he asked after only a few seconds.

"As long as it takes. A while," said Nimue with a shrug. "I'll be back to tell you when you've sat here long enough."

"All right…" sighed Lancelot. "And then you'll tell me what I'll do next?"

"Oh, I can tell you that right now."

"Wonderful! What is it?"

"Sit some more."

Nimue shrugged and began to walk away. She hadn't gotten far when:

"So I'm just supposed to sit here then?"

Nimue nodded.

"There's no monsters or villains or cataclysms headed in this general direction?"

Nimue shook her head.

"You just want me to sit here and…?"

"And relax."

With that simple request, Nimue turned and left.

"No problem…" said Lancelot with determined calm in his voice. "It'll be my pleasure to finally have a chance to sit peacefully and relax…"

But barely a minute had passed when Lancelot sighed heavily. Discomfort was already creeping over him.

An hour passed.

Lancelot flopped down on his back.

Night fell.

Lancelot softly pounded the back of his head against the lush grass.

If possible the meadow was only more beautiful beneath a blanket of stars and a bright shimmering moon. But Lancelot literally writhed on the ground. He punched his one good fist upon his forehead. He toed impatiently at the earth with his bare feet after having tossed his boots aside hours ago in a fit of boredom.

Hours into the night, Nimue finally returned.

"Thank goodness! You're back!" cried Lancelot, leaping to his feet at her approach. He all but flew off of the ground as he added, "Tell me, what now?!"

"Hold your horses there, big man…" she said as she watched Lancelot bouncing from foot to eager foot. "When was the last time you just sat still?"

Lancelot thought for a moment, then said with shrug, "I almost died a few years ago. Lost my arm, and nearly all of my blood. I could barely move for months. Does that count?"

"Well, if you survived that, this should be easy," Nimue pointed out.

"It's horrible! Tell me we can do something else."

Nimue nodded, and Lancelot actually skipped with excitement.

"Sleep," Nimue said.

Lancelot's face fell. Horror crept over his handsome features, and he found himself struggling to breathe.

"You're kidding me, right?"

"Go on, Sir Knightly," said Nimue. "Lay down. Go to bed. Count some sheep. Take a snooze. Get some shut-eye. Sleep!"

"Sleep?! You honestly want me to sleep!? All I've done is sit around all day."

"And now I'm telling you to lie around all night."

With a sweet smile that Lancelot considered devilishly evil, Nimue turned and left Lancelot all alone again. Even though it seemed to take an extreme effort, Lancelot dropped back to the ground and reclined in the grass. He grumbled and frowned, but told himself that he could do this. He was the greatest knight in the land; there was no challenge he couldn't overcome. He had fought armies single-handedly. He had tamed dragons. He had looked death in the face and come through on the other side. If Nimue wanted him to sleep, then he would snooze better than any man had ever rested in the history of relaxation.

Three hours later, Lancelot still laid on his back staring at the moon with wide murderous eyes and he growled at the twinkling stars:

"I despise you all."

Things would only get worse.

For the next several days and even weeks, Lancelot napped, he reclined, he lay about, and he hated every minute of it. Periodically, Nimue would arrive and lead him to another part of Avalon and then with her brutal, merciless, vicious cruelty, she would instruct Lancelot to continue his desperate toil with passivity.

In the fruit groves, Lancelot slumped against tree trunks.

"Please, can't we do something?!"

"Sure, we can. Sit. Relax."

Beside the shimmering lake, Lancelot sat cross-legged.

"There must be a sea monster in there that needs slaying or something!"

"Just clear your mind."

After a fortnight, something remarkable happened. Sitting atop the gently sloping hills, for a single moment, Lancelot finally began to appreciate the sun on his face and the breeze through his hair.

"You know, I must admit... This is somewhat nice."

"Isn't it, though?" Nimue agreed gently. "Enjoy."

And for the first time in his life, Lancelot sat comfortably beneath the sun in a soft luscious field and he thought of nothing. He simply relaxed.

Five seconds later, it was gone.

Quickly, Lancelot sank back into painstaking boredom. And he stayed there for another twenty-four hours. However, after another full day, Lancelot was able to embrace another period of calm and serenity, and this time it lasted a full fifteen seconds. Little by little, as the clouds passed overhead and the sun rose and fell in the sky, Lancelot began to master the beast within his heart. He wrestled with his demons and sent them on their way. He released the power that years and years of toil held over him.

The mighty Lancelot, after a lifetime of war, finally began to savor his taste of peace.

Longer and longer periods of time would pass in which Lancelot was able to simply sit, clear his mind, and just enjoy his little spot in the sun. Even Nimue was beginning to be impressed.

35

One day, she found Lancelot settled into a lotus pose, his strong, limber legs twisted up comfortably beneath him. His eyes were closed, and he had been sitting still for nearly two hours. Nimue silently crept up alongside him. Lancelot took no notice of her approach. She crouched near him. He stayed frozen and still.

Ever so gently, Nimue blew into his ear, and within seconds:

"AAAAHHHH!"

Lancelot waved his arms wildly. Concentration broken. Peace gone. Simple as that.

"That is not fair!"

"Would you just relax?!" she laughed with a mischievous grin.

Lancelot glared at her with eyes of fire, but the feeling quickly faded away. There had been a time, not all that long ago, where he would've lashed out and carried the frustration upon his back for hours, if not days. Instead, he let it go, and Lancelot laughed along with Nimue. He was starting to get the hang of this relaxation thing.

Amongst the gently rolling hills, Lancelot flopped on his back.

In the middle of the wide plains, he snoozed under the warm sunshine.

Up in the thick tree limbs, Lancelot dangled his legs freely.

Beside the crystalline waters of the lake, Lancelot reclined quietly. Eyes closed. Face calm. Body impassive. Peaceful.

This time when Nimue came along and blew in Lancelot's ear, nothing happened.

She leapt at him with a shriek.

"Boogedy!"

Still nothing.

"Lancelot, look out! It's a six-foot porcupine!"

No reaction.

"We're under attack! The lemmings are coming! You have to save us!"

Cool as an autumn evening.

Nimue nodded in satisfaction.

"Not bad…"

But as she started to walk away:

"You realize you're a terrible person, right?" Lancelot called with a mere flicker of a smile in his voice.

And Nimue knew she was succeeding in the impossible task of taming Sir Lancelot.

After Lancelot had been at the lakes of Avalon for so long that he had lost track of the days and the outside world seemed far removed, he took a walk with Nimue through the orchard. The sun was setting and the horizon had turned delicious shades of pink, gold, and orange. Lancelot gazed in amazement at the skyline, as he bit into a crisp apple, and savored its delicate tartness.

"How're you feeling now, tall, dark, and sun-tanned?" asked Nimue.

"Good," said Lancelot simply. He almost left it at that, and for several moments he did, but he finally felt compelled to add, "For moments, everything goes quiet. I forget about my past. I don't worry about my future. All the pain goes away. And I'm just… Here. Now."

"Oooooh. I love it when that happens! Isn't it the best?"

"I never thought I could feel like this," admitted Lancelot.

"Most people never do," said Nimue. "They get so caught up in their toils. Or their missions. Or their quests. They forget to just stop and recognize that in every moment there can be peace, if they just stop and look for it. Most people never take the time. Not even for a second."

"I'm not sure I'll ever be the same again," said Lancelot.

"Ooooh, stop and marvel at the profundity! Feels good, doesn't it?" laughed Nimue. "But you'd be surprised how quickly it can slip away. And you willingly re-embrace the pain."

Lancelot shook his head.

"Well, well, well, look at the enlightened guru!" she said with just a hint of mocking. "I guess you've found nirvana. You've slipped out of the realm of consciousness, huh?"

"Well… maybe not… I'm not sure I'd put it exactly like that," muttered Lancelot, taken off-guard because he didn't even know several of the words Nimue had just used. "I just mean I've found something wonderful. Why would I give that up?"

"The world has a frustrating habit of being, well, frustrating," Nimue pointed out.

Once more, Lancelot shook his head definitively.

"No. I've tried things the other way. Ever since I was a boy, I've sought out struggles to wrestle with and challenges to overcome and battles to fight. And what's it gotten me? A lonely life of pain and war. But from this day forward, I turn my back on all of that. I, Sir Lancelot, vow to be a man of peace. It feels good just saying it!"

Nimue smiled at Lancelot's grand pronouncement. She didn't have to the heart to tell him that he was wrong.

~ ~ ~

CHAPTER 3

The Dream

In his favorite spot in the middle of the meadow where a perfect breeze danced over his brow, Lancelot slept beneath the wide expanse of perfect blackness overhead. Since his arrival in Avalon, he'd begun to sleep in a way he never had before. His muscles loosened. His face relaxed. His breathing calmed. He really slept.

But this night his eyes stirred behind their lids.

In his dream, Lancelot walked through the same field that he laid in in reality. The soft grass stretched on forever, and pale moonlight shone down from above. The warm, fragrant air tickled his skin, and he felt unencumbered and relaxed.

And Guinevere strode with him.

For a long time, they simply walked side by side, her simple dress rustled in the breeze and her long braided hair bobbed along behind them. Lancelot's left arm swung close to her right. They didn't touch, but they were very aware of their proximity to each other. The rhythm of their limbs wasn't quite in sync; Lancelot knew it was tantalizingly close, though, as he tried to match her steps, but he couldn't seem to find the right cadence.

"Why can't I get you out of my mind?" he asked.

"And why would you ever want to get me out of your mind?" Guinevere asked right back. "I'm a part of you now, Lancelot. I may be the only one who can ever really understand you."

"But I barely know you!" cried Lancelot. "We've spent only a few days with one another. Yet you seem so deeply ingrained in me."

"Yes, I know," she said, glancing over at him, and for a single shining moment, her beautiful brown eyes locked with his. Just as quickly, the gaze was broken. "Isn't it wonderful?"

"It certainly is," Lancelot said, not really sure that it was. He felt compelled to add, "But we're not good for each other, are we?"

Guinevere stopped walking, and Lancelot paused beside her. They finally turned and looked upon one another fully. Guinevere reached out her hands, touched Lancelot's face, and gently traced along the creases of his face with her soft fingertips.

"Maybe we're the only thing that's good for each other..."

Lancelot gazed upon her face bathed in the moonlight. She was almost impossibly beautiful, and his heart ached at her touch. As if obliging his heart's desire, Guinevere began to move toward Lancelot. They leaned toward one another.

Inches away from a kiss.

Centimeters.

Millimeters...

A shorter distance than can be measured when:

RUMBLE!

CRASH!

The soft glow of the moon and stars vanished as oppressive storm clouds filled the skies, and shook the heavens with their thunder and lightning. Lancelot and Guinevere pulled away from each other as rain streaked down upon them. Lancelot took Guinevere's arm and prepared to sprint through the storm to find a warm quiet place that they might wait out the weather, but:

A harsh rattling noise filled Lancelot's ears.

He looked around, and to his astonishment he found that he and Guinevere were surrounded by an army of dark soldiers. All as one, they rapped their swords against their shields, and they grumbled and bellowed beneath their helmets as they called for Lancelot to come and fight them.

Guinevere squeezed Lancelot's arm.

"Kill them all," she whispered. "Keep me safe."

And she slipped a sword into his left hand.

There was a pit in Lancelot's stomach as her words dug into him, and he said, "But I don't want to fight anymore."

Guinevere actually laughed. "But Lancelot, that's all you're good for!"

Lancelot stared at her with pain in his eyes. And there was only harshness behind hers.

Suddenly, the army charged. They were only feet away, but Lancelot wouldn't raise his sword.

"I don't want to do this!"

The army rattled closer. They raised their weapons.

42

"Please... Lancelot! You must fight!" Guinevere cried as the army closed in.

They were inches away. Ready to slash. Ready to kill.

And Lancelot fought them.

He spun and dodged and slashed with all of his considerable might. Blood spilled freely upon the ground. All who came close to Lancelot were felled. But he knew there were too many of them. He could kill a dozen men, but the thirteenth would land a blow, and Lancelot's back would bear a new wound. He could dodge a hundred swords, but then one would slip through, and Lancelot's leg would pour with blood. As hard as he fought, Lancelot could tell it was a losing battle.

In really no time at all, Lancelot stumbled and the massive army crowded in upon him. They raised their blades as one. They drew back, prepared to strike when:

A blinding flash of light split the skies.

And King Arthur charged to the rescue.

In armor flecked with gold and wielding a sword the likes of which Lancelot had never seen before, the golden-haired king overtook the strength of the dark army. Despite the storm clouds overhead and the gray tones of the army's shields, Arthur was somehow bathed in light. Lancelot watched with astonishment as Arthur, infused with incredible strength and power, dispelled the dark army in a manner of moments.

Then Guinevere rushed to her king's side.

Lancelot lay upon the ground. Wounded and aching with the pain of his many wounds, Lancelot reached out to Arthur and Guinevere and begged, "Please, my friend... I tried…"

"Ah yes, you fought like you always will," said Arthur, ignoring Lancelot's outstretched hand. "But you never could've succeeded, Lancelot. It's not in your heart. You will always fight. But you can never win."

"You can't have peace," added Guinevere.

"You can only bring pain," agreed Arthur as he looked down on Lancelot lying in the mud. "All you're good for is doom. And destruction. And death."

Then Arthur and Guinevere turned to one another and embraced. They passionately entwined into one another's arms. Their lips met. And it was like two proper halves meeting to make one perfect whole.

Lancelot's head fell in anguish, and he closed his eyes to try and block out the sight of them. When he opened his eyes once more:

They were gone.

And Lancelot lay upon a rough wooden table. Mud and blood were still caked upon every inch of his body, and he felt overwhelmed with exhaustion, pain, and despair. His eyes cast around on his new surroundings and he realized that he was back in the simple hut of the old healer woman, Morgana, who had saved him after his most hopeless battle. He had lain upon this table for months after his defeat at Tintagel Castle. After he had lost his

44

right arm and nearly been crushed by an army of Saxons, Lancelot had clawed his way out of death's clutches in this very hut. The poorly laid roof seeped with rain. The decrepit walls creaked against the wind. A large cauldron sizzled and popped in the corner as it emitted thick waves of orange steam. Morgana, hunched over with age, shuffled around Lancelot and waved her gnarled fingers over his wounds as she took in the sorry state of him with her milky, nearly white eyes.

"Leave me be…" gasped Lancelot, struggling to rise from the table, but finding no strength to do so. "I don't want you to heal me…"

"Don't worry, my sweet Lancelot," the old woman cooed. "I can save you. I can make you whole again."

"Stop… Don't… Please…"

The orange mist wafted from the cauldron and swirled around Lancelot, filling his nostrils.

"You're mine, my sweet. Mine."

Morgana moved to Lancelot's side, and lifted a potion to his lips, but he wrenched his head away from it.

"I don't want to drink…"

"You must," she said, holding it insistently to him.

"Not like this…"

"You can be the greatest knight the world has ever seen," she whispered. "But you must choose to drink."

Finally, Lancelot consented. He opened his lips and let the hot liquid burn its way down his throat. He drank with a dying man's thirst. He embraced the escape it promised.

"You will be the greatest. And the most terrible," the old woman whispered as she poured every last drop into Lancelot's mouth. "And mine."

"No…" coughed Lancelot as he realized the consequences of his momentary weakness. He tried to spit the potion back out, but it was too late. It seized hold of him and flooded his veins with boiling hot fervor. He screamed with pain as blinding orange light enveloped him. Mist and visions swirled around him, and then he heard it:

A voice from his past.

Soft, slightly foreign, beautiful.

And screaming.

Piercing through the madness. Terrified. Aching. Blood-curdling.

"LANCELOT! PLEASE! HELP ME! WE'LL ALL DIE WITHOUT YOU!"

~ ~ ~

The sun had barely risen the next morning and Lancelot had already gathered his few meager belongings as he prepared to head out. He was piling several apples into his shoulder bag to help him along his journey, and Nimue waddled along in his wake, desperately trying to talk sense into the determined knight.

"You're not ready!" she insisted as she tried to keep up with him. "You've barely tasted peace. If you go out there, you'll just fall into the same patterns of pain and despair. Maybe even worse."

"I can't leave her like that."

"Oh, you're such a typical knight! So determined to rush off to the side of the damsel in distress," Nimue groaned. "Get over yourself, you brave bonehead, it was only a dream!"

"It wasn't a dream," said Lancelot, shaking his head. The vision had seized hold of him, and it gripped him down to his bones. He couldn't explain why, but he knew it was real. "I felt it like I've never felt anything before."

"All the more reason for you to ignore it!" shouted Nimue. "You're on the verge of something here! If you go off to chase some vague premonition that came from who knows where, it could tear you apart!"

"You think this is just some dark spell trying to manipulate me?" scoffed Lancelot.

"Of course, you handsome fool!"

"You don't know what you're talking about."

"Hello! Mystical protector of a magical lake here!"

"Why would it come upon me now? When I'm finally starting to feel some peace?"

"Because you're finally starting to feel some peace! For exactly that reason!" cried Nimue in exasperation. "You're an uncommon warrior, Lancelot. Maybe unique throughout all of history. It's not surprising that powerful forces might not be thrilled about you throwing down your sword forever."

Lancelot paused as these words penetrated him and he nodded. "You're right."

"Thank you—"

But Nimue's relief was short-lived, as Lancelot continued, "I am an uncommon warrior. Maybe unique throughout all of history."

"That's what you're focusing on from what I said?!"

"And I can overcome this."

Lancelot tugged on the boots that he hadn't worn in weeks, and turned to give Nimue a soft hug as he said, "I'll be back. I promise."

But Nimue simply shook her head and muttered, "You won't come back the same, you foolish, stubborn beast of a knight."

"Have a little faith in me," said Lancelot with a charming wink, as he stooped to pick up the weapons that had lain untouched since his arrival in Avalon. Nimue put her foot down on the blade that Lancelot had fashioned into a sword arm to lash upon his missing hand.

"At least leave your weapons," she said.

"Are you mad?! Who knows what I may face out there. I need my sword arm!"

"Are you an uncommon warrior unique throughout history or not?"

With a reluctant grumble, Lancelot nodded.

"Then prove it. By choosing not to fight. Find another way."

Lancelot stared at Nimue for a long moment and weighed her challenge. Deep down, he felt that whatever lay ahead of him would be monstrously difficult. It was unpredictable what he might come up against. Generally, he knew it was foolish to go into any unknown circumstances without some means of protecting himself. However, he could tell by the look on Nimue's face that this was important, and he had come to respect her wisdom. If she felt that he was in a more profound danger with his weapons than he would be without them, then he would have to accept her opinion. He straightened up and left the blades upon the ground. Then, to show he was serious, Lancelot placed his hand over his heart and said solemnly:

"I give you my word as knight. No fighting. Only rescuing."

And with that, Lancelot turned and left Avalon behind him. Nimue watched with her short arms crossed against her wide chest and worry all over her usually carefree face.

Lancelot had barely gone a hundred meters when he heard Nimue call, "Give sweet ole Guinevere my regards!"

"Oh, it's not Guinevere I have to save!" called back Lancelot. Then he whispered to himself, "It's a woman who's even more trouble…"

~ ~ ~

CHAPTER 4

Back to the Beginning

Of course, it wasn't the first time Lancelot had turned his back on Lakes of Avalon.

It wasn't even the first time he left there without any weapons.

When Lancelot had been only twelve years old, just after his victory over the Copper Knight, he had journeyed off into the wild uncertainties of the many kingdoms. Back then, he had even less going for him. He had no formal training. He had no prospects for a proper master who might guide him. He didn't even have a sword, a fact which he chided himself for since he easily could've claimed the fallen Copper Knight's weapon as his own.

Fortunately, the last bit could be easily remedied.

It was true that a real sword was an expensive proposition, and Lancelot had no coin in his pockets. Nonetheless, he had always been an industrious boy, and not easily discouraged. As he travelled through the forests, Lancelot came across plentiful wood, rocks and vines. While he walked to his unknown destination, he slowly and painstakingly used jagged rocks to shape sturdy pieces of wood until they became passable blades, hilts, and finger guards. He twisted the vines tightly over and over until the pieces were lashed securely together. At last, Lancelot wielded his homemade first sword, and he was confident that it would bring him to greatness.

"*That's* no sword, boy!"

Lord Umberland was less impressed.

After having constructed his wooden sword, Lancelot set about finding himself a master. However, this too was no easy task. The vagabond wayfarers that Lancelot met along the road were usually not terribly skilled themselves, and Lancelot couldn't hope to learn much from them. The local champions of the small towns and villages weren't interested in apprentices who might one day try and take their place. And proud knights of the kingdoms took no notice of a filthy boy from the streets. Yet Lancelot wasn't one to be deterred, and he eventually turned to more unconventional methods.

He went to sign up for Umberland's Um-believable Um-broglio!

On the outskirts of a kingdom in the lawless lands, it was common for unbound swordsmen and warriors to compete for a bit of gold and a chance at glory. All manner of competitions sprang up where men could test their daring on horseback or with a sword or in a raucous melee. They were terribly dangerous and unruly, and many a young brawler ended up with their head cracked open or in the bottom of an unceremonious grave.

Lord Umberland ran the most chaotic event of all.

The Umberland family had been given a scrap of land generations ago by the legendary Ambrosius Aurelanus for unflinching loyalty and services rendered to the king. However, as time moved along and the land was passed from one hand to another, the purity of the Umberland family was diluted. The latest in a long line to bear the title "Lord Umberland" had come to enjoy games and sport and he dedicated his plot of land to just such an endeavor. Men and women came from all over the kingdom to watch the events, where combatants would crowd into a cramped wooden ring and proceed to wail upon each other until only one man was left standing and oftentimes all the others were dead. The crowd would cheer for their favorite champions, groan in delight at the bloodletting, and exchange spectacular amounts of gold all under Lord Umberland's greedy nose.

Lancelot wanted in.

"Don't waste my time. There's no money in watching boys getting their heads hacked off," scoffed Lord Umberland as he tried to brush Lancelot away.

Lancelot was barely a boy any longer, though. He had been on the verge of thirteen when he arrived in Avalon. Amidst his hard scrabble journeys, over a year had passed, and now Lancelot was fourteen. He was nearly as tall as any man in the wooden arena, and while he wasn't nearly as broad or filled out, it was undeniable that there was a hungry strength that surged through his youthful muscles.

"There's not a man here who could cut me down," said Lancelot. "I want to compete."

"Oh, do you?!" laughed Umberland. "You want to get your heart bashed in and your back broken is more like it. Now shoo; I've got a battle to start."

With that, Umberland turned his back to Lancelot and faced the crowd as he bellowed:

"LADIES AND GENTLEMEN! WELCOME TO LORD UMBERLAND'S UM-BELIEVABLE UM-BROGLIO!"

The crowd cheered in delight even though most of them had no idea what the words that Lord Umberland was mangling meant. Nonetheless, they lapped it up as they whistled and roared and placed odds on their favorite fighters.

"TODAY, WE HAVE TWELVE OF THE BRAVEST—"

"Thirteen!"

Lancelot tried to push his way forward again, but Umberland shoved him aside again.

"—AS I WAS SAYING, TWELVE OF THE BRAVEST—"

"Not brave enough to face me!"

Once again, Lancelot tried to inject himself into the proceedings, and Umberland's face, which was usually red with drink, was now growing red with frustration. He spun to glare at the brash young man.

"You get out of here, boy! Before I set all of these brutes loose to teach you a real lesson!"

Umberland waved a hand at the twelve heavily armored men waiting in the ring. They were all shapes and sizes. Tall, fat, slightly wheezy, and furious. Lancelot wasn't concerned in the least.

"That's what I want! Let me in there with those brutes. Maybe I'll teach them all a lesson!"

"You haven't a scrap of armor or a sword," growled Umberland.

"I do too have a sword!" protested Lancelot, brandishing his rough-hewn wooden weapon.

"That's not a sword! It's a couple of tree branches held together with moss!" laughed Umberland. "You'd be dead in under a minute, and dead boys drive business away. These gamblers are a superstitious lot, and I don't want to give them any reason to go someplace else. Now, get out of here and let me start my game."

"But I want to compete!"

Umberland looked like he was on the verge of erupting when the shouts started coming from the assembled crowd.

"Eh, let him fight, if he's so determined to get himself killed!"

"Go ahead, Lord Umberland. He looks like he can handle himself!"

"I'll put 5 to 1 odds on the boy!"

"I bet 10 to 1!"

As gold started passing amongst the spectators, Umberland's eyes began to twinkle. His palms sweated eagerly. He licked his lips with desire. Finally, he turned to Lancelot and nodded.

"It's your funeral, boy," said Umberland. "I'm going to make a killing off of your killing." He nodded to the men in the ring and added, "Try to leave enough of the boy to bury."

Then with a shrug, Umberland motioned to his assistants, who adjusted the odds and began collecting bets from his gathered gamblers. Lancelot bounded into the wooden ring, vaulting his legs easily over the four-foot-high wall, and faced off with the assembled group of warriors hoping to make a name for themselves. While Lancelot was the only one with a wooden sword, there was a varied collection of weapons overall. Some of the combatants had polished swords, but others gripped axes, spears, and spiked clubs. All of them had some degree of armor, with the obvious exception of Lancelot, but many of the suits were ill-fitting or incomplete. Bare arms or bellies protruded through gaps in the metal, and dented helmets clearly impeded the sight and movement of several men. Lancelot quickly took in all of the challengers, he noted the chinks in their armor, he sized up the most likely to stumble, and he prepared his plan of attack. Lancelot had just settled on the first man he would attempt to take down when Umberland roared:

"LET UMBERLAND'S UM-BELIEVABLE UM-BROGLIO BEGIN!"

And Lancelot leapt into battle.

There was a rattle of armor and a clash of steel as all of the men piled together into a massive shuddering mess of violence. Each of the challengers had experience in battle, and most of them had fought each other at one point or another. They'd pummeled one another over their heads. They'd cracked bones. They'd knocked their friends senseless. Each of them had spent days and even weeks recovering from various injuries, wounds, and near-death experiences, and none of them was too eager to repeat it. As a result, even as they fought they had a certain amount of caution.

Lancelot had no such hindrance.

With his boundless confidence, fearless speed, and unfettered recklessness, Lancelot was a force of nature in the crowded, chaotic ring. He swung his wooden sword with all of his strength into the gaps in armor, knocking the air out of many men's stomachs. He would dodge a swing from a sword or a blunted ax and instead send it careening into another man's dented helmet. There was no one that Lancelot wouldn't attack. And he dared any of them to come back after him.

The crowd had never seen anything like it.

And they cheered like thunder for their new favored champion.

In record time, all of the combatants were down. Most of them were unconscious. A few were simply too broken to stand. One man claimed to be dead, although he shouted it in such a ringing voice that only a few people believed him. Lancelot alone remained standing. He raised his wooden sword in triumph, and everyone in attendance screamed with delight. Everyone except for Umberland, who stood off to the side with his jaw hanging wide with astonishment. He had lost a lot of gold on the cocky young man that the crowd loved so much.

A few moments later, dripping with sweat, Lancelot stood just outside the arena and met his now-adoring fans. They patted him on the shoulders, they ruffled his hair, they shook his hands. Some of the women, who were definitely too old for him, even eyed

Lancelot with clear interest. Lancelot grinned and winked back at them all and sent the young women rushing away in fits of giggles. However, the more people Lancelot met, the more disheartened he became. The gamblers counted their winnings, but no one offered a coin to their champion. The spectators finished the last of their food and drink, but none of them invited Lancelot to a feast. Even seasoned fighters who had just come for the show didn't seem inclined to welcome Lancelot into their confidences. It seemed like Lancelot was going to leave in the same position he arrived in until a gruff voice called to him:

"Get over here, lad."

Searching for the source of the voice, Lancelot turned and found a man with wild manes of shaggy hair on his head and face. The wild man beckoned Lancelot to join him on the far end of the arena, and as Lancelot approached, he took in the man's strange appearance. He wore dented, war-beaten armor that was painted with faded runes and foreign symbols. His long hair and beard were braided with talismans, trinkets, and what appeared to be a shark's tooth. Lancelot didn't know who this man was, but he felt certain that he was a man who had seen his share of the kind of adventures that Lancelot was hoping to see himself one day.

"Not bad, boy," said the wild man. "Not bad at all."

"What, you mean that minor skirmish? Oh, that was easy." Lancelot shrugged. "I've taken on knights twice as tough as them."

The man didn't bat an eyebrow. Clearly, the grizzled warrior didn't believe Lancelot's boast, but Lancelot couldn't help but push it as he asked, "Want to try your luck, old man?"

Lancelot took out his wooden sword once more, and squared up to fight. But the man just laughed.

"I'm not here to fight you, boy," he said with a disbelieving shake of his head that rattled the exotic beads woven into his beard. "I'm here to ask you a simple question: Is this really what you want?"

"Take a swing, and I'll show you," replied Lancelot. "Just like I showed those others."

With amazing speed and strength, and without a hint of warning, the man struck out and slapped Lancelot's wooden sword right out of his hands. Unfazed and defiant, Lancelot clenched his fists. He was still prepared for a fight.

The wild man didn't take the bait as he sighed and asked, "Do you really want to go down this road? You'll never be able to rest. You'll never be sure if today is your last day. Being a knight is a glorious life. But it's also a hard one. Always fighting. Always struggling."

"Always helping," pointed out Lancelot. "Goodness. Glory. Heroism."

"Pain. Death. Destruction."

"Sounds like just the job for the mighty Lancelot."

"The mighty Lancelot…" chuckled the man. "The one thing I can promise you is this: You won't always feel mighty. The life of a knight won't come easy. And it won't come for free. So I'll ask you again, boy, and let's try to answer the question this time; don't just give me boasts and quick wits: Are you sure this is what you want?"

"More than anything."

The wild man only nodded silently and fell into deep thought as if Lancelot had just given the most troubling answer possible.

"Who are you?" asked Lancelot quietly, after the grizzled knight had stood in silence for several long moments. "What court do you belong to?"

Grumbling slightly, the wild man dug into a pouch on his belt and drew out a small pendant.

"Sir Gawain," said the knight, slapping the pendant into Lancelot's hand. "Of the court of King Uther Pendragon."

Lancelot gasped as he took in the words and examined the pendant.

"Come see me when you're ready, lad," said Gawain. "I may be able to set you up with an apprenticeship."

"With you?" gaped Lancelot.

Gawain barked out a laugh. "Goodness no! I'd never be able to put up with a hot-head like you. We're far too much alike."

"Take me with you. I'm ready now," stated Lancelot firmly. "Can't I go back to Tintagel with you?"

"No," said Gawain simply. "You're a bit too young yet, anyhow. So, do me a favor: go out and see the kingdoms a bit. Have some adventures, such as they would be. Get roughed up. Get knocked down. Get into a few scrapes that you're not quite sure how you'll get out of. Make sure you understand what you're asking for."

And with that, Gawain turned to leave. Lancelot took in the experienced knight's words, and silently vowed to himself that he would prove himself beyond Gawain's wildest expectations. The only problem was, he still had no weapons, no gold, no food. Almost as if in answer, Gawain stopped and turned back to Lancelot.

"Oh, I almost forgot…" And Gawain drew the sword off of his hip and stabbed it into the ground at Lancelot's feet. "You'll be needing a proper sword, I expect."

Lancelot stared at the weapon in astonishment. Then, just as amazingly, Gawain took the leather pouch from his belt and tossed it to Lancelot. It jangled heavily with gold as Lancelot held it.

"What's this?" said Lancelot.

"Your winnings," said Gawain as he turned to leave once more. "I figured you were a good bet. Now, go and have your adventures. And I'll hope that I never see you again."

~ ~ ~

CHAPTER 5

A Welcome from Wildelions

In the many years after his meeting with Sir Gawain, Lancelot certainly would have his share of adventures. He learned to hunt by moonlight with the Cat-men who lived in the forests of Arden. He practiced tricks of the sword under the tutelage of ruthless assassins from the far east, and barely escaped with his life when they inevitably turned on him. At the age of twenty, much to Gawain's dismay, Lancelot arrived at Tintagel Castle and pledged his sword as a knight under King Uther Pendragon, and then Lancelot lost his arm for his trouble. He had even ridden into glorious battle on the back of the White Dragon.

And now, as a battered man of thirty, he was headed back to the land where he had had one of his earliest and most memorable adventures.

After leaving Avalon, with Nimue's warnings still ringing in his ears, Lancelot had travelled for over a week with little rest. He walked for two days and two nights to the seashore. He bartered passage upon a small ship. He struck a deal for a horse. He rode through forests and fields until he finally came upon a place that he hadn't seen since he was a young man.

At a steady trot, Lancelot beat a path toward the tiny kingdom of Corbenic. He hadn't thought that he'd ever return, but as the sunshine showered down upon him, and he traversed through wide fields of sprouting corn, wheat, and grain, Lancelot began to feel a certain comfort. Without even meaning to, a smile crept across Lancelot's face and he couldn't deny that it felt good to be here once more.

Until the wildelions came bounding at him.

Lancelot had seen his share of beasts in his many adventures, yet nothing compared to the pair of wildelions charging across the field straight in his direction. To begin with, they were absolutely massive, at least five times the size of a normal lion. Their fur seemed to be sloughing off in great clumps, as if they were shedding winter coats for the warmth of spring, and thick patches of hanging hair only added to their wild appearance. Their mouths bulged with saber-teeth that could be more accurately described as tusks, and the long, jagged fangs made the beasts seem all the more ferocious and hungry. Nonetheless, despite their intimidating appearance, Lancelot was ready to take them on.

His horse, however, was not.

As the wildelions sprinted across the field, they opened their massive jaws and each emitted a roar that could've knocked down a tree. The roars sounded more like the blasts from cannons with the prolonged resonance of a gong being struck. Lancelot's horse panicked at the sound and reared back onto its hind legs. Try as he might, Lancelot couldn't keep his seat, and he careened off of the horse and slammed to the ground with a painful crash. While Lancelot drew a deep, strained breath, his horse charged off and left

Lancelot to face the hungry beasts on his own. Quickly rising to his feet, Lancelot watched the wildelions cutting across the wide field in a few mere pounces. They'd clear the distance and bear down on him in no time at all.

He suddenly wished he had insisted a bit more strongly on bringing his sword.

"It wouldn't be fighting…" Lancelot assured himself. "I would just be surviving…"

The massive paws pounded upon the earth. They'd reach him any moment now.

Lancelot planted his feet and prepared to engage them.

They were seconds away from reaching him.

He looked from one to the next. It was easy to dodge one beast. Two was another story.

They opened their mouths and bared their teeth.

Lancelot gritted his jaw.

And the wildelions pounced.

With all of the speed and agility he could muster, Lancelot dove and rolled out of the beasts' paths. He just barely avoided the swipe from a massive claw before a hind leg struck out at him. In a flash, Lancelot twisted and leapt again as he narrowly stayed out of the way of a jutting fang. Again and again, the two wildelions sprang and bit and slashed, and each time, Lancelot was just able get out of their way. Nonetheless, as tireless as Lancelot was, he knew that he could only keep up this dance for so long. His mind raced through its options. If he had a weapon, he would've tried to slay the wildelions, but that wasn't the case. There was no shelter in sight, and it was unlikely that Lancelot could've outrun the animals to it anyway. And it was looking more and more likely that Lancelot would slip up before these predators did. Just as the merest suggestion of despair crossed Lancelot's mind, he heard a soft, polite voice call out:

"Would you mind terribly if I gave you some help?"

As Lancelot ducked out of the way of another swipe from a heavy paw, he saw that a young boy, who couldn't have been older than thirteen, stood some twenty feet away. He clutched a leather bag in his hands, yet seemed to be trying to maintain a respectful distance as Lancelot fought for his life.

"Get out of here, boy!" shouted Lancelot. "Save yourself!"

"Oh, they can't hurt me," said the boy.

"What?!" cried Lancelot, with little time for confusion at this unusual pronouncement as he ducked another pounce from one of the wildelions.

"But I could distract them, if you'd like?" said the boy with utmost sincerity.

"They'll eat you alive!" warned Lancelot.

"I don't mean to argue, but don't you think you stand a better chance with some friendly assistance?"

"Go!" insisted Lancelot as one of the wildelions whipped him with its tail and sent him spinning to the ground.

As Lancelot stumbled, the boy sprung into action. With incredible speed, the boy sprinted closer and seemed intent on joining the fray as he stated simply, "I beg of you not to be mad at me, but I think I had better lend a hand!"

In the blink of an eye, the boy dove and rolled into the midst of Lancelot and the two wildelions. It immediately proved to be helpful as the wildelions, who had been ready to feast upon Lancelot, now seemed uncertain which prey to go after. In the brief moment it took Lancelot to regain his balance, he marveled at the agility and grace with which the boy moved. He could've been a cat himself as he bounded between Lancelot and the two wildelions. With complete ease, the boy pushed off of Lancelot's shoulder and leapfrogged high into the air, performed a perfect mid-air flip, landed lightly upon the ground and dashed off again.

The wildelions seemed as bewildered as Lancelot.

As they all took stock, the boy shouted, "Please, get ready to run! That is, if you don't mind?"

"No," said Lancelot, still a little confused. "Whatever you say, boy..."

The boy ripped open his leather bag, dug a hand in, and produced a large bloody hunk of meat. He flung it high into the air.

And the wildelions both leapt for it.

"Run!" yelled the boy as the wildelions snapped their monstrous jaws at the bait. "I mean, if that's still agreeable to you."

Still trying to make sense of things, Lancelot watched the boy tear off across the field, and Lancelot immediately chased after him. Once more, he had a hard time believing the boy's quickness. It had been a long time since Lancelot lost a foot race, but it was looking like today he would have to concede. Nonetheless, Lancelot sprinted after the boy, and they both pumped their legs with furious determination.

"Who are you?" asked Lancelot, panting slightly, as he ran in the boy's wake.

"Not to be rude," said the boy, and Lancelot was surprised to notice the boy wasn't even a little out of breath despite his impressive pace, "but we don't have much time."

Sure enough, at that moment, a furious roar erupted from behind them.

The wildelions had finished their morsel, and, their appetites far from satiated, were now resuming their hunt of Lancelot and the boy. As quick as Lancelot and the boy were, they still only had two legs, and they were no match for massive four-legged beasts. With several long bounding strides, the wildelions cut the distance in their pursuit. Lancelot added a burst of speed, and the boy kept up without any problems. The wildelions were nearly upon them, but they had reached the edge of a downward sloping hill. The beasts sprang in a final pounce.

"Jump!" called the boy, and quickly added, "Please!"

The boy dove, and Lancelot followed his lead. The grizzled knight and the young boy fell into a small dugout hole in the side of the hill and the wildelions overshot them. Lancelot scrambled around in the hole, and tried to prepare for the wildelions' next attack.

But he didn't need to worry.

The wildelions had already forgotten all about him.

Down the short hill, a herd of cattle was grazing amongst a wild patch of clover, and the wildelions charged straight for them. The cattle tried to scatter, but it was no use. The wildelions were too quick and too vicious and too hungry. The hunt was over in no time.

Emerging from their hiding spot, Lancelot watched the carnage in the meadow below.

"Should we help the cows?" asked Lancelot.

"How?" asked the boy with just a hint of sadness in his voice.

As the wildelions rampaged, Lancelot knew the boy was right. There was nothing that could be done. Not without weapons. Not without risking their own lives.

"The wildelions will eat a dozen or so of them," stated the boy. "And then they'll go to sleep again for about another month. Everyone will be safe until then."

Lancelot turned to the boy and asked, "And then what?"

"And then I'll lead them away again. Just like I always do," said the boy with a shrug. "Is that bad?"

For the first time, Lancelot was able to properly appraise the boy. He wasn't terribly tall, even for his age, but he was thin as a reed. An unruly mop of curls flopped just above his round, slightly dimpled cheeks. There was nothing imposing or remarkable about the boy, and yet Lancelot had just seen that he could unmistakably take care of himself. The most unbelievable thing of all was that the boy didn't seem to have a scratch on him, smooth and unblemished despite the dangers that he claimed to constantly be facing.

"Why do you do this?" asked Lancelot. "Why risk your life like this?"

"It's the right thing to do," said the boy without pausing. "Isn't it?"

Lancelot nodded. "I suppose I can't argue with that."

The grizzled, maimed knight shared a smile with the strange, unblemished boy, and then with a quick courteous nod, the boy said, "Well, please don't consider this rude, but I really should be going."

And with his dazzling quickness, the boy darted away.

"Wait! Who are you?" shouted Lancelot as the boy sprinted off. "What's your name?!"

"Galahad!" called the youth over his shoulder, without breaking his stride, and within moments he disappeared back into the trees and was gone.

~ ~ ~

CHAPTER 6

Waterfalls and Hot Springs

Lancelot had found his horse cowering amongst the trees, and truth be told, Lancelot couldn't blame the shaken animal. He ran his fingers many times through the horse's bristling mane until it calmed enough to follow.

Still smarting from his unusual encounters with the wildelions and with Galahad, Lancelot was happy to simply lead his horse by the reins along a narrow dirt path down a forest trail. After a short journey, they came to a small babbling stream. Pausing to rest, Lancelot allowed his shaken horse to duck its head and drink from the clear bubbling waters. Once again, Lancelot gently stroked the horse's back. Lancelot could tell that the animal's heart was still beating furiously in fear, and so Lancelot gave it a gentle, soothing pat on its flank.

"Drink deeply, my friend. Cool yourself and relax," said Lancelot. Then he took a few steps along the stream as he muttered to himself, "Enjoy it while you can... who knows what else we might come across."

Walking against the flow of the creek, Lancelot followed the snaking waters through the forest. Now that he had arrived back in Corbenic, Lancelot knew that he was approaching his destination and he felt that he should explore more fully. As he walked,

Lancelot heard the strengthening of water up ahead. For several minutes, he followed the noise of the water, and finally he emerged through a clump of trees to find a towering waterfall gently cascading over a cliff face down into a large pool amongst the rocks. The pool was wide and deep enough to swim in. It had several large flat rocks that created small islands on the surface of the water.

And in the center of the pool, barely disturbing the serene waters, a beautiful naked woman was swimming.

From the tree line, Lancelot watched her gently paddling through the calm waters. He couldn't help but be entranced as she emerged onto one of the largest rock islands in the middle of the pool and began to wring out her wet hair. She stood naked and comfortable without a hint of abashment as she lightly stretched her back and arms. Quietly, Lancelot turned to leave so as not to disturb her privacy, but—

SPLASH!

Lancelot slipped on a slick rock, and his foot dunked into the creek.

In a flash, the woman spun around and spotted Lancelot. Shock and surprise flashed across her face, but not a hint of embarrassment, and she didn't even think to grab anything to cover herself. Instead, she squinted slightly and stared with apparent astonishment as she cried out:

"Lancelot?!"

"Hello, Elaine."

Sheepishly, Lancelot stayed rooted in his spot along the edge of the pool and raised his left hand in a meager wave. Elaine didn't return the gesture as she angrily put her hands on her full and lovely hips.

"What are you doing here?!" she shouted from her stone island, her voice lilting slightly with her foreign accent.

"Don't you want to...?"

Lancelot trailed off as he became uncommonly soft-spoken. It was Elaine who raised her voice.

"Excuse me? I cannot hear you," called Elaine. "Would you mind speaking up?!"

"Don't you want to...?" Lancelot trailed off again at first, but finally spoke up loudly enough to be heard over the waterfall and the distance. "Don't you want to cover up?!"

"What?!" cried Elaine, and then as if she finally noticed her nakedness, she sighed. "Oh, for goodness sake... All right..."

More out of propriety than embarrassment, Elaine picked up a thin robe that lay crumpled upon her stone island and began pulling it on.

"You never did know a good thing when you saw it..." said Elaine under her breath.

"What was that?" called Lancelot.

"I said," shouted Elaine clearly, "you never did know a good thing when you saw it!"

Lancelot pointed his gaze away respectfully, and once Elaine had tied her robe shut, she called out to him once more.

"Well? Would you care to let me know what you are doing here?" asked Elaine as she once again placed her hands on her hips.

"I'm here... to save you..." said Lancelot, rather lamely.

Elaine cocked an eyebrow at him.

"I had a hard time hearing you again. Would you care to repeat that?"

After a moment of hesitation, Lancelot began, "It's rather an interesting story. You see, I had a vision of you —"

"Oh wonderful..." cut in Elaine. "The mighty Lancelot has had another vision..."

"It's not like last time!" said Lancelot. "This was a literal vision. Of you. In danger. Terrible, terrible danger."

"From where I'm standing, it looks as though you might have been hit over the head one too many times since last I saw you. Are you sure it was a vision? Not a hallucination?"

"I'm perfectly fine in the head, I assure you. I was just... I was concerned about you. I wanted to check that you were all right is all."

"Thank you for your concern. As you can see, I am perfectly all right!"

Which was when the first boiling bubble rose and burst upon the surface of the pool.

Instantly, both Lancelot and Elaine surveyed the waters. The edges of the pool had begun to sizzle, and within moments more and larger bubbles formed and burst all along the surface. The pool churned and roiled, and quickly steam wafted from the once-cool water. Now on alert, Lancelot stooped and held his hand out to the water. A bubble burst and sprayed him with scalding water, and he wrenched his hand away quickly. The water fell onto the rocks and hissed along the edges of the pond.

"Did you do this?!" demanded Elaine. "Just so you could play the hero?!"

"I can't make water boil, Elaine!"

Elaine inched toward the edge of her stone island, but the boiling water splashed menacingly at her. She leapt back, trying to shield her bare toes from being scalded.

"Would you care for some assistance?" called Lancelot, a little more pompously than he probably should have considering the danger.

"What? Are you going to fight the hot water?"

"Actually, I recently made a vow not to fight anymore."

"How convenient for me!"

"But this wouldn't be fighting," insisted Lancelot. "This would be rescuing. Shall I?"

"Oh, of course I would like you to rescue me!" Elaine shouted back, with a little more exasperation than she probably would've used on anyone but Lancelot. "Just because I don't like you, doesn't mean I am a fool!"

"Fair enough," muttered Lancelot, and he leapt into action.

In his years as a knight, ever since his first melee, Lancelot had learned to quickly take stock of his situation before doing anything too brash. As his eyes darted around the pool and watched as the boiling water rose higher and higher, Lancelot realized he didn't have much time. The hotter things became the sooner they would overtake even the few stones that rose above the surface. Lancelot charted a course from his bank to Elaine's island, and he quickly determined a clear path of stones. With smooth deft skips, Lancelot bounded from one stone to the next. More than once he nearly stumbled and tipped into the boiling waters, and it became clear that he had no room for error. Lancelot set his face with calm determination, and steadily moved from one stone to the next, until he finally made it into the middle of the boiling pool. Standing alongside Elaine on the rapidly heating stone island, Lancelot gave the lady a small respectful nod of the head.

"It's nice to see you again, Elaine," said Lancelot.

"Yes, yes, you too," said Elaine quickly. "Don't you think we should be going now?"

"Do you mind if I—?" And Lancelot mimicked lifting Elaine up in his arms.

"Suddenly so bashful," said Elaine in mock surprise. "There was a time when you never would've asked."

"I'm doing my best to show you that I've changed," said Lancelot.

Not bothering to give a response, Elaine slung her arm over Lancelot's shoulder and lifted her legs to allow him to scoop her up into his powerful left arm. For the first time, she seemed to take in the extent of his many injuries, and she noticed that while Lancelot's left arm supported her from beneath, the right arm that steadied her from behind the back came up short just beneath the elbow.

"You truly have changed…"

"Don't worry about that. It's nothing," said Lancelot as he hoisted Elaine up into his strong arms. "Ready?"

Elaine nodded.

"Right then. Hold on tight."

Once again, Lancelot leapt from stone to stone across the boiling waters. Near the halfway point, he landed uneasily on a narrow rock, and began to wobble precariously and tip nearly to the edge of the boiling pool. With a supreme effort, Lancelot wrenched himself upright and regained his balance. Elaine gasped at the near miss, and looked down to see that boiling water was now splashing around Lancelot's feet. Lancelot grimaced, but didn't say a word of complaint from the overwhelming heat.

"Look, you've been very noble," said Elaine as she prepared herself for the worst. "You don't have to do this for me."

"Just… getting… my… balance…" said Lancelot through gritted teeth.

And then he leapt again to the next rock. And the next. And the next. And the next.

Finally, after several more close calls, they made it back to the edge of the pool. Lancelot placed Elaine back upon the ground and they both distanced themselves from the searing water. They stood in awkward silence amongst the trees for a long moment, until Elaine finally said with a softness that had eluded her thus far:

"Thank you, Lancelot."

"You're very welcome, Elaine," said Lancelot, and then he added quietly, "It's nice to see you again."

"You as well," she said with surprising tenderness.

Lancelot's eyes looked away, and he found himself oddly struggling with that feeling of being a young boy unable to quite make eye contact with the beautiful girl that he liked. Finally, he sputtered, "I have a horse! Somewhere... Would you like a ride back to your castle?"

Elaine shrugged and extended her hand to Lancelot. He took it and began to guide her through the trees. They had only walked a short distance when Elaine said in a tone that was nearly impossible to read, but which caused Lancelot's insides to contract:

"I'm sure my father would love to see you."

~ ~ ~

CHAPTER 7

Corbenic Castle

Seated awkwardly together on the back of the single horse, but looking as if they were both doing their best to touch each other as little as possible, Lancelot and Elaine rode along a small dirt path. It emerged out of the forest and into the distant edge of a large golden field of wheat. Following the rocky path, Lancelot continued toward a tiny castle off in the distance.

"So are you planning on staying around for a while?" Elaine asked, with an attempt at sounding casual, as they jostled along.

"Trying to get rid of me already?" said Lancelot, pretending to be offended.

"Of course I am," admitted Elaine.

"But I came a long way to see you!" blurted Lancelot, starting to feel genuinely offended.

"A long way?! From what I've heard, you're not the one to complain about long adventures and grand distances. Besides, unless the stories I've heard are exaggerated, which wouldn't surprise me in the least, you have a White Dragon to ride, do you not? Why didn't you just bring it here?"

Lancelot gritted his jaw so tightly that a vein bulged along his left temple. He was getting sick of being asked about the White Dragon.

"Word of your *'greatness'* has even reached these distant lands," continued Elaine. "You weren't kidding when you left. You have certainly have made quite a name for yourself."

"A lot can happen in thirteen years."

"Yes, it can. For you…"

"I never forgot about you, Elaine," Lancelot said softly. "That's why I've come. I had to see that you were all right. And I promise you that I will stay as long as I have to in order to make sure that's the case."

Elaine sighed, although there was a slight reddening of her ears at Lancelot's words. "And I promise you that you don't have to stay, you brave buffoon. Everything here is wonderful. This kingdom is wonderful. My life has been wonderful."

"Wonderful," agreed Lancelot. "Mine too."

"Glad to hear it," Elaine said.

"In fact, I couldn't be better!"

"Neither could I."

"It's true, I did nearly die a few *dozen* times," said Lancelot, dropping his voice ever so slightly. "But that's to be expected for a great knight!"

"And I've had a frustrating run of suitors," Elaine admitted with a dismissive shrug of her shoulders. "But that too is expected for a princess."

"If you'd like, I'd be happy to rough them up a bit for you," offered Lancelot.

"Oh, that wouldn't do much good. They're already dead."

Lancelot gaped at her in surprise. *"They're dead?!"*

Elaine winced. She clearly hadn't meant to let that slip.

"All right... You win," said Elaine with a sullen frown. "Our kingdom's been overrun with monsters. They've been rampaging through our villages and killing our people, including anyone foolish enough to become close to me. Happy?"

"Really? Monsters?!" said Lancelot with wide eyes, and then a smile broke out across his chiseled features. "Sounds fun!"

~ ~ ~

The kingdom of Corbenic was only a kingdom by the loosest of standards.

In actuality, it was more like a collection of farms with a small village or two mixed in. If anyone had bothered to count, they would have probably discovered that there was more livestock than people making up the inhabitants of the small kingdom. Nonetheless, the dozen or so farms stood united around the wise old King Pelles and his modest but mighty castle.

It wasn't always that way, though.

Just sixty years earlier, all of the farms stood alone, scraping their way along in almost complete isolation from one another. It was a disaster. One farmer could successfully grow a field full of wheat, but he couldn't tell the difference between a cow and a chicken to save his own life. Another farmer had mastered irrigation, but it didn't matter because he didn't know how to properly seed his own fields. Yet another could build the best farmhouses, but couldn't seem to understand why he shouldn't grow fruit trees inside of them. Worse of all, as farmers are prone to be, they were all too stubborn to seek the assistance of each other.

Until Pelles came along.

The young industrious man was the son of a farmer himself, but his father, while an expert at tilling the soil, couldn't manage to grow anything besides root vegetables. By the time Pelles was fifteen, he'd eaten so many potatoes, carrots, beets and turnips that he feared he would soon start sprouting roots from his feet and vines from his head. So he began sneaking onto the other nearby farms to try and learn their secrets. He learned how to tend to the animals. He gleaned information on growing wheat and corn. Most important of all, Pelles discovered that if all of the farms could simply work together, they might all prosper and have a chance to lead richer, fuller lives. With some smooth talking, Pelles managed to gather all of the families and laid out his brilliant plan. He was laughed out of the room.

The other farmers simply wouldn't take him seriously.

So Pelles built a castle.

The young man realized that he needed a greater authority to get the other farmers to listen to his grand scheme. So over the next two years, with every spare moment he could find, Pelles set about scouring the fields and forests for any stone he could lay his hands upon. Slowly but surely, he built up a modest castle that put every other home in the lands of Corbenic to shame. Once he was done with that, he dug a wide moat one shovelful at a time. When he gathered the other farmers once more, they were much more interested in listening, because things simply sound more intelligent when they come from someone who lives in a castle.

Thus began a great age of prosperity for all of the people who lived in those parts. The dozen or so farms all worked in harmony and shared their various bounties and different areas of expertise. Everyone was fed and healthy, and eventually a few small villages even sprang up nearby and populated themselves with blacksmiths, seamstresses, and merchants who were interested in dealing with the successful farming community. Unfortunately, the growth and riches also attracted the attention of rival lords who wished to take the newfound food, drink, and gold for themselves. Pelles, who was now nearing thirty, rode out to face any challenger who wished to conquer his and his friends' lands. He was remarkably strong, as anyone would be who had built a castle with their bare hands, but the greedy villains weren't impressed and all vowed to kill him and take what they wanted anyway.

The rival lords simply wouldn't take him seriously.

So Pelles raised an army.

Riding from one farm to the next and through each of the small villages, Pelles gathered every able-bodied man he could find, and even a few who were of questionable use. He scrounged up steel and wood so that he could fashion swords and shields for all of them. Finally, he trained tirelessly with each and every one of them until his small fighting force became feared and respected for miles around. With Pelles riding at the front, the small Corbenic army threw out anyone who tried to conquer them, and they easily dispersed any invaders. They ran out any raiders. They massacred any marauders. And they peacefully went back to their farms.

The prestige and reputation of Corbenic spread until the community was known even by distant lords and ladies. The name of Pelles had also preceded him, and it carried a great respect by all who spoke of him. Nonetheless, when it became necessary for Pelles to visit neighboring kingdoms to request supplies and to forge new trading alliances, the rulers of those lands would look down on Pelles for his calloused hands and dirty fingernails, and they quickly showed him the door.

The nearby kings simply wouldn't take him seriously.

So Pelles found a queen.

By this time, Pelles was nearing fifty, but he was handsome and rugged from his decades of hard work and battle. More than a few princesses would have happily accepted his offer for marriage, but Pelles wanted the most exotic lady he could find. He sailed across the seas and quested into distant foreign lands. Finally, he arrived on the ancient islands where civilization began and he found a breathtakingly beautiful princess with olive skin and exquisite curls. Pelles brought her back to Corbenic, and all who met her were entranced by her kindness and foreign charm. Simply being married to a woman of that caliber lent Pelles an air of refinement that he never could've managed from toiling in the fields. Finally, the other kings and lords were willing to do business with Pelles. And people were no longer dismissing Corbenic as a little farming community.

With a castle, an army, and a queen, it was undeniable that Corbenic had become a kingdom. And Pelles had become a king.

The problem was that Corbenic was a kingdom that had been almost entirely built on the shoulders of King Pelles. The farmlands flourished beautifully. The trade partnerships produced ample wealth and prosperity. The army maintained order and peace. The queen shined grace and respectability. However, without King Pelles at the center of it all, it would all easily have come crashing down. Unfortunately, producing an heir turned out to be the one task that Pelles couldn't seem to manage. His beautiful queen quickly gave him a daughter, and all of the citizens of Corbenic adored the new princess, Elaine. Yet try as they might, for many years after, King Pelles and his queen couldn't conceive another child. It seemed that Elaine's birth had left the queen unable to bear anymore children, and Pelles's vigor was finally starting to fail him. The citizens of Corbenic continued to dote upon the young princess, but a daughter just wasn't the same as a son. And the sad truth was, the years were brutally piling up upon Pelles, and he had no prospects to sire himself a prince.

The ravages of age simply wouldn't take him seriously.

And Pelles became an old man.

Over the course of a few years, his wife passed away from illness. His once prodigious strength faded. His clear-eyed leadership dimmed.

And then the monsters came.

The beasts flowed in from all corners of the world and dug out habitats throughout the tiny kingdom. Many men tried over the years to drive the creatures away, and so defend the glory of Corbenic, but they all met their demise at the hands or teeth of one of the vicious creatures. And poor old King Pelles could only sit and watch as the kingdom he had worked so hard to build teetered on the verge of collapse.

The monsters simply didn't take an old man seriously.

Until Lancelot came to the rescue.

More than six decades had passed since Pelles had united those first farms through the sheer force of his own will when Lancelot followed Elaine into the modest throne room where they found the once mighty King Pelles peacefully snoozing in his well-cushioned throne. It was fairly adorable. There had been a time when King Pelles was a paragon of strength and vitality. Now, he was an ancient man, hunched over by the years and toils. He had less hair on his head than he would've liked, and more coming out of his ears than he would have chosen.

Elaine delicately approached the throne and softly cleared her throat as she said, "Father?"

"Hmmm…" he grunted, and it was clear that he had woken up although his eyelids were still struggling to catch up to his mind. "What's that? Where am I?"

Finally, the old king pried his eyes open, and it seemed to take him a moment to recognize his own daughter. He shook his head to disperse the sleepiness, and his thin crown slid sideways on his rumpled white hair.

"Ah, Elaine, my dear!" he said, straightening himself up in his seat, and then he cleared his throat as if to give the impression that he hadn't been asleep at all. "I've heard everything you've just said. And I will give it due consideration, before I give you my final judgement. Let me mull it over and let us speak no more of it at this time."

"Very good, Father," Elaine said with a slight smirk, clearly unwilling to embarrass her father. Then she gestured to Lancelot and added, "In the meantime, allow me to present Sir Lancelot."

Once again, King Pelles seemed befuddled by confusion, but his eyes locked on the tall, rugged knight who stood a few mere feet in front of him.

"...you can't be serious..."

But after a moment of astonished examination, King Pelles's long beard rose along the edges of his mouth and he broke into a wide grin. A small laugh escaped his lips, and King Pelles reached out his thin hands and pulled Lancelot into a tight hug. Lancelot seemed shocked at the unexpected embrace, and Elaine couldn't help but look on with a smile.

"The mighty Sir Lancelot!" King Pelles croaked happily. "Bless my soul! It's wonderful to have such a mighty presence in my humble castle."

"It warms my heart to be in your kingdom, King Pelles," said Lancelot, and then he snuck a knowing glance at Elaine before adding, "For the first time."

King Pelles squinted and once again took in Lancelot's scarred and wounded appearance. The old man's eyes lingered for a long moment on Lancelot's right arm.

"I must say, though, it seems like there's less of you than I would've imagined," remarked the old king.

"I've had many great adventures and fought many valiant battles." Lancelot shrugged. "It doesn't come without a price."

"Oho! I know that well," said Pelles with a delighted grin as he puffed up his frail body, and rearranged a soft pillow so that he could sit straighter upon his tall throne. He leaned forward to whisper conspiratorially to Lancelot, "It's been a long time now, my boy, but in my youth I too had my share of trials, tribulations and triumphs."

"I have no doubt, my lord."

The old king beamed at Lancelot and seemed to sit a little taller. But Lancelot also noticed that Pelles was already breathing a little heavily. Just the simple effort of boasting was taking it out of the old king. Nonetheless, King Pelles smiled warmly at Lancelot.

"I was once very much like you, my lad," said Pelles wistfully. "I know, it's hard to believe now. But it comforts me to have someone of your stature around. I hope you like my kingdom."

"I'm sure I will, sire," said Lancelot. "It's a beautiful place you've built. I look forward to exploring it further."

It was King Pelles's turn to shoot Elaine a knowing wink as he said, "Yes, that would be wonderful. Who knows? There may be a place for you here."

Lancelot and Elaine exchanged a glance and smirk. Clearly King Pelles didn't know the half of it.

"Your daughter was telling me all about the problems you're having here in Corbenic," said Lancelot. "Ogres, trolls, and wildelions running wild all over the place."

"Yes, yes, a nasty business."

"I thought perhaps I could help with that, my lord. And slay every last one of them for you."

Elaine's eyes went wide with surprise, and she coughed slightly as she said, "You mean you're staying?!"

Lancelot just winked at her.

"Yes, yes!" cried Pelles in an excitement that quickly got the better of him. He hiccuped and wheezed for a moment, before saying, "We could really use your help. Oh, yes! And the help of that White Dragon of yours! Say... Where's it gotten to?"

Lancelot gritted his teeth again as he thought, *Would people give it a rest with the dragon?!*

"I don't think it'll come to needing the White Dragon," he said in his best attempt to sound dismissive.

"I don't think it'll come to needing you at all, Lancelot," cut in Elaine. "It's very kind of you to offer, but you can be on your way."

"Nonsense!" said Pelles, cutting in himself. "How often do we have a true hero at our disposal?"

87

LANCELOT OF THE LAKE

"Unfortunately, Lancelot recently informed me that he made a vow never to fight again," said Elaine, doing her best to sound disappointed. Then she turned to Lancelot. "But thank you for visiting, Sir Lancelot. I guess you cannot help us. Too bad..."

"Of course I can help!" laughed Lancelot.

"But you made a vow!"

"I won't be fighting!" said Lancelot. "I'll be protecting."

King Pelles grinned. His eyes twinkled with joy as he looked upon the undeniable youth and vigor of Lancelot. But even as Pelles's eyes sparkled, his eyelids began to droop over them.

"Wonderful! It's... settled then! It all sounds wonderful... Very wonderful... Most... perfectly... wonder…"

And King Pelles's head slumped softly as he fell asleep once more.

Lancelot was a little taken aback by the king's unexpected napping, but he shrugged it off with a good-natured smirk. He turned to look at Elaine, and saw that her face was far from sharing the amusement. Without saying a word, Elaine locked eyes with Lancelot, then beckoned for him to follow her from the throne room.

"But what about your father?" asked Lancelot.

Elaine just waved a careless hand. "It happens all the time…"

Then she stormed out of the room in a way that made it clear that she expected Lancelot to follow.

Moments later, Elaine led Lancelot into a secluded hallway, and they had barely rounded the corner when she spun on him with a fury in her eyes.

"Just what exactly do you think you are doing?!"

"You said you had monsters," said Lancelot. "And it so happens that I'm very good at killing monsters. It seems like an easy match."

"My father and I do not need you here."

"From the way your father welcomed me with open arms, I guess he doesn't know about my last visit?"

"Don't flatter yourself," huffed Elaine, but there was a slight redness around her ears again. "There have been many men since you left."

"Many?!" sputtered Lancelot.

"Many."

"Well... All right then... There have been many women too."

"Who asked?!" shouted Elaine. And with that, she turned and stormed off, and left the usually unflappable Lancelot bewildered and at a complete loss for words.

~ ~ ~

CHAPTER 8

Plucking Wild Roses

Of course, it wasn't the first time Lancelot had been bewildered by Elaine.

And it certainly wasn't the first time she had left him at a loss for words.

It had been thirteen years since a much younger Lancelot had stumbled into Corbenic for the first time. Literally stumbled. In the two years since he had won Umberland's challenge and met Sir Gawain, young Lancelot had seen things that most grown men could only dream of. He had trekked north with fur traders who rode on sleds pulled by dogs. He had learned new skills with a sword at the hands of travelling samurai. He had even taken a short but thrilling ride on the back of a wild winged horse that had gotten lost in its migrations from Olympus. All in all, Lancelot had embraced the kinds of adventures that he had dreamed about from his earliest days as he sat with his books.

But even the greatest crusaders have to eat.

And Lancelot had been having some trouble on that front lately.

Being on the road, travelling from kingdom to wildland to seashore, didn't provide the most reliable food sources. At sixteen years old, Lancelot had grown into a tall, strong young man. He had reached his full height, and his strength had grown almost to its fullest extent. However, he often was hungry. He often lay awake at nights as his stomach growled for food. He often had to get by with handfuls of wild mushrooms or even just boiled roots.

When he heard about a kingdom of farmlands, it was like a dream come true.

So on the verge of starvation, Lancelot entered into the bountiful lands of Corbenic. At first he darted carefully from one farm to the next, and took only snatches of food here and there. He only intended to stay in Corbenic long enough to replenish his strength, and then he would venture back out onto the open roads.

Then Lancelot heard about the treasure housed in the center of Corbenic Castle.

The riches that were contained within the modest castle seized upon Lancelot's imagination, and he could barely slow his feet from journeying there. In the past few years, Lancelot had been within reach of mountains of gold and priceless ancient artifacts, but in his present condition, the bounties contained in Corbenic Castle held far more appeal than anything he'd heard of before.

In the still of the night, Lancelot crept toward the castle that was situated in the middle of the many farms. As the guards changed posts, Lancelot slipped over the drawbridge and in through the gates. With deft quietness, Lancelot navigated the deserted hallways. He trained his ears, eyes, and nose to lead him toward his desired goal. Finally, he emerged into the cool night air beneath a blanket of stars and laid eyes upon his treasure.

A garden.

The lovely place was lush and overgrown with a decadent assortment of fruits and vegetables from all over the world that made Lancelot's mouth water just from the sight of it.

Lancelot couldn't help himself as he attacked a collection of leafy greens and succulent tomatoes. Even when he had taken crops from nearby farms over the past few weeks, it had been nothing like this. The fresh, ripe vegetables burst with sweetness that was made all the more exquisite by Lancelot's immense hunger. In a matter of minutes, he devoured a cucumber, two onions, several handfuls of lettuce, and an entire eggplant. He had just wrenched a carrot out of the dirt and taken a generous bite when a soft voice demanded of him:

"And just what do you think are you doing in *my* garden?"

Tossing aside the half-eaten carrot, Lancelot spun around and did his best to not look guilty. His eyes locked upon Elaine for the first time, and even in her nightgown with her hair haphazardly pulled up into a bun, Lancelot was stunned by her beauty.

"I wasn't stealing anything!" he cried.

"Really? The seeds and juices dripping down your front seem to tell a different story," said Elaine as she fixed a stern gaze upon Lancelot.

Lancelot brushed at his shirt but mostly just managed to smear the dirt and juices further. He lowered his eyes and said, "I'm sorry, m'lady. I wouldn't have taken it if I had known it was yours."

"But you would've happily stolen it if you thought it was someone else's?"

Sputtering slightly, Lancelot opened his mouth to respond, and the best he could come up with was, "I didn't mean to steal. From you or anyone else. Please believe me. I would never do anything to offend a lady. I hope to be a proper knight one day!"

"Is this the training for knighthood now? Climbing over castle walls, and digging through princess's gardens?"

"No… I… It was just that… I was hungry… and… I made a mistake, m'lady. I beg your forgiveness." In simple supplication, Lancelot dropped to one knee and bowed his head to the lovely young woman with her strange accent. Lancelot said, "I place myself at your mercy."

Elaine strode forward and appraised Lancelot, but then her lips split into a smile and she laughed, "I was merely playing with you. Of course, you are forgiven. There is no harm done. There's more than enough food here to share, and you look positively famished."

Lancelot looked up at her in surprise, and they locked eyes for the first time. In the pale moonlight, their gazes sparkled and they had to struggle to look away from each other.

"Please, eat," she said softly.

"You're sure?" Lancelot said, not daring to move without her permission.

"Of course," Elaine said as she plucked an apple from a nearby tree and offered it to Lancelot. "If you wish to be a knight one day, then I daresay you will have to keep up your strength. It would be my honor to help you in your quest."

Gratefully taking the apple and biting into it with relish, Lancelot said, "Thank you, m'lady," and once again he dug a carrot from the ground, brushed it off, and began to eat.

As Lancelot filled his belly, Elaine watched the young man with equal hunger. Even at his relatively young age, Lancelot was tall and handsome, but that wasn't what intrigued Elaine. She could tell just by looking at him that he had travelled far and wide, and there was a pure wildness about him that enchanted her.

"Here," she said, holding out a strange off-white vegetable with long twisting roots. "Try the kohlrabi."

Lancelot took it, and bit off one of the crisp juicy stems. Favor flooded his tastebuds as he chewed upon the exotic plant, but he examined it with apparent amazement.

"I've never seen food like you've got in this garden," he observed as he took another bite.

"My father is a great lover of the soil," said Elaine. "He's imported seeds from all over the world to grow. The soil here has been carefully cultivated so that it might support any vegetable or flower. His desire is that any foreign transplant might flourish here." Then she added with a hint of sadness, "Even me."

She quickly waved a dismissive hand even as Lancelot shot her a confused glance. She shook her head as if she was being silly, and then addressed Lancelot, "What is your name, brave sir knight?"

"Sir Lancelot," he said, and then quickly corrected himself, "I mean, just Lancelot."

"I'm sure it will be *'sir'* very soon," Elaine said with a sparkle in her eye. "In any case, Lancelot, I can tell you're very hungry. And that cannot do in your quest to become a knight. So I propose a bargain. If you will help me, then I will happily give you all the food you can carry."

"You would do that for me?"

"I am the princess of this castle. This garden was made for me. I can do whatever I wish with it," said Elaine. "But I must ask for something in return."

Once again, a confused look crossed Lancelot's face, but Elaine simply smiled.

"You are a knight, correct?"

Lancelot nodded uncertainly. "I am. Or at least I will be. I believe I have the heart of a knight."

"Wonderful," said Elaine. "Then I need you to take me on a quest."

~ ~ ~

A short time later, Lancelot and Elaine crept up to the edge of the moat that surrounded Corbenic Castle. Lancelot had suggested that the best way to exit the castle was across the drawbridge, but Elaine had quickly dismissed that idea. It was far too likely that they would be caught, she had argued.

"However, water is brought in daily for the plants," she said as she led Lancelot to a small wooden door in the stone garden wall.

The door was hidden behind several large blueberry bushes. Elaine pushed the wooden door open and said with a smile, "And where the water can get in, we can get out."

Just beyond the door was the edge of the castle moat, but Lancelot still wasn't convinced.

"We can't go this way," he protested. "Come on, I'm certain I can get us through the castle hallways undetected."

"Oh, don't be silly..."

And without another word, Elaine dove into the water. A moment later, her head broke the surface, and she quietly paddled in the shimmering surface of the water. She giggled and waved for Lancelot to join her.

"Well, come on then!" she called after spitting out a mouthful of water.

Duty-bound as a hired knight, Lancelot dove in after her.

Moments later, still dripping from their swim, Lancelot and Elaine raced out away from the castle and through the nearby fields. Elaine sprinted ahead, wild and free, and spread out her arms so that her fingers could brush through the tips of the soft wheat. A few feet behind, Lancelot chased after her and watched as her soft wispy curls bounced along and tickled the back of her neck.

"Wait, my lady!" called Lancelot. "Slow down!"

"Says the boy who gets to live his whole life wild and free!" laughed Elaine, and she added a burst of quickness. "You speed up!"

96

With a grin and a laugh, Lancelot pressed forward and easily passed Elaine. Elaine gave a good-natured growl and then overcame Lancelot once more. Farther and farther they ran from the castle. They darted into a cornfield, and ducked in and out of long rows of tall corn. They dodged around each other, skipping and dancing and laughing as they did so. Finally, they emerged on the edge of the field along a tree line and found what Elaine had been looking for:

A wild rose bush.

Elaine stared at it silently, utterly entranced by the tall gangly stems, the ragged thorns, and the lopsided red blooms that bobbed along with the night's gentle breeze.

Watching Elaine's fascination, Lancelot pointed out, "But surely you already have every kind of rose in your garden."

"No, not like this," said Elaine without taking her eyes off of the flowers. "Those are all perfectly tended to. Meticulously shaped and pruned. This is more beautiful by far, precisely because it is so wild."

With a quick movement, Lancelot drew the sword off of his hip. It was the one that Gawain had given him years ago, but it was now well notched and not nearly as sharp as it once had been. Nonetheless, with a sure slash, Lancelot cut a rose from the bush and held it out for Elaine.

"For you, m'lady," he said tenderly.

But in an instant, Elaine's eyes filled with tears, and she almost screamed, "Why did you do that?!"

97

Lancelot gaped in confusion as he mumbled, "I thought you wanted… I was doing it for… It was supposed to be a gift!"

"It was alive and vibrant and peaceful," shouted Elaine. "And you destroyed all of that! You killed it! What is wrong with you?!"

Suddenly, without another word, Elaine sprinted back into the cornfields. Lancelot tossed the rose aside and chased after her, but she didn't spare him a backward glance. Once again, Lancelot chased Elaine through the fields, but there was none of the playfulness of before. They emerged out into a wild stretch of uneven grasses, clovers, weeds and saplings. Gasping for breath, Elaine finally stopped running, and sat down in the overgrown field. Lancelot stood beside her at a respectful distance.

"I'm sorry, m'lady," said Lancelot.

But she shook her head. "You couldn't have known what was in my heart. Nevertheless, we will have to see if we can find a way for you to make it up to me. Please, sit."

She patted the ground beside her, and Lancelot sat. Elaine gazed up at the stars. She drank in the wide expansive sky and once again seemed mesmerized.

"I could get lost up there. Never-ending. Forever. Always a new star to seek out."

"Always a new adventure," said Lancelot.

Elaine didn't respond, but Lancelot was sure that she was wishing for the same thing.

As a warm breeze danced over the field and caressed each of their faces, Elaine turned to Lancelot, and looked into his eyes with the same eager exploration that she had just used to search the starry sky. Slowly, she moved toward him. Lancelot didn't move away. They both closed their eyes at the same instant. And they kissed. It was soft and gentle and it left them both gasping for breath. Although neither of them could have known it, it was the first kiss for both of them.

After another moment gazing into each other's eyes, Lancelot said softly, "I should get you back to your castle. I'd be a poor guardian if I failed to—"

But Elaine silenced him with another kiss. This one became more curious, more uninhibited, more passionate. They explored each other for several long moments before they finally broke apart, each of them shaking ever so slightly.

"You wish to be a knight, do you not?" she asked.

Lancelot nodded.

"Knights and ladies and quests and kingdoms. Sir Lancelot, will you join me on another adventure?"

Hesitant but eager, Lancelot nodded again.

They came together once more in a kiss. This one was strong, passionate and confident. And this time, they fell down into the tall grasses.

Sometime later, the skies began to turn gray as the morning sun crept closer and closer toward the horizon. The air was warming as the day grew near, and Lancelot and Elaine slipped once more through the small wooden door into the safety of the garden.

LANCELOT OF THE LAKE

They gazed upon each other without speaking for a long moment, then finally Elaine said, "Thank you for the unforgettable adventure, my good and noble knight."

"At your service, my lady."

Lancelot took her hand and kissed it. Elaine glowed. Finally, somewhat clumsily she remembered and said, "How silly of me... I owe you your payment. I would say you have earned it."

For the next several minutes, she combed through the garden and plucked all manner of fruit and vegetables. She piled them into a sack and held it out for Lancelot.

Lancelot took the bag, examined its contents, and couldn't help but ask, "How is this any different from my cutting the wild rose?"

"These were grown to be plucked," said Elaine as she gazed at the slightly torn earth.

The first rays of the morning sunshine began to peer overtop the castle walls. Lancelot spotted them and gave Elaine a courteous nod as he headed for the door. "I must go, m'lady."

He had barely gone more than a few feet when he was caught by Elaine's passionate words.

"Wait! Lancelot! Please, don't go."

Lancelot spun and searched her longing eyes as he said, "But I don't belong here."

"But you could," she insisted, and she gestured to the bountiful variety of plants that surrounded them. "Anything can flourish here. Even you. You could find a place in Corbenic. Amongst our soil." Then with her eyes shining, she added barely above a whisper, "With me?"

Lancelot moved closer to her, and he softly brushed a tear off of her cheek with his rough right hand as he said, "I'm sorry, m'lady, but I'm afraid I must refuse your most generous offer. You see, I have a vision. A vision of a grand life."

Then he kissed her one last time and said quietly as though it brought him no pleasure,

"I'm off to become the greatest knight in all the world."

And he headed for the garden wall, ducked through the small door, and was gone.

~ ~ ~

Thirteen years later, Lancelot stood on the balcony of his bedroom in Corbenic Castle. He couldn't help but reflect on how different his circumstances were now in comparison to when he had been a young man. Back then, he had snuck into the castle under cover of darkness; now, he was welcomed in with open arms by the king. Now, he was honored with a comfortable room and a soft bed; however, in his first visit, he had been thrilled to lie amongst the tickling grasses in an overgrown field. All those years ago, he had been a wide-eyed young man with the optimism of a lifetime ahead of him; now, he was an older, battered knight with a collection of scars that sat both upon his skin and his soul. As the memories from a lifetime ago danced through his mind and filled him with joy and sadness, Lancelot looked out into the gently rustling fields and he gazed up into the twinkling stars of the night sky.

Then he looked down, and to his surprise, he saw Elaine.

In the still of the night, Elaine stole out across the drawbridge. Lancelot watched her rush away as she followed a dirt path that led away from the castle and down toward a village in the distance.

For a moment, Lancelot stirred and his mind filled with a desire to follow her. He remembered chasing her through cornfields as her curling tendrils bounced along in her wake. But that was another time, another life. Now, Lancelot shook his head, and did his best to dispel the lady from his thoughts.

"Leave her alone, Lancelot," he said to himself, thinking of all the pain he'd already caused her. "She's not your concern. And you've got to get some rest tonight… You've got a date with a troll tomorrow…"

~ ~ ~

CHAPTER 9

The Troublesome Troll

Many years earlier, in a land far away, there was a boy whose best friends were all rocks. The types of rock made no difference. Large, small, smooth, coarse, the boy loved them all. He struck up conversations with stone. He befriended boulders. He palled around with pebbles.

The other children didn't quite know what to make of it all. They would find the boy having heart-to-hearts with limestone, or telling jokes to statues, or playing games of catch with granite walls. As children are prone to do, they dealt with the strange boy the only way they knew how: they made fun of him. It started with teasing, it grew into jeering, and eventually exploded into beating.

However, it only made the boy more determined to show them what they were missing.

Driven on by the abuse of his fellow children, the boy sought out ways to make them see what he saw in all of the rocks. He put on puppet shows with rocks acting as the heroes. The other children slapped him around for it. The boy performed amazing feats of juggling with his smooth stone friends. The other children whacked him with sticks. The boy stacked the rocks into beautiful displays of art, but the other children just tore them down and ground the boy into the piles of rubble.

Eventually, the boy turned to magic.

For years, the boy pored through thick books of the mystical arts. And slowly but surely, he mastered the craft of enchantment. First, he taught his rocks to roll on their own. It wasn't enough to impress the other children. Then the boy bewitched the rocks to pile one atop the next. Still not enough. So the boy bound the rocks together. He taught them walk. He taught them to punch. He taught them to destroy.

And the troll was born.

With savage pleasure born from years of abuse, the boy sent the troll to terrorize the leader of the children who had antagonized him. The twenty-foot-tall body of melded stones stomped its way across the village, pounded upon the door, and then proceeded to demolish the home. The bully and his parents could do nothing but stand by helplessly as the massive pile of moving rocks methodically ground their house down into dust. The troll was almost painstakingly slow, but that only made it worse. It was like a slow-motion disaster. One stone fist after another after another after another. It took almost two full days, but the troll finally flattened the home into finely mashed pulp.

After that, one by one, the boy sent the troll to each of the homes of the children who had made his life miserable, and one by one, the troll reduced every house to rubble. The other children and their families begged the troll to stop, but the boy ignored them just as they had ignored him, and he continued urging his monster forward. It took weeks, but eventually every one of the homes was pummeled down into bits.

The boy couldn't have been more pleased.

What he hadn't counted on, however, was the troll turning on him too.

Having been created to destroy, the troll sought out every solid thing it could find. Once it had leveled all of the homes of the children who had picked on the boy, it turned to the houses of their neighbors. Then it set its sights on the common areas and meeting halls. Finally, when there was only one structure left standing, the troll trudged toward the boy's own home. He tried to stop it, but while the boy had spent countless nights learning how to bring the stones to life, he had never bothered to learn how to stop it. With mindless dedication, the troll demolished the boy's house and the boy was buried along with the debris.

In the end, the entire village lay in ruin, and every single inhabitant was forced to run for their lives. They spread out into nearby villages, or journeyed for months to put as much distance between themselves and the troll as possible. The children who had once taunted the boy grew into adults themselves, and they all taught their own children to be kind to even the strangest of people lest they risk creating their own worst nightmare.

However, even though the boy was gone, his troll still remained.

It slowly marched across the countryside and demolished anything that stood in its path. It uprooted trees. It trudged through lakes and swamps. It dug through mountains.

And eventually someone pointed it in the direction of Corbenic.

Over the past several years, the troll had tromped around the farmlands of Corbenic. It ruined farmhouses. It flattened fields. One time, it even demolished an entire village. Anyone who tried to stand up to the troll was quickly squashed into jelly, and so the citizens of Corbenic had learned to simply stay out of its way. When it stomped toward a stable, the farmers would clear out their horses and wait while the troll pummeled the place. Then once the monster moved on, the farmers worked together to build a new structure to replace the old one. They had even employed this exhaustive strategy with the village that the troll had hobbled. The one thing everyone had learned was:

When the troll was coming, get out of its way.

Until Lancelot changed all that.

He found the troll slowly working its way across a field with its sights set on knocking down a farmhouse that it had already crushed four or five times; the farmer couldn't quite remember how many. Lancelot stepped into the troll's path, and faced off with the monster.

"I give you this last chance!" roared Lancelot. "Leave Corbenic forever. Or face me."

The troll simply swung its massive stone fist at Lancelot.

"*Aaaarrrggghhh!*" bellowed the troll, which Lancelot took to mean, "*I will happily crush you, puny little man!*"

If Lancelot had been foolish, he would've tried to fight the troll outright and probably would have found himself quickly mashed into jam just like all the others who had stood up against it. But Lancelot wasn't foolish. He easily dodged the slow, clumsy swing from the troll. Then, Lancelot took out the large sledgehammer he had borrowed from the castle's blacksmith. When the troll tried again to smash Lancelot beneath its broad rocky hand, Lancelot leapt out of the way and then ran up the troll's arm.

And Lancelot's work began.

One swing with his hammer at a time, Lancelot chipped away at the troll's stone shoulder. Lancelot found he could get in a dozen blows or so before the troll would make another slow strike with its free hand. Lancelot would dodge out of the way, like a fly avoiding the swish of a horse's tail, and then the knight would go back to work. Another dozen chips, another dodge, and back to work.

"It's not fighting," Lancelot told himself as he continued chipping away at the monster. "It's just sculpting."

And Lancelot continued to work.

Chip, chip, chip.

Dodge a slow blow.

Chip, chip, chip.

The sun rose high in the sky. And Lancelot kept chipping away.

Chip, chip, chip.

Dodge.

Chip, chip, chip.

Dodge.

The sun fell toward the horizon. Lancelot continued his steady progress.

As the many hours passed, Lancelot whiled away the time by imagining a conversation in his head with the massive stone beast.

"Curse you, Sir Lancelot. I will spread your blood across my bread!" shouted the troll. But really all it said was, *"Aaaarrrggghhh!"*

Chip, chip, chip.

Dodge.

"I shall not rest until I've utterly defeated you!" screamed the troll. But really, *"Aaaarrrggghhh!"*

Chip, chip, chip.

Dodge.

Night fell, the moon overtook the sky, and Lancelot still hammered away. After nearly an entire day and night, there was a decisive crack and:

One of the troll's stone arms fell away at the shoulder.

"I'll make you pay for that, cursed Lancelot!" Or really, *"Aaaarrrggghhh!"*

Wiping sweat from his brow, Lancelot moved across the troll's shoulders and set to work on the other arm. With its remaining arm, the troll continued to clumsily try and swat Lancelot away, but it was harder for it to get a clear swing now. Lancelot could get in a few dozen chips now before having to dodge a blow.

Chip, chip, chip, chip, chip, chip.

Dodge.

The sun rose the next morning, and there was more hammering from Lancelot. Breakfast time passed, and there was more hammering. Lunch blew by; more hammering.

Chip, chip, chip, chip, chip, chip.

Dodge.

"I rue the day I met Sir Lancelot!" or *"Aaaarrrggghhh!"*

As night fell on the second day, there was another rumble, and the other arm crumbled and fell off. The troll wasn't finished yet, though, and it continued to stomp and twist its armless torso. It did its best to dislodge Lancelot from between its vast stone shoulders, but the knight held on. Then, with a deep tired sigh, Lancelot began hammering away at the back of the troll's neck.

The troll's neck was twice as thick as either of its arms, and Lancelot had to continually spin around it to find the best targets. It took a maddeningly long time. The sun rose and fell. The moon appeared and vanished. Day after day, night after night, and Lancelot was exhausted and covered in sweat, but continued hammering on and on.

"End it already! End this madness!" cried the troll in utter exhaustion, although what came from its mouth was just, *"Aaaarrrggghhh!"*

As the sun fell over his fifth evening of work, Lancelot was about to fall over with exhaustion. But he kept hammering away.

Chip, chip, chip.

Dripping, pouring, stinking sweat.

Chip, chip, chip.

Aching, screaming, tired muscles.

"I'm done for. No, really. Done for. Truly. I'm done. I am done."

Really just:

"Aaaarrrggghhh!"

And then finally:

The troll's head cracked and rolled off of its shoulders. The massive stone body tipped over, and Lancelot leapt away as the collected rocks collapsed in a heap. Lancelot sighed an enormous breath of relief, knowing that his long toil was finally over and the battle was won, when:

He noticed the head continuing to roll around.

It bit and roared and fought on as it yelled:

"You can't leave me like this, you coward!"

But really:

"Aaaarrrggghhh!"

On the verge of tears, Lancelot walked over to the head and, with a heavy sigh, started hammering away at it. Night crept over the land, and the sun rose again, and night returned once more, yet Lancelot continued to crack away at the troll's stone head.

Chip, chip, chip, chip... never-ending chip!

"Aaaarrrggghhh!" roared the troll, and Lancelot couldn't even bring himself to give it words anymore.

"Oh, would you just be quiet already?!"

Pausing just for a moment to wipe his sweat-covered forehead, Lancelot looked off to the distance and noticed a strange thing. At the edge of the field, a young man stood silently watching Lancelot's tireless work. With a squint, Lancelot recognized the boy.

It was Galahad looking on from a respectful distance.

It was impossible to be sure, but Lancelot suspected that Galahad had been standing watch for a good long while. Lancelot even guessed that Galahad might've been standing guard since Lancelot had begun his long, exhausting work all those days before. Galahad seemed to want to be on hand just in case Lancelot needed it. Lancelot gave his silent sentry a nod of thanks, and Galahad returned it.

Then Lancelot turned back to finish his work.

Chip, chip, chip.

"Aaaarrrggghhh!"

"Shut it!"

Chip, chip, chip…

Crack!

With a final mighty swing, Lancelot's hammer cleaved a crevice that finally threatened to crumble what was left of the troll's head. It continued to bite and growl, but the look in its monstrous eyes knew that the end was near. Lancelot raised his hammer high over head, and said:

"Go to sleep, my friend."

And he brought the hammer down with a last burst of strength. The stone head split and crumbled to bits. With a jolt of surprise, Lancelot had to spring backward as a spurt of glowing orange lava burst forth and oozed from the remains of the troll. The fiery liquid seeped through the remains of rock, singed its way through the grass, and sunk into the earth.

The troll was finally vanquished.

The sun was dropping back behind the horizon at the end of the sixth day, and Lancelot dropped his hammer. His legs shook from weakness, his back shuddered with exhaustion, and his arm screamed at its nearly week's worth of abuse. Lancelot was ready to stumble back to the castle for some well deserved food, drink, and rest when:

"Hooray for Lancelot!"

"Hooray for our savior!"

"Hooray for our champion!"

Lancelot had barely taken a few steps when a crowd of men, women and children began to flood toward him. They were all laughing and cheering and carrying armloads of food and drink, and they seemed intent on celebrating their freedom from the terrible troll.

However, Lancelot tried to wave them away, as he said weakly, "No, no, I just did what I could to help. I'd love to go sit down now…"

But the villagers didn't seem to hear him as they thrust wine and bread into his hands. Someone drew out a guitar and began to play. In moments, music rang out. A party was underway.

Lancelot was tired. But he wasn't dead.

He shrugged and said, "I suppose a little celebration never hurt anyone…"

The people cheered and welcomed him with open arms. The grateful villagers shared their best mead, and Lancelot happily partook. He was given sumptuous hunks of lamb to help replenish his strength. One farmer even tried to offer Lancelot his daughter's hand in marriage, and although the girl did seem to be a charming young lady, Lancelot properly declined. Night fell, but the party showed no signs of slowing. As the celebration roared along, Lancelot looked amongst the faces of the many people and tried to find Galahad, so that he might thank the boy for his vigilance throughout the long trial.

But the young man was nowhere to be found.

~ ~ ~

CHAPTER 10

A King's Request

Several hours later, stumbling somewhat from a combination of his tussle with the troll and his four rounds of drinks at his well-deserved post celebration, Lancelot returned to Corbenic Castle. He had every intention of heading straight to his comfortable bed, collapsing fully-clothed into it, and sleeping a good long sleep in preparation for his next encounter with one of Corbenic's resident monsters. However, Lancelot decided to make a stop first. Even though his mind reeled with exhaustion, Lancelot shuffled into the castle's throne room and found King Pelles settled atop a pile of over-sized pillows. Lancelot couldn't be more envious. Startling out of his sleepy haze at Lancelot's arrival, though, the old king wriggled himself into a straight-backed, upright position and waved for the knight to come closer.

"Ah, Lancelot, my boy!" croaked King Pelles, grasping Lancelot's hand and shaking it with all the aged strength he could muster. "Well done! Well done, my good man!"

"I was simply happy to help. That troll was nothing," said Lancelot, although in fact he thought he really was quite something. "Nothing at all."

The old king chuckled and wagged a finger at Lancelot. "And so modest! I have a feeling that with your help we'll be free in no time from all these beasts that have plagued us for these thirteen long years."

"Thirteen years...?" asked Lancelot as this number struck a chord with him. "Is that really when it started?"

"Hmm? Why, yes," said King Pelles. "Thirteen long years. You would've still been a young man then, barely older than a boy. I, however, was already being overcome with age."

"Not you," said Lancelot kindly. "You've still got years' worth of battles ahead of you."

"No, no. I am the past," said Pelles with a hint of sadness, and his mind seemed to drift off as he added, "But with your help, I think we may finally be on course for the future."

Lancelot looked at the king with a questioning glance and a slight smirk, and when Pelles spoke once more, it brought a jolt of seriousness to the knight.

"I hope that you can bring us peace, Sir Lancelot."

The words rung deeply in Lancelot's ears until, humbly and with uncharacteristic modesty, Lancelot replied, "It will be my pleasure to serve you, King Pelles. I hope to be able to do right by Corbenic before I go on my way again."

Once again, King Pelles seemed troubled as he put his hands on Lancelot's shoulders and said, "We are certainly glad to have you. For as long as we may convince you to stay, I hope you will consider Corbenic to be a worthwhile home. We may be a small kingdom. Not as grand as some of those you have served. But there are treasures here that might be worth your while, Lancelot. And we are grateful to have such a brave and noble and... noble and... brave... and... brave…"

Despite being mid-sentence, King Pelles's eyelids began to droop. As much as he struggled, the old king seemed to be losing his battle with drowsiness, and Lancelot gingerly leaned King Pelles back in his throne amongst his pile of pillows. Within moments, the king rattled with soft snores, and Lancelot arranged the king's arms in a comfortable position across his lap. Thinking of his own comfortable bed, Lancelot nodded at the sleeping king and said:

"I hope I don't disappoint you, my friend."

~ ~ ~

Of course, it wasn't first time Lancelot had pledged his service to a king.

And, although he'd never admit it, it wasn't even the first time he'd worried about being a disappointment to that king.

Ten years earlier, Lancelot knelt before a grander throne in a much more magnificent castle. At that time, he was undeniably in his prime. Lancelot was tall and strong with full, unvarnished hair and a mouth full of gleaming, unbroken teeth. His face and body only bore a few scars, and they served to simply make him all the more ruggedly handsome. Greatest of all, Lancelot was the most formidable knight in the kingdom. He had been mentored by the best knights, and eventually he surpassed them all. He had slain griffins, hellhounds, and even a tiger-shark that was an actual mix between a tiger and a shark that a sorceress had set loose near a children's swimming hole. Throughout the kingdom and probably

116

the entire world, there wasn't another man who could match Lancelot with the sword, especially when Lancelot used his dominant, unblemished right hand.

It was inevitable that King Uther Pendragon would bring Lancelot into his service.

Witnessed by hundreds of fellow knights, as well as court advisors, foreign lords, and even Uther's personal wizard, Lancelot proudly strode up to the foot of Uther's tall golden throne. Lancelot bent his knee, bowed his head, and presented himself at the feet of the mighty king of Tintagel Castle, which was inarguably the greatest kingdom of that time.

Dressed in his most beautiful armor flecked with gold, King Uther Pendragon extended his sword. He dispensed a few ceremonial taps onto Lancelot's shoulders and head, and then Uther proudly declared to all the people gathered there:

"Here rises Sir Lancelot. May his bravery and love serve to strengthen our lands and all the lives he may touch. May he bring honor to me, this kingdom, and all he now serves. May he seek to always work in friendship with any whose hearts are also pure and righteous. And may he strike down any and all who might strive to bring suffering or malice to those weaker than themselves. Now, stand and join our ranks, Sir Lancelot!"

Lancelot rose and turned to face the crowded throne room. He was met with a bellowing roar of applause. Men of all ages clapped for him. Women, young and old, smiled at him with bright love and affection. The few children that attended, including Uther's teenaged son, Arthur, looked on with admiration for the mighty knight who now presented himself to the court. However, no one was grinning more broadly than Lancelot himself, and he gave a bow to the cheering crowd.

Without a doubt, it was the highpoint of his life.

Lancelot felt a strong hand on his shoulder, and then the voice of Uther Pendragon whispered in his ear, saying, *"I hope that you can help bring us peace, Sir Lancelot."*

For a brief moment, Lancelot's smile faltered, because deep down there had been a secret that he had borne in his heart for nearly his entire life, ever since he had looked upon the broken lifeless body of the Copper Knight, and it was a secret that he dared not speak aloud although he feared that it must be true:

No matter how much he might wish it, peace wasn't something Lancelot was meant for...

~ ~ ~

Back in his bedroom in Corbenic Castle, Lancelot dragged one foot after the other with no other desire than to reach his bed, collapse into it, and sleep for many glorious hours if not several long days. He was only feet away from his feathery reward when he heard a rustling noise outside. The sound of footsteps crossing the drawbridge drew Lancelot's curiosity, and he couldn't help but move to his balcony for a quick peek.

Elaine was once again darting away from the castle and into the night.

From his balcony, Lancelot watched the beautiful woman pull the hood of her cloak over her head and then dash down the dirt path away from the castle. Once again, Lancelot felt an urge to follow after her. Yet this time his utter exhaustion easily won out. Lancelot shook his head, stumbled back to his bed, and dove into it without so much as a pause to take off his boots.

Within moments, Lancelot was fast asleep.

Although even in his dreams, he was preparing for his battle with an ogre.

~ ~ ~

CHAPTER 11

Of Onerous Ogres

Many years earlier, in a land far away, there was a contest amongst magicians to see who could create the most magnificent beast.

The obvious problem was that *"magnificent"* is an imprecise term and no one could agree on what would constitute the winning creature. Fortunately, most of the competitors sought to concoct monsters of breath-taking beauty or heart-aching sweetness. One wizard colored a peacock with feathers of shimmering gold and bestowed it with a voice that would make the Greek sirens weep with love. There was a mage who had created a puppy that would never grow old and squeaked a tiny bark that sounded adorably like it was woofing, *"I wuv you…"* A priestess had birthed a living cloud that could transport its rider to any location on earth within hours without a hint of motion sickness. And one sour-faced witch simply presented a common housecat, arguing that there was no improving on perfection.

All manner of beast was created that day, and all sorts of combinations were tried. Some were good. Some were bad. Some were just head-scratchingly strange. One way or another, though, no one seemed to pay any attention to the fact that they might be doing something that shouldn't have been done in the first place. They gave themselves all sorts of excuses like:

"This is moving the human race forward!"

"Surely this is a benefit to the world."

"But it's a puppy that says, *'I wuv you...'*"

They should have known that someone would bring to life a creature of utter destruction.

And so the ogre was created.

One magician felt that his contribution to the contest would have to combine all of the sorts of strength he could muster. He brought together a bear, a bull, a boar, and buffalo, because he really had an affinity for animals that started with the letter *"B."* However, as he was trying to decide if the name for his new creation should be *"bubbabob"* or *"boabibbubbey"* or something equally nonsensical that incorporated even more Bs, the creature broke free of its cage. It trampled its creator and then charged amongst all of the other magical folk.

Very quickly it received the name that would stick as one terrified fairy woman screamed, *"Oh!"* and the monster responded *"Grrr!"* and from then on everyone simply called it the *"ogre."*

The ogre stormed around the competition and made quick work of all the other creatures that had been formed that day. The golden peacock was crushed. The eternal puppy was flattened. And the wonder cloud was dispersed. All of the sorcerers, mages, priestesses, and magicians ran for their lives and vowed to never meddle with the forces of nature again, which of course they promptly forgot all about as soon as they made it to safety. For her part, the sour-faced witch always considered herself the winner since common housecats are the only creature still in existence today.

However, the ogre proved to be an absolute menace that no one was prepared to deal with. It charged for miles in any direction and demolished anything that it came across. For years, it laid waste to anything that stood in its way. Individual brave men were trampled beneath its mix of hooves and paws. Teams of adventurers were bowled over by its tusks and teeth. Entire armies were crushed by its rampaging bulk. Nothing that tried to stand up to the ogre could stop it. And, though it would've been to its creator's dismay, the beast's name became legendary.

It stampeded through lake towns.

"Ohhh!" cried the townspeople.

"Grrrr!" growled the beast.

It devastated alpine villages.

"Ohhh!"

"Grrrr!"

And eventually someone pointed it toward Corbenic.

For some reason, the ogre finally found a home amongst the farms of Corbenic. And for a beast of its unpleasant nature, home meant a place to permanently rip apart. It trounced from one field to the next, tearing up the soil and trampling the crops. It ground down homes as it charged through villages. It offset irrigation and terrified livestock. However, the farmers finally managed to corral it into one remote field, although it came at a terrible cost. The farmers had to constantly toss food to the terrible beast to keep it satiated, but even that simple task often led to dismemberment or death. They had no choice, however, because anyone who had tried to fight the ogre had quickly found themselves mashed into the mud.

Until Lancelot changed all that.

One bright day, the mighty knight strode toward the ogre's field, he bounded over the mostly ineffectual stone wall that the farmers had built in a misguided attempt to contain the monster, and he prepared for battle with the beast.

"Ohhh, I think it's time to put an end to this monster," said Lancelot.

"Grrrr!" responded the ogre. And Lancelot, employing his usual habit of interpreting a beast's bellows, imagined it saying, *"An epic duel we shall have, Sir Lancelot!"*

After having slept for nearly a week following his struggle with the troll, Lancelot had all but leapt out of bed that morning and headed out to face the ogre. It wasn't hard to find, since everyone knew the field that it had called home for over a decade now. The soil had been ripped and torn and dug up hundreds of times. Great mounds of earth lay scattered about. Hunks of grass were overturned. Rocks and trees had been tossed in every direction. Most ominous of all, human bones and leftover animal carcasses were strewn all over the bloody field.

Nevertheless, Lancelot urged the ogre to charge.

And charge the ogre did.

The beast stormed closer.

Lancelot waited.

The ogre pounded across the field in several long bounds.

Lancelot waited.

The ogre opened its jaws to feast and roared its stinking breath.

And as it came within inches of the knight, Lancelot leapt high into the air. With his good left hand, he flung a coil of rope and it caught around the ogre's neck. Lancelot yanked quickly and landed on the massive hairy back of the ogre, because Lancelot didn't plan to fight the ogre.

Lancelot was going to ride the ogre.

When Lancelot had been much younger and travelled through the forests of Arden, he had learned how to tame the wildest stallions. When he had travelled to the deserts to the south, he had mastered dancing with bulls. And, of course, he had recently ridden on the back of the White Dragon even as it engaged in a midair battle with the ferocious Red Dragon.

But the ogre was unlike anything Lancelot had ever sought to conquer before.

As Lancelot landed onto the ogre's back it opened its jaws and emitted a bear-like roar that Lancelot translated to roughly mean, *"As sure as the mountains will one day be ground to dust, so too will I crush you!"*

Lancelot admitted he was attributing quite a philosophical bent to the beast.

The ogre bucked and kicked and wrenched itself violently, but Lancelot held on tight. He used the rope that he had thrown over the ogre's head, and lashed himself onto the wide hairy back of the beast. Straining all of his muscles, Lancelot drew in the slack and the rope cut into the ogre's neck.

"Like a storm cloud blocking the sun's own rays, you are a worthy foe, Sir Lancelot!" said the ogre, but it was really just a boar-like snort.

So the battle of wills was underway. The ogre continued to charge and pounce and even roll about on the ground. Lancelot held tight even when the ogre reared up like a bear upon its hind legs, and attempted to reach and slash at Lancelot with its razor-tipped forepaws. Whenever he had a chance, Lancelot pulled his ropes tighter, and threw extra loops around the monster. Lancelot never let up, he never slackened his grip, and after several hours, the ogre finally began to tire as it struggled for breath.

"Aye! I fear that as surely as the sun must set, the day of my life risks turning into night," cried the ogre, but really it just gave a bull-like wheeze.

Although his back and shoulders ached, and every inch of his skin had been ripped by the biting of his rope, Lancelot pulled tighter and tighter. As the ogre finally stumbled, Lancelot leapt off of its back, and wrapped the ropes around the beast's hind legs and forepaws. With a mighty heave, the ogre tipped over and Lancelot quickly lashed the rope to bind up the beast's limbs.

"Cursed be this day…. But I must accept the inevitability of my demise just as the leaves upon the trees in the autumn must accept that one

day they will turn colors and fall..." But this time it actually just gave a groan like a tired old buffalo.

Stirring feebly in its bindings, the ogre cast a wide, reproachful eye up at Lancelot. He was exhausted and pained and ready to be done with it. He shuffled over to the stone wall where he had left a sword at the ready. Lancelot hadn't dared keep it at his side, just in case the ogre had managed to impale Lancelot upon it with a well-timed roll. Now that the ogre was bound, however, Lancelot picked up the weapon that he had borrowed from the castle's armory, and he prepared to finish his task. As Lancelot took up the sword, though, something strange caught his eye.

Galahad watched from the edge of the field.

Once again, it seemed as if the boy had come to observe Lancelot's struggle against the mighty beast. And, once again, Lancelot wasn't entirely sure why. Most curiously, however, a look of grim concern seemed to be etched across Galahad's face, and at first Lancelot assumed it was for himself. However, a strange thought flashed through Lancelot's mind as he wondered if the young man was actually more worried about the beast.

Putting it from his mind, Lancelot approached the feebly struggling ogre. Lancelot raised his sword and pointed it directly at the monster's head.

"If I must die, I am glad it is at the hands of the mighty Lancelot. This was an excellent fight," which was really more of a pained wheezing gasp.

"This wasn't fighting," protested Lancelot, although he knew deep down that he didn't believe it, since it was he himself that gave the ogre its words. "This was... It was... I wasn't..."

But Lancelot couldn't bring his blade down.

This was certainly fighting.

And it would certainly be killing.

There was something desperate and pleading about the look in the ogre's massive eyes. Then Lancelot turned once more and saw Galahad in the distance, and Lancelot saw the same wounded gaze. There seemed to be connection between the pain in both the boy and the beast. Finally, Lancelot looked around the field until his eyes fell upon another strange sight.

Amongst the torn ground, a small lopsided rose bush flourished.

Lancelot stared at the unfettered flowers with their long stems and jagged thorns. He looked down at the bound and gagged ogre. Then Lancelot made a difficult decision. He tossed his sword aside.

"You there, boy!" called Lancelot. "Give us a hand!"

Without a moment's pause, Galahad sprinted toward Lancelot. In the space of a breath, the unblemished young man leapt over the stone wall and reached the side of the scarred, aching knight.

"What're you going to do with it?" asked Galahad, looking down at the beast.

"I've got a foolish idea... Probably my dimmest one ever..." sighed Lancelot. "And it's going to take a bit of work."

~ ~ ~

After many long hours of exhausting toil and several close calls where it looked like the ogre might escape to rampage once more, Lancelot addressed a large group of villagers and farmers who had gathered from the nearby villages to see what the great knight had accomplished.

"I wasn't fighting!" Lancelot announced. "I was taming the wild ogre!"

With that, he swept his arms to show that behind him the ogre was now rigged up to a massive plow. An enormous harness of heavy, iron chains connected the beast to a ten-foot-high plow made of jagged boulders and steel. Yet despite the hugeness of the rig, the ogre still managed to trudge forward, although it was now at a slow controlled pace of only a few inches at a time.

"And not only have I tamed the untamable beast, but I've brought you a way to bring back your fields!"

It was true. For as the ogre dragged the plow forward one inch at a time, it left in its wake a row of beautiful tilled soil. It was perfect for planting.

"I predict this will revolutionize your farms, and lead to greater crops than you've ever enjoyed before."

The crowd erupted into wild cheers.

"Hooray for Lancelot!"

"Hooray for our Savior!"

"Hooray for our Noble Warrior!"

Lancelot waved to them as he tried to give his best impression of modesty. He grinned broadly but then added with alarm flooding his voice:

"But whatever you do... In the name of all that is good... If you value your lives at all... Do NOT take off those chains!"

The crowd fell silent for a moment at this grave warning. However, Lancelot quickly waved away their fears as he laughed and shouted:

"Now who's ready for a party?!"

~ ~ ~

CHAPTER 12

Moonlight in the Garden

As night fell, the celebration moved into the castle. Corbenic's gates were thrown open and its stores of wine, meat and cheese were shared by all. Men and women dressed in their finest garments. Musicians broke out their instruments and played their favorite tunes. And everyone cheered for Lancelot's triumph over the ogre.

Lancelot himself, arms laden with gifts and food, stood before the throne as King Pelles twisted his long beard in delight and heaped effusive praise upon the dashing knight.

"I cannot tell you how pleased I am, my boy! How very, very pleased."

"It was nothing… Please, stop," said Lancelot, hoping that King Pelles wouldn't stop.

"And still so humble!" said Pelles. "You remind me of myself when I was young. You know, I had quite the reputation as a slayer of beasts!"

"You don't say?"

"Ah yes. I was something of a warrior of conquest. A vanquisher of evil. A bringer of justice." But then Pelles's voice began to taper off. "Yes, those were the days. Yes, indeed… Why I was… known… for…"

But King Pelles's head tipped forward and he drifted unexpectedly to sleep.

Lancelot stood awkwardly in place for a moment. He wasn't sure what to do. Should he leave? Was that rude? The man was still a king...

Suddenly, King Pelles emitted a snore loud enough to jolt himself awake, and as he tried to get his bearings, he asked, "Hmmm? What was that, my boy? What were you saying...?"

Lancelot had to admit, he was caught off-guard; after all, he wasn't saying anything.

"Uh, you were telling me about the brave exploits of your youth, King Pelles," said Lancelot, doing his best to fill in, so as not to embarrass the king too much.

"Yes, yes. Many beasts. Many battles. Many conquests," said Pelles, and he looked slightly ashamed as he added, "Never grow old, my boy. Never grow old... "

Lancelot smiled and gave a respectful nod, but secretly the thought nagged at his mind. Was there an alternative to growing old? Was it better to die young?

Dispelling the unpleasant thought, Lancelot looked out amongst the gathered crowds of people. Everyone was smiling. There was an abundance of laughter. There was vibrant life all around. It warmed Lancelot's heart just to see it all.

Then his eyes fell on Elaine and his heart warmed all the more.

"Go, my boy. Go. Enjoy the feast. Enjoy your celebration," said Pelles as he patted Lancelot on the shoulder, and then added with a wink, "I've got my eye on you."

Lancelot bowed to King Pelles and then moved away from the throne and began to work his way through the crowd. Several people hugged Lancelot or kissed him upon the cheeks. More than once, he stopped and shared a long drink with an admiring fan. Finally, he arrived at the side of Elaine, who was gossiping with several other women. They all fell silent at Lancelot's arrival, and Lancelot couldn't help but acknowledge a few lusty glances.

"Excuse me, my lady," Lancelot whispered in Elaine's ear. "May I have a word?"

After a moment of surprise, Elaine nodded. It was the most charming mixture of eager and unsure. As Elaine broke away to follow Lancelot, several of the other women shot her envious glances that couldn't all be considered congratulatory. Lancelot and Elaine worked their way through the crowd, and eventually emerged out into a quiet hallway together.

"What may I do for you, Sir Lancelot?" she asked with a playful formality.

"Come with me, my Lady Elaine. I have something I'd like to show you."

Lancelot led the way, and he was surprised at how well he remembered the castle hallways from that one night so long ago. Moments later, Lancelot and Elaine emerged into the cool night air and stood in Elaine's garden. Once again, it was a beautiful night under a clear sky filled with a blanket of stars. The garden was just as luscious as ever. Flowers, fruits and vegetables of every shape, color, and variety bloomed in a dazzling array of nature's bounty and scented the air with delicious fragrances.

"I appreciate the thought, Sir Lancelot," laughed Elaine as she shivered slightly in the cool night air. "But it didn't end so well for us last time we were here."

Lancelot shook his head and laughed. Elaine had such a disarming way of being so charmingly blunt.

"I brought you something, my lady."

And with a flourish, Lancelot presented a small rose bush that had recently been planted into the freshly dug soil. It was lopsided and only bore a few red blossoms, but it was elegant and enchanting.

"I rescued it from the ogre's field," explained Lancelot.

Elaine laughed as she said, "It's very kind of you, Lancelot. However, I think you missed the lesson from our last adventure. It's the wild roses born of nature that I prefer."

"But these are wild, my lady!"

"I think that ogre must've jostled your head! If the roses are to reside in here, then they most certainly are not wild anymore."

"Of course they are!" cried Lancelot, and with a wave of his hand he gestured around the fine garden filled with its luscious varieties of wondrous plants. "It's just a smaller wild."

Elaine smiled at the thought of that. Falling silent, Elaine allowed her eyes to rake across the garden. She took in the trees, bushes, and short rows of crops. The green leaves rustled gently in the night's breeze, and for a moment, Elaine saw the garden with a new sense of appreciation.

"A smaller wild…" whispered Elaine as a flicker of a smile crossed her soft lips. "I like the sound of that. Thank you. Here's hoping that they might flourish."

With that, Elaine turned to leave, but Lancelot caught her by the arm. Her skin rippled with gooseflesh as his fingertips tickled her arm.

"Come now. I had to go through a lot to bring those roses to you," Lancelot said playfully.

He showed her a small scratch on his right forearm, or what was left of his right forearm. It was only a bit of blood, but the tiny streak of red stood out noticeably on the mangled, unnaturally short limb.

"I got that wound from one of its unforgiving thorns. It was a trying ordeal."

Elaine smiled and, in the bright moonlight, it was a breath-taking sight. She seemed to catch on to Lancelot's insinuations and she said, "Ah! Does the noble knight wish for a kiss of appreciation from his grateful lady?"

Lancelot grinned and shrugged. "Only if you insist, my lady."

Elaine giggled, but she began to move toward Lancelot. The moonlight sparkled in her eyes as she grew nearer. Her warm sweet breath danced beneath his nose. Her eyes closed. Their lips met.

Many long tender moments passed between them before they finally broke apart.

Elaine sighed in a voice that was barely above a whisper, "I've missed you, Lancelot."

"I've missed you too, *Guinevere*."

The spell between them broke.

Both Lancelot and Elaine lurched apart, and any love that was there, even for an instant, vanished like fog on an early morning wind.

"I meant, *'Elaine,'*" stammered Lancelot. "I mean, I've missed you very much, Elaine. And I've missed kissing you very much. That is to say, I would like to kiss you again, my lady, if you please."

But the damage had been done.

"I think I should go back to the celebration," said Elaine.

"Please, Elaine, forgive me," said Lancelot. "Guinevere is no one. Just a woman that I crossed paths with once, but she doesn't mean anything."

"You need not explain yourself," cut in Elaine, because she knew Lancelot wasn't doing himself any favors. "You've been very sweet tonight, Lancelot. Thank you for the roses. But it's late now, and—"

Suddenly, Elaine fell silent and it seemed like she had awoken from a strange trance.

"What time is it?" she asked abruptly.

Without waiting for an answer, Elaine looked to the sky. She examined the moon, then turned to rush out of the garden.

"I have to go."

And, with barely a glance back at Lancelot, she hurried away. For a moment, Lancelot struggled with the question of whether or not to follow her. Finally, he shrugged to himself.

"How much worse could I make this evening?"

And he chased after Elaine.

~ ~ ~

CHAPTER 13

The Lady and the Boy

As silvery wisps of cloud stole across the night sky and obscured the crescent moon, Lancelot silently tracked Elaine's path. It was surprisingly hard. Elaine apparently knew how to cover her tracks, and she left nary a footprint or a broken stalk of grass in her wake. Lancelot secretly doubted that he could have matched the level of stealth. Nonetheless, Lancelot was, well, a very accomplished knight. Despite the surprising challenge, he followed Elaine's flight along the dirt road that led out of Corbenic Castle, through the sparse forest, across the tiny stream, and into the meager village.

Lancelot held back, but glimpsed Elaine's fluttering travelling cloak as she approached a small hut on the outer edge of the town. He watched as she rapped upon the wooden door and was soon greeted by an old man and woman who, to put it politely, looked eternally grumpy. They were both small and slightly hunched and their faces seemed to be contorted into ever-present scowls. After a moment, however, they moved aside and a young man appeared in the doorway. After just a glance, Lancelot gasped. How could he not have seen it before?

Galahad was Elaine's son.

Quietly moving closer, Lancelot examined Elaine and Galahad side by side. They shared the delicate ringlets that bounced softly across their foreheads even at the slightest movement. Their skin glowed in the moonlight with the same pale smoothness. They each had the same oval-shaped faces with soft dimples in their rounded cheeks.

Lancelot watched as Elaine led the boy around the back of the hut, and Lancelot couldn't help but follow. With building fascination, Lancelot crept up to the hut, and quietly circled around to the back. Being careful to stay hidden, Lancelot heard the crackling of a small fire, and saw Elaine and Galahad seated upon stumps of wood, bathed in the firelight, and chatting softly.

"I will talk to them again," said Elaine as she tenderly brushed Galahad's hair away from his eyes. "They assured me that they would be kind to you."

"And they try to be," said Galahad. "It was my fault. I did break half of their dishes."

"Clearly by accident. And I can replace them with ease. Heavens knows that I've helped to provide for you and them for all these years. They shouldn't be so angry."

"You can't force them to like me, Mother!"

On hearing his suspicions confirmed, Lancelot tried to move just a bit closer to overhear the hushed voices when:

CRACK!

Lancelot cursed his clumsiness as he trod upon a twig.

Elaine and Galahad spun at the noise, and the young man rose to his feet, placing himself in front of his mother. Lancelot observed the boy's protective instincts and Lancelot grinned. This boy never ceased to impress him. Knowing that he was caught, Lancelot stepped out of the shadows, prepared to calm the boy down.

But it was Elaine who was quick to confront Lancelot as she demanded with firelight blazing in her eyes, "Lancelot?! What are you doing here?!"

"I followed you."

"How dare you!"

"I wanted to make sure you were safe. You know, there are monsters all about."

"Yes, there's one standing in front of me at the moment."

"Am I not your sworn protector?"

"Please, don't try to be cute."

Quietly, Galahad cleared his throat as if he didn't want to be disrespectful, and then asked in a polite voice, "Um... Mother?"

With a jolt of surprise, Lancelot and Elaine turned to Galahad. They had almost forgotten he was there. Stepping aside, so that she could gesture to both Lancelot and Galahad, Elaine introduced them both with a tone that showed barely a hint of emotion. "Galahad, this is Sir Lancelot. Lancelot, this is Galahad. My son."

"Oh, we've met," said Lancelot.

However, Galahad's eyes went wide with terror, and the young man shook his head subtly but with vigor at Lancelot, who quickly realized he'd stepped into something.

"You've met him? When?" asked Elaine as her eyes narrowed with menace.

"I mean, we haven't met!" Lancelot all but shouted. "That is to say, I thought he looked familiar. But now that I look closer, no, I actually haven't met him at all. Certainly not. I've simply met so many people recently at celebrations that I got confused. But him? Nope."

Elaine fixed Lancelot with a hard appraising look, but seemed to accept the explanation as she said pointedly, "It certainly wouldn't be the first time tonight that you confused two people."

Lancelot's stomach clenched at Elaine's jab.

Rallying, the knight extended a hand to Galahad and the young man shook it as he said, "Galahad, is it? It's a pleasure meeting you."

"Thank you," said Galahad in his softest, most polite voice. "You're too kind. The pleasure is all mine, Sir Lancelot."

"Well, Elaine, you have a son. That's excellent," said Lancelot with a slight tremble in his voice. "He seems to be a fine young man. Although not that young. But certainly not old. Say, how old is he?"

"Thirteen," said Elaine.

"THIRTEEN!" cried Lancelot, almost choking on the word.

For a moment, Elaine looked terribly confused, until she finally realized what had been Lancelot's real reason for asking, and she all but shouted, "No! He's not your—you're not his— oh, no. No, no, no."

In the faint firelight it was difficult to tell, but both Lancelot and Elaine seemed to have turned deep shades of red. They wouldn't have noticed, however, since they couldn't seem to manage to look one another in the face. Finally, Galahad cleared his throat courteously once again.

"Ummm... Would it really be that terrible?" asked Galahad, for he clearly had put it all together too.

Lancelot and Elaine looked to one another in panic. Neither seemed sure what to say, so they both blurted out at the same time:

"No!"

"Yes!"

They both spoke so loudly and forcefully, and at the same time, that it was hard to tell who had said what. But it was pretty clear they both would be hard-pressed to give a good answer.

"Thank you for clearing that up," said Galahad with a slight frown. "Or at least trying to..."

"Galahad, you know that your father's name was Sir Bromell," said Elaine, then she turned to Lancelot. "Although I admit, I met him very soon after I met you, Lancelot. Unlike you, he was a perfect gentleman."

"Apparently not a perfect one."

Elaine pretended not to hear Lancelot as she continued, "He and I were due to be married — until he died suddenly."

Lancelot shot her a look of surprise, then mouthed, "Monsters?"

"Yes. It was the monsters," said Elaine quietly. "He was the first."

Elaine shrugged as if it were nothing to worry about, as if it was perfectly natural for her suitors to meet their untimely demise at the hands or jaws of otherworldly beasts.

"Maybe now Lancelot could be my father?" chimed in Galahad.

Once again, Lancelot choked on the very air he was breathing.

"Is that bad?" asked Galahad with wide questioning eyes. "I only meant *like* a father. A suitor for you is all I meant, Mother."

It was Elaine's turn to choke on thin air as she sputtered, "No! Lancelot would be a poor choice."

"Why?" asked Galahad.

"Yes, why?!" demanded Lancelot.

Elaine glared at him and leaned forward as she said, "Do you really want me to answer that question?"

"He seems like a brave and noble knight," pointed out Galahad. "He's all the people in the villages have been talking about lately."

Lancelot puffed up his chest in satisfaction.

But Elaine quickly said, "He's not that brave. Just a short while ago, he was complaining about being scratched by a rose thorn."

Lancelot's chest deflated.

"That's not what I heard, Mother. I heard he was a great warrior. Unparalleled with a sword," said Galahad as he pointed to the sword on Lancelot's hip. "Could you show me something with it?"

"Of course!" said Lancelot, beginning to draw the blade that he had borrowed earlier that day to slay the ogre. He hadn't even realized that he had failed to return it.

"Absolutely not," said Elaine, reaching to force the sword back into its sheath.

"I didn't mean to upset you, Mother," said Galahad with gentle bow of his head. "It's just that most of the other boys have some training with the sword."

"Come, Elaine, most of the other boys have some training with the sword," parroted Lancelot as he stepped past Elaine and drew the sword again. "You don't want Galahad to fall behind, do you?"

"I thought you weren't supposed to be fighting," said Elaine through gritted teeth.

"It's not fighting. It's training!"

Elaine crossed her arms angrily, but stepped aside. Lancelot grinned and flipped the sword so that he could offer it by the hilt to Galahad. The young man gripped the weapon and gazed upon it in awe. As Galahad gave the sword a few tentative slashes through the air, Lancelot went to a wood pile, searched, and selected a long, thin tree branch which he held like his own sword.

"Excellent! This will be fun. Now, we'll start slow. First thing to remember is—"

But without warning, Galahad sprung at Lancelot. The young man shifted his weight and took a natural fighting stance. With surprising confidence and skill, Galahad cut at Lancelot. However, Lancelot was still a formidable knight, and it wasn't that easy to take him off-guard. He deflected the attack with his tree branch, but Galahad didn't stop there. The young man swung, cut, and hacked with surprising speed, smoothness, and improvisation. Try as he might to hide it, Lancelot struggled to keep up with the boy.

"Not bad! Not. Bad. At. All..." said Lancelot, trying to sound casual as he deflected a dizzying combination of hacks and slashes from the boy. "Of course, it would be only to easy to disarm you, by doing—"

And Lancelot locked his branch up with Galahad's sword, and twisted with a fancy maneuver.

"—THIS!"

Nothing happened. The maneuver failed. Galahad still had his sword. In fact, Galahad just looked confused by the whole thing. Elaine looked like she was struggling to restrain her smile.

"All right. Well done," admitted Lancelot as he gave credit where credit was due. "But really, you should first learn defense. Because, if I were to attack—"

Suddenly, Lancelot pressed forward. With all of his many years of training and skill, the seasoned knight brandished his tree branch as if it was the finest of swords.

And Galahad defended against it perfectly.

"—you would be helpless..."

Lancelot had to smirk and admit that Galahad was a natural. The two of them circled one another, and even as Lancelot tested the boy, Galahad easily deflected Lancelot's attacks.

"Hmmmm…" said Lancelot. "Well, I suppose if I'm to actually teach you anything, I need to see what you can really do."

With that, Lancelot launched into a full-scale attack on Galahad. Sure, Lancelot's tree branch was unwieldy and the balance was terrible, but he knew it would serve to put Galahad through his paces. Lancelot unleashed a volley of blows, parries and thrusts that drew into his vast knowledge of skirmishes, duels, and fights to the death. Galahad defended it all. Easily. Forcing a grin to give the impression that he simply found this all to be an enjoyable game. Lancelot secretly was starting to feel a little less special. Suddenly, Galahad locked his sword against Lancelot's branch and twisted in a dexterous maneuver.

And Lancelot's branch went flying out of his hand.

Lancelot's jaw dropped and he asked in a whisper, "How did you know how to do that?"

"I just did what you just did," replied Galahad simply, as if it was the most obvious thing in the world.

"That is not what I just did."

"Well, I changed it a little," said Galahad. "I hope you don't mind. I thought yours could've been more effective."

Lancelot gazed at the boy in shock and amazement. To be honest, his pride was a little wounded, but he forced a laugh as he said, "Extraordinary, Galahad! Who trained you?"

"Trained?" asked Galahad with a look of utter confusion.

"Where did you learn how to use a sword?"

"This is the first time I've ever held one."

Lancelot's jaw hung open and his eyes went wide with astonishment. He really didn't feel special anymore. Galahad shrugged and asked in his small, unassuming way:

"Is that bad?"

As a new smile crept across his face, Lancelot shook his head and he threw an arm around Galahad's shoulder. Lancelot couldn't deny that he liked this boy. Then he looked over at Elaine, and she was absolutely beaming.

~ ~ ~

As the sky began to turn gray just before the sunrise, Lancelot and Elaine crossed the drawbridge over the moat and slipped back into Corbenic Castle. They had talked the whole way back, and their entire conversation had focused on Galahad. Lancelot found the boy to be fascinating, but that raised even more questions about the strangeness of his whole situation. After some delicate prying, Elaine began to explain.

"I have to keep Galahad a secret," she said. "It would be a scandal if people knew I had a son before I had a prince."

"People can be backward like that," acknowledged Lancelot.

"I so wish I didn't have to leave him with those grumpy old people. I wish I could give him the life of a prince that he so deserves. But for the time being, his guardians are honest. And I see that they're all well provided for."

"He's a remarkable boy, Elaine. I'm sure King Pelles would understand."

"Don't be fooled by my father. He can be very sweet and kind, but he can also be very proud. He very much believes in ceremony."

"I'm sure you could find a suitor."

"Yes, I am the marvelous daughter of —" She suddenly caught herself as she added with a hint of abashedness, "Forgive my lack of modesty, but I am marvelous."

Lancelot nodded. "It's true. You are."

"And I am a princess. And a beautiful one at that. In a successful comfortable kingdom. It's true, I've never had any lack of suitors."

"Then what's the problem?" asked Lancelot.

"The monsters," said Elaine. "You see, they have a terrible habit of killing anyone who dares to woo me."

"How many have been killed?" Lancelot tried to ask gently.

"Twelve," Elaine replied without a hint of sadness.

"Twelve?! Twelve suitors?"

"I told you I was marvelous."

Having entered into the castle, Lancelot and Elaine crept quietly through the still sleepy hallways. The scent of fresh baked bread for the morning's breakfast wafted into the corridors from the kitchens below.

"And you say all of your suitors have met their demise by these monsters?" asked Lancelot.

"Or some strange unnatural disasters like the boiling pool that you rescued me from," Elaine replied. "But mostly, yes. The ogre. The troll. The goblins."

"There's goblins too?"

"Oh yes, they're the worst."

"Well, I guess I know what I'll be fighting next…" said Lancelot, before quickly correcting himself. "Not fighting! I meant conquering. No, I mean dispelling. Don't worry about the precise wording. Just rest assured, I'll rid this kingdom of them too."

Elaine came to a halt in front of an ornate carved door.

"These are my chambers," she pointed out, and then added just in case it wasn't perfectly clear, "You cannot come in."

"I assumed as much," Lancelot said, but then he added seriously, "Elaine, I promise you, I will put an end to all of these monsters. I'll make it safe for you and your son and… whomever becomes lucky thirteen."

It was nearly impossible to tell in the faint morning light as the last candles burnt down, but Lancelot thought that Elaine blushed ever so slightly.

"So you're still my sworn protector?"

"If you'll still have me."

In silent agreement, Elaine gave Lancelot a slight bow of the head, then she quickly gifted him with a kiss on the cheek. Without another word, or even another look, Elaine opened her chamber door and disappeared inside. Lancelot heaved a deep sigh, and his mind drifted to wondering who might be that lucky thirteen.

~ ~ ~

CHAPTER 14
Grappling with Goblins

Many years earlier, in a land far away, there were people who loved gold above all else. That, in and of itself, wasn't so uncommon. What was remarkable about these people was the lengths to which they were willing to go to obtain mass amounts of their prize.

They ransacked nearby towns. But it wasn't enough.

They overthrew wealthy castles. But it wasn't enough.

They combed through deep mines. But it wasn't enough.

The last bit was what ultimately led to their disappearance. The insatiable raiders plunged deeper and deeper into the earth in their ever-hungering search for more gold. They scoured through rocks and cast aside worthless boring minerals like diamonds and silver. Legend has it that they eventually stumbled upon a vein of gold so rich that they decided to live in it. They molded their mine into an underground city of gold. They hoarded the precious metal they had collected, and then sequestered themselves in the city they had built and vowed never to give it up. Their skin became rough and scaly from the conditions below ground, but still they wouldn't leave. Their eyes grew massive and bulging to combat the oppressive darkness in the caves, but still they didn't leave. They ceased to be people at all and instead transformed into monstrous beasts, but still they couldn't give up their gold.

They became the goblins.

Over the centuries, many men and women went off in search of that mythical city of gold, but they were all doomed to never return. The city of gold was rumored but never found, and the goblins guarded their underground world with a merciless cruelty. Their race flourished until their golden halls were filled with goblin men, women, and hideous children.

Yet even amongst goblins, oddballs had a way of cropping up.

Every so often, a member or two of this greedy race would blasphemously turn their back on the love of gold, and venture out of the cave in search of a new treasure. As is so often the case, some of the goblins ceased to want the treasure that they held in abundance and instead hungered for something more.

In these goblins' cases, the thing that drove their hunger was, well, hunger.

They wanted better food.

Living beneath the ground, even in a city of gold, didn't offer many options by way of meals. There are only so many recipes for bats and blind-eyed fish that a creature can try before getting restless. So, from time to time, a few goblins would leave their underground city of gold, journey to the surface, and begin gobbling up any of the delicious varieties of meat, cheese, bread, and wine that they could get their clawed fingers on.

They feasted upon roasted ducks and turkeys. But it wasn't enough.

They engorged their bellies with barrels of beer. But it wasn't enough.

They even chewed up the bones of any poor soul who dared to get in their way. But it wasn't enough.

And eventually someone pointed them toward Corbenic.

A land of farms was too good for hungry goblins to resist, and so a trio of the meanest, filthiest, most ravenous ones made their way there. They gobbled through fields of wheat. They gobbled down goats and chickens. They even gobbled up Maid Rosemary and her pies, and she was generally agreed to be the worst cook in the county. They gobbled and gobbled and gobbled some more until it seemed like, given enough time, they were bound to gobble down the entire kingdom.

Until Lancelot changed all of that.

He found the trio of goblins napping in a nearby rock quarry. Even though they were out of the caves, the goblins still preferred to sleep on boulders and jagged stones. They were very sleepy after a particularly large meal of dairy in which they gorged on cheese, guzzled down cream, and gobbled up the milkman. However, Lancelot had no intention of letting them rest. With a roaring battling cry, Lancelot charged into the goblins' midst as he declared:

"This is your last chance, foul creatures! Leave this place, or face the mighty wrath of Sir Lancelot!"

But the goblins had other things on their minds.

"I'd rather face a mighty lunch!" belched Toblin, the fattest goblin, as he pushed himself to his feet.

"Me too! I'm starving!" squeaked Yoblin, the female of the bunch, who was much shorter but just as massively fat.

"Ooooh, I know! We could go gobble through the sunflower fields," suggested Boblin thoughtfully, since he was generally considered the thinker of the bunch.

"Um… That's not really what I came to discuss…" said Lancelot, looking a little put out that his dramatic entrance was less than well-received.

"You fool, sunflower seeds'll just stick in our teeth!" said Toblin, as he continued to seem unaware that Lancelot was even there.

"Here's what we'll do! We could find a pack of porcupines to gobble on after so wes can pick our teeths too," offered Boblin.

"Um, hello there? Perhaps you lot didn't hear me before," spoke up Lancelot. "I'm here to cast you out of Corbenic. Never to return again."

"Porcupines give me a stomachache," complained Toblin.

"Can we stop squabbling and start gobbling?" added Yoblin. "I'm famished!"

"You won't be able to eat anything once I'm through with you, you troublesome fiends!" shouted Lancelot, who was now missing the days when he filled in his opponents' inner dialogue for them.

"I've got it!" shouted Boblin, still ignoring Lancelot. "We could gobble up a nice crispy roast pony!"

"And where are we supposed to get a pony? Does this look like birthing season to you?" demanded Toblin.

"I'm faint with hunger..." sighed Yoblin swooning.

"Oh for goodness sake!" cried Lancelot, throwing his hands up in despair. "Can you even hear me?"

"I know just the thing!" declared Boblin, and with shocking speed and strength the goblin spun and seized Lancelot with his monstrously strong arms. "We can just gobble him up right here and now!"

Cursing his foolishness for falling into the creatures' trap, Lancelot tried to free himself from the goblin's grasp. Yet struggle as he might, Lancelot's strength was nothing compared to Boblin's, who had grown up cracking rocks in search of gold.

"So you could hear me all along?" grunted Lancelot.

"Oh yes," said Boblin. "Wes could smells you too."

"He should hit the spot nicely," said Yoblin, licking her lips and baring her pointed teeth.

A grin spread across Toblin's scaly face and he retrieved a pick ax, saying, "We can hacks him up into three pieces and have ourselves a little feast."

The three goblins converged on Lancelot. Toblin raised his pick ax, Boblin held Lancelot tight, and Yoblin eagerly smacked her lips. They seemed prepared to enjoy quite a meal. As he struggled hopelessly against the goblin's strength, Lancelot's mind reeled and rattled through his options in such a dire situation.

When a solution came out of thin air.

"I would like to help you, Lancelot! If you don't mind!"

Like a blurred human battering ram, Galahad flung himself into the midst of the goblins. They were all taken off-guard by the new arrival, and the young man used the moment of surprise to leap through the air and throw his shoulder forward so that he slammed into the open jaws of Boblin. The tall goblin staggered and released Lancelot, who dropped to the ground and quickly leapt into action. As Toblin swung his pick ax, Lancelot caught it, twisted it and buried it right into Toblin's own generous belly. One goblin down.

The fight had just begun, though, as Lancelot and Galahad teamed up against the two furious goblins that remained.

"Yummers, yummers, yummers," said Yoblin, as she rushed toward Galahad. "Even more delicious snackers."

But now it was Lancelot and Galahad's turn to ignore their assailants.

"I'm sorry I didn't wait for your permission, Sir Lancelot," said Galahad with his usual politeness, as he dove away from the lunging outstretched arms of Yoblin. "I hope you can forgive me. But I thought you might want my help. Are you mad at me?"

"I suppose I can forgive your rudeness just this one time," said Lancelot, feigning disappointment, as he cracked Boblin over the head with the butt of the pick ax.

As Lancelot tussled with the towering bulk of Boblin, he watched Galahad dealing with Yoblin, and once again Lancelot couldn't help but be impressed by the boy's unnatural skill.

Galahad's agility and speed was astonishing. Lancelot found himself thinking that Galahad strongly resembled a cat. The boy leapt, landed, and took off again with feline grace. Then the boy could pounce with the suddenness and precision of a leopard. It was a remarkable display.

Being a seasoned knight, Lancelot made short work of his goblin and quickly sunk the pick ax into the heart of Boblin. Then Lancelot turned and shouted, "Here you go, boy!"

He tossed the pick ax through the air, and with cool assuredness, Galahad dove through the air and caught it. Lancelot was surprised, however, when Galahad chose not to use the pointy end and instead cracked Yoblin in the forehead with the blunt butt of the ax. Nevertheless, it did the trick, and Yoblin collapsed with a thud. Galahad landed lightly atop the wobbling fat of her wide chest and raised the pick ax high over his head, preparing his killing stroke.

But Galahad paused.

The pick ax stood at the ready, all Galahad needed to do was bring it down. Lancelot was sure that the boy possessed the strength and the aim. It was the will that was missing. In all the times Lancelot had met Galahad, the young man's face had always been remarkably impassive and open, but now his brow was furrowed and his dimples disappeared to be replaced by a grimace. Lancelot realized with a lurch in his stomach that this would be the first time that Galahad had ever killed anything. It had been so long since Lancelot had ended his first life, and so many men and beasts had met their demise at his hand that Lancelot had all but forgotten what it must feel like.

A few moments' hesitation was a few moments too long, though, and Yoblin stirred back into furious life. Galahad still couldn't bring down the pick ax, and Lancelot rushed forward.

"Galahad!" Lancelot shouted. "Give it here!"

Seizing the wooden handle, Lancelot wrenched the weapon from Galahad's frozen grip. Then, with the unflinching practice that came from a lifetime of bloody battles and grim war, Lancelot plunged the point of the ax into Yoblin's beastly head and the goblin struggled no more.

Even after the skirmish had ended, Galahad stood over the fallen bodies of the goblins. Pain wailed behind the boy's eyes as he looked at the crumpled forms. Lancelot moved to Galahad's side and placed his hand on the boy's shoulder.

He said, "You did the right thing, Galahad. It was them or you. And they would've killed me if you hadn't come along."

Deep down, Lancelot believed he still would've found a way to triumph even without Galahad's help, but he felt that it was best to try and boost the boy's spirits.

The words seemed to have their desired effect as Galahad's furrowed brow softened and he said, "They were amongst the most terrible monsters, weren't they?"

"That they were."

"And they've left countless dead in their wake, haven't they?"

"That they have."

"And… the world is safer without them in it, isn't it?"

"That it is, my boy."

Galahad nodded and finally tore his eyes away from the fallen goblins as he said, "Then I'm glad I was able to help you in your fight."

"It wasn't fighting. It was — " Lancelot began to protest, but then he looked to the mangled corpses of the monsters and had to concede, "I suppose it was fighting."

And it was Lancelot's turn to grimace under the weight of it all.

Leaving their fallen foes behind, Lancelot and Galahad left the rock quarry and began to head back in the direction of the villages. As they walked, Lancelot patted Galahad on the back.

"I must admit that I'm glad to see you here, Galahad," said Lancelot. "But how did you know where to find me?"

"You've killed most of the other beasts," said Galahad. "These three seemed the most likely to be next on your list."

"And you knew where they were hiding?"

"Oh yes. For as long as I can remember, I've known where all of the monsters have dwelled," said Galahad, then before the strangeness of that statement could settle in, he added quickly, "Please don't tell my mother."

Lancelot laughed. "You can trust me to keep your secret. But it must've been dangerous. Tell me, why would you follow around all of these beasts like that?"

Galahad fell uncharacteristically silent, and once again Lancelot noted that there seemed to be something strange in the relationship between Galahad and the beasts. However, Lancelot felt it would be ungrateful to push further, so instead he ignored the boy's silence.

"I can't tell you how impressed I am by your skills, Galahad," said Lancelot. "I had no idea I was even being followed. And, forgive my immodesty, but it's not easy to sneak up on me."

"I'm sorry!" said Galahad, with panic flickering across his face. "I hope I didn't embarrass you. When I saw you were in trouble, I knew I had to leap in and rescue you."

"Rescue?" Lancelot said, flinching at the term. "Is that really how you'd put it? Assist me, maybe... Let's just keep that between us."

"Don't worry. I won't tell my mother," said Galahad with utmost sincerity. "I would be in much more trouble than you would if she found out."

"I very much doubt that," said Lancelot, and it was his turn to sound panicked as he added, "And, yes, absolutely, positively, without a doubt, do not tell your mother about this!"

Galahad nodded.

"Come now, let's get back to the village," said Lancelot, throwing his arm around Galahad. "With any luck they'll throw another celebration for us!"

Once again Galahad's eyes went wide, and Lancelot could've been imagining it, but he thought they were wide with alarm this time. The idea of a party seemed to frighten Galahad more than a skirmish with a trio of bloodthirsty goblins.

Lancelot tried to put the boy at ease as he asked with clear interest, "By the way, who taught you to wield an ax like that? Remarkable!"

"I've never picked one up before," said Galahad simply.

"Amazing..." was Lancelot's equally simple reply.

"Is that bad?" asked Galahad.

"No, it's not bad at all," said Lancelot. Although he wasn't honestly sure.

~ ~ ~

CHAPTER 15
Galahad's Greatest Challenge

Sure enough, another celebration was underway.

The villagers, who had had precious little to celebrate for years, seemed thrilled to have any opportunity to rejoice now. Many of them had carefully hidden away stores of food and drink in the hopes that they might survive the insatiable hunger of the vicious goblins. Now that the goblins were gone, the villagers and farmers unearthed their hidden stockpiles and happily spread around the bounty. Mouth-watering varieties of salted meats were shared. Hunks of cheese surfaced and were scraped across crisp fluffy loaves of bread. Succulent vintages of wine, mead and beer flowed plentifully. Anyone who fancied themselves a musician had pulled out harps or hand-carved lyres. Music and dancing and happiness filled the tiny village as men, women and children hooted and laughed and felt freer than they had in a long, long time.

Galahad was terrified.

Lancelot guided the young man through the crowd of revelers, and Lancelot couldn't help but marvel at Galahad's unease. In the past few weeks, Lancelot had seen Galahad evading wildelions, helping to tame an ogre, and even assisting in slaying murderous goblins. Yet it seemed as though the prospect of making small talk was a task that the boy feared above all. Lancelot did his best to help Galahad along, and to Lancelot's surprise, it seemed like very few people in the village even knew who Galahad was. The boy had grown up there, he'd been living near these people all his life, and yet it appeared as though Galahad had kept himself hidden away the whole time.

"Come on, Galahad, loosen up," said Lancelot as he threw his arm around the boy and tried to shake him a bit. "This celebration's for you too. I know we can't tell anyone. Your mother would kill us faster than any beast ever could. But, Galahad, you're a hero. You deserve to enjoy this too."

"No," Galahad said as he turned a deep shade of red. "I should probably go home. I shouldn't be here. I can't enjoy this..."

"Of course, you can!" laughed Lancelot as he guided Galahad into the throng of celebrating villagers. "Get my young friend here some food!"

Almost out of nowhere, food and drink were forced into Galahad's hands.

"Go ahead, my boy! Have a little drink!"

"Oh, no, no, no! I couldn't..."

"Just a little sip won't hurt you. It's a party!"

Galahad fell silent as he stared at the drink with concern. Lancelot shook his head in disbelief. He had seen the boy bravely squaring off with monsters, but now he seemed utterly flummoxed at the prospect of a drop of wine.

"Do you really think I should?" asked Galahad. "I don't think I should. Should I? I've never tasted any of this before."

"It's just a taste," said Lancelot as he helped to tip the goblet up to Galahad's mouth.

Lancelot had only meant to nudge the boy along, and maybe help him to relax a bit. However, Galahad's nerves kicked in again, and the boy lifted his goblet up, and in several large gulps he chugged the entire contents of the cup. Lancelot was impressed; Galahad had managed to only dribble a little down his cheeks.

"Uh... well... Perhaps it's a bit more than just a taste," laughed Lancelot, and then he declared, "Is there anything this boy can't do?!"

A twinge of green coloring crossed Galahad's face and made it pretty clear that maybe this was a challenge that Galahad wasn't up to. Lancelot seemed unnerved for a moment, when suddenly, Galahad erupted with a loud belch. Instantly, the young man seemed more at ease and a hint of pink appeared in Galahad's cheeks.

Very quickly, his rich burp was matched by an outburst of giggles.

Lancelot and Galahad turned to see a group of young girls giggling at Galahad's belch. They all seemed to be right around Galahad's age, and without a doubt, they all seemed to be checking out Galahad with great interest.

"Well, go ahead," said Lancelot as he nudged Galahad toward the group of young ladies. "They're calling to you, boy."

Galahad began to turn a shade of purple, and Lancelot chuckled at the range of colors that seemed to be overtaking the young man's face.

"Oh no, no, no... I couldn't…" stammered Galahad.

"Of course, you can!"

With a quick stride, Lancelot led Galahad over to the group of girls.

"Quick advice," Lancelot whispered to Galahad as they approached the girls, who seemed to giggle ever more greatly with every step Galahad took. "If you get lost, compliment their eyes. Women love that. It's the perfect fall-back."

And just like that Galahad was face to face with a pretty girl.

Lancelot moved away to let the boy work, but there was no denying that Galahad looked considerably more terrified than he did when he was battling the three goblins. He seemed so frightened, in fact, that he immediately blurted out:

"I like your eyeballs."

The girl's smile faded. She didn't seem sure what to make of that.

Lancelot tried to come to the rescue as he said, "No, no, that's not what I meant when I said to compliment her eyes."

"They're nice and round," Galahad jabbered on as if he couldn't even hear Lancelot. "And they're a very pretty color."

The girl began to soften a bit, and now her eyes were gazing dreamily at Galahad. Galahad grinned bashfully, and Lancelot noted that Galahad's dimples were doing a more than admirable job to win this battle for Galahad. Lancelot smiled as he thought that Galahad just might manage to pull this off after all.

"The black part in the middle is like nighttime," explained Galahad. "And the white part is quite nice too."

Lancelot sighed. Maybe Galahad wouldn't pull this off...

Without a doubt, the girl was looking more and more confused, to the point that she was bordering on downright affront. Her gentle smile and mooning gaze was gone now. Yet Galahad didn't seem to notice as he continued to ramble on.

"Your eyes are like milk. Or paper. Or clouds. Not rain clouds. But regular clouds. Nice daytime clouds."

The look of confusion had spread to all of the young girls, and they all looked at Galahad with slightly hanging jaws. Galahad smiled at them all, but no amount of dimples could save him now. Lancelot stepped up alongside Galahad and kindly took him by the shoulder.

"Well, we'll see you later, ladies…" said Lancelot as he led the boy away.

Lancelot couldn't get Galahad out of there quickly enough. Finally, when they were a safe distance out of earshot, Galahad spun and terror overtook his face.

"Was that bad?"

"Yes. Yes, that was bad," was all Lancelot could say because he didn't think he could manage a good enough lie to say otherwise. But then he shrugged. "Come on. Let's get you another drink! We've got another big day tomorrow!"

CHAPTER 16
With Wretched Wildelions

Many years earlier, in a land far away, there was a lion without a pride.

More precisely, it was born with a pride; it just quickly outgrew it. Literally outgrew it. At its birth, the cub was by far the largest of the litter. Within a few months, it was bigger than all of the females. After a year, it was the most massive lion for a hundred miles in every direction.

Unfortunately, the lion's impressive size invited many, many challenges.

Fortunately, out of necessity, the young lion quickly learned to love the fight.

As it grew to ever more remarkable size and weight, the lion faced down any fellow lion that dared to take it on. Its muscles attained remarkable strength as it fought the alpha males of its birth pride. Its roar deepened into an explosive bellow as it repelled aggressive hunting females. Its claws sharpened into devastating blades as it struck down entire rival prides. The lion swelled in size. Its mane thickened to the point of dragging continually on the ground and became clumped and dreadlocked. Its teeth lengthened until they were like saber-toothed tusks. Within a few years, not another lion in the land was foolish enough to bother with the hulking beast. It could've been the king of all the prides, but through its many battles and challenges, the massive lion had learned to spurn all other cats and it had come to prize the fight above all else.

It chose to strike out alone.

Even though it was the most dominant lion in the history of lions, it refused to take the head of one of the prides. It rejected or killed the other lions that tried to take refuge with it. It wanted no friends, no family, no allies. The largest of all the lions prowled alone, far and wide, and there was no animal or beast that it didn't seek to conquer.

It charged down bull elephants.

It outraced cheetahs.

It mud-wrestled with hippos.

Eventually, it seemed like even death itself was too scared to take on the indomitable lion, because the beast lived well beyond the lifespan of any other animal of its kind. Years stretched into decades as the massive lion roamed across the savannahs and through the deserts in search of its next challenge. It encountered rhinoceroses, land squids, and even the three-headed dog that had been put out for the night at the gates of Hades. The lion conquered them all.

And still it always chose to be alone.

It was at this point that it finally received the name that would stick with it for all the days left in its life. There was a scholar whose parents had been so stunningly accomplished that the young man felt constantly lost in their shadow. The scholar desperately yearned to make a discovery that might stand the test of time, and earn him the same respect that had been achieved by his staggering geniuses of parents. One day, the young scholar caught word of the legend of a majestic lion who put all others to shame. The scholar left his homeland and scoured the world in hopes of finding the mythic creature. After years of searching and after spending every last bit of his considerable inheritance, the scholar's hard work was finally rewarded and he caught his first glimpse of the lion, which by this time had grown to nearly five times the size of a normal lion. Its coat was shaggy and wild. Its jaws bulged with twice the normal number of teeth, and its tail could whip with the force of a hurricane. Upon seeing this magnificence, the scholar determined that it would be a disgrace to simply lump this tremendous beast along with other common lions. Thus the scholar dubbed the animal: the wildelion. It was without question the greatest achievement of the man's life, and he was certain that this discovery would ensure his place in the history books for all time.

The man was quickly eaten.

And his name was forgotten.

However, his journal lived on and was found soon thereafter, and the title of the wildelion stuck. Rumors of the wildelion spread throughout the world. Word tickled the ears of circus performers travelling through the east. Whispers blew across the oceans and reached the roaming natives in the Americas. The stories sparked the imagination of pilgrims from all races and nationalities.

LANCELOT OF THE LAKE

Migrants came from all over the world just to catch a glimpse of this strange and amazing beast.

They were all eaten.

So, eventually, just as it wished, the wildelion was left alone.

Until the day when it finally met its match.

While trekking deep into the jungles, where it proved itself to be more adept at navigating the trees than tigers, leopards, and the screeching vampire monkey, the wildelion became aware that it was being tracked. Nothing like this had happened in years. No other predator had been foolish enough to approach the wildelion since a thirty-foot python had tried to strangle the wildelion and gotten itself slurped down like a spaghetti noodle for its trouble. The wildelion thrilled at the opportunity. It sought to turn the tables on the foolish creature that was doing its best to stay concealed. However, the wildelion was far too skilled to be put off, and it quickly caught the other creature's scent. It was initially confused, because it found that it had never smelled another beast quite like it. Nonetheless, the wildelion and its quarry hunted one another through the oppressive thickness of the jungle. Finally, the wildelion closed on its prey, it pounced through a curtain of vines, and it laid eyes on the astonishing beast that had been tracking it.

It was another wildelion.

The two massive beasts lurched in astonishment, but they each knew not to let their guard down, even for a moment. They set about circling one another. Each of them rumbled with threatening growls. Both wildelions flexed their massive muscles and bristled their shaggy manes. They circled and circled and circled as they each studied for a point of weakness, an opening for attack. Finally, the moment came when one of them must spring.

Neither of them did.

The moment passed.

The two wildelions backed down from one another. Each of them had spent their entire lives fighting; there wasn't another creature that they feared, but they weren't sure about each other. Instead, they began to travel together side by side. The pride of wildelions was formed, and the world was the worse off for it. Armed with a companion, the wildelions roamed far and wide. They left the confines of their home climate and continent, and hunted in every corner of the globe.

They battled with polar bears in the arctic.

They crushed armies of barbarians to the east.

They even dove into the oceans and gnashed teeth with shivers of sharks.

However, through all of their battles, they never dared to challenge each other.

And eventually someone pointed them toward Corbenic.

Of all the beasts and monsters that had taken up residence in Corbenic, the wildelions were by far the most feared. Anyone who stumbled upon them quickly became their next meal. Any animal that the wildelions desired was immediately eaten. The only saving grace was that, in the manner of all lions, the wildelions spent much of their time sleeping so as to digest their massive meals. The wildelions would awaken approximately once a month, gorge themselves upon cows, goats or school children, and then settle themselves down for a few weeks to process the meal. The poor citizens of Corbenic could only do their best to avoid the wildelions when they awoke and then count their blessings during the weeks while they slept. For in the many years that the wildelions had lived there, no one had faced the beasts and survived to tell the tale.

Until Lancelot changed all of that.

In his first day back in Corbenic, Lancelot had obviously come face to face with the wildelions, and only by the intervention of Galahad did either of them escape. However, after having heard the stories of the devastation wrought by the terrible beasts, Lancelot knew it was only a matter of time before he would have to go back to face the wildelions once more. And once more, he would have Galahad to help him. Although, Galahad wasn't quite at the same prime as he had been before.

"I don't think I should've had that second drink yesterday…"

One of the wildelions pounced at Galahad, but the boy darted out of the way. Even at less than his best, Galahad was possessed of unnaturally quick reflexes. He was still more nimble than almost any fully grown man, although he did seem less sure on his feet than usual. And the key to his and Lancelot's strategy was to stay out of the wildelions' way until the proper moment presented itself.

"Now?" asked Galahad as he tensed and readied to dodge another pounce.

"Not just yet," said Lancelot as he also narrowly avoided a vicious attack from the other wildelion that had set its sights upon him.

Lancelot and Galahad stayed on the move, but made no attempt to strike back as they continued to discuss the celebration from the day before.

"But tell me the truth," scoffed Lancelot. "You've really never had a drink before?! You're a natural at it. You're telling me that was the first time you've imbibed?"

The other wildelion roared at Lancelot. Almost casually, he slapped it across the face, and then Lancelot moved with all the speed he could muster to get out of the beast's way.

"Most certainly I haven't!" cried Galahad. "I wouldn't have dared to have a drink before. My mother wouldn't have liked it."

"Yes, but there've been men around sometimes. Surely some of them must've shown you the ropes."

"I'm sure they would have. Many of them were very nice. It's just that pretty quickly they all ended up, you know, dead."

As if in display of the dangers the suitors faced, Galahad ducked and rolled out of the way as a wildelion leapt over him.

"Now?" asked Galahad.

"Soon. Not yet," replied Lancelot.

The two of them kept up their dance with the wildelions.

"I suppose having your father figures slain does make it harder to bond," said Lancelot, continuing the conversation as if he hadn't just had a close call with the pointy end of a saber-toothed tusk.

"But you also have those guardians that you live with. Are you telling me that they never showed you a good time either?"

One of the wildelions swiped its massive paws at Galahad again and again. The young man dodged expertly and barely lost his train of thought as he explained, "They never liked me too much. It's not their fault! They're old. They wanted their lives to settle down. And I have a bad habit of, well, breaking everything."

"I'm sure it's not that bad," said Lancelot.

"Oh, it's quite bad," insisted Galahad as he darted out of the way of another vicious swipe by the larger wildelion. "My mother always replaced things for them. But it still must be terribly frustrating for them. Bad things tend to happen when I'm around."

As a wildelion pounced, Galahad darted out of its way, but he hadn't taken stock of Lancelot's position. The wildelion landed and had a clear view of Lancelot. It swiped at Lancelot, struck him in the chest, and sent him flying. Lancelot hit the ground hard, but quickly rolled out of the way before the wildelion could pounce on top of him.

"I hadn't noticed…" groaned Lancelot.

"For the most part, I just try to stay out of everyone's way," said Galahad as he got out of the way of the other beast.

"Ah, that's a noble thing to do, my boy," said Lancelot, barely managing to duck beneath the whipping tail of the first wildelion. "To think of others in such a selfless way. But that's no way to live a life."

"It is the only way to live a life when most people who get close to you tend to end up, you know, dead."

Suddenly, Lancelot saw the moment he had been waiting for and he shouted:

"Now!"

And in perfect rhythm, both Lancelot and Galahad leapt aside just as the two wildelions pounced simultaneously toward the knight and his young companion. The massive wildelions struck one another violently for the first time in the battle. For the first time ever, in fact. Over the many years that they had spent together, the two beasts had welcomed combat with any man or monster, but they had avoided one another out of fear and respect. Now that they had been finally forced to blows, neither of them could let the offense pass. The beasts roared ferociously at one another and bared their mouths full of teeth and tusks. With the devastating ferocity of an earthquake mixed with a thunderstorm, they attacked. The wildelions devolved into a mass of slashing claws, ripping teeth, and flying fur.

It was an epic battle between the two kings of kings.

Lancelot and Galahad simply stood aside and let the duel play out.

"But you must have friends," Lancelot said to Galahad as they watched the wildelions trying to bite one another in the necks.

"Nope."

"Not even at school?"

"I don't dare go. One of my mother's suitors tried to tutor me once. But he ended up, you know —"

"Dead?"

"Yes. That's right."

The two wildelions were both deeply gashed by now, and blood dripped from their jaws and flanks. Yet they continued their fight. Neither of them had ever lost a battle before, and they didn't seem willing to do so now.

"But that couldn't have had anything to do with your schooling."

"He was teaching me mathematics when he was attacked and eaten," said Galahad, a little too off-handedly. "That was the first time I saw these wildelions."

Galahad motioned to the monsters which were finally weakening from their struggle. They both hobbled in different ways as they tried to protect wounded paws or hind legs. It was clear to Lancelot, though, that they were both on the verge of collapse.

"He was eaten by these things right in front of you?!" cried Lancelot. "How are you not terrified of them?"

"Well… He wasn't the first I'd seen," said Galahad. "Several of her suitors were killed while I was nearby. I was more scared of the goblins, because they hacked up my mother's fourth suitor. But then I saw the troll smash the fifth. And the ogre gored the sixth and seventh. After a while, it just didn't shock me so much."

"I'm sorry to hear that, Galahad," said Lancelot, and a vicious swipe from one wildelion into the face of the other helped to cover for the lameness of Lancelot's response.

"It's all right," said Galahad, and he truly didn't sound at all upset. "I don't want to put people in danger. And it's not a bad life. Considering there's monsters all around."

Finally, one of the wildelions lay dead in the field. And the other was so wounded that it couldn't manage to lift itself from the ground. Lancelot walked up to the mangled monster, and he gazed down upon it as the barely surviving wildelion struggled and wheezed.

"Should we kill it?" Galahad asked. "The fight's over."

"We weren't fighting," said Lancelot, but he wasn't sure who he thought he might convince at this point. "They fought each other."

The second wildelion laid its bloody head down on the ground. Lancelot was silently thankful that the beast seemed ready to succumb to its own wounds, and that he wouldn't have to raise his own hand. He watched as the wildelion gave a final, rattling breath and expired. Lancelot and Galahad watched as the two kings of all the kings from the jungle lay in a silent, dead heap.

At least they were together.

"We didn't fight at all…" said Lancelot.

~ ~ ~

CHAPTER 17

Elaine's Desire

In the last hours before the sun set, Lancelot returned to Corbenic Castle. He was dirty and bloodied and tired, but he didn't seek to wash himself or take a rest. Instead, he sought Elaine. Lancelot found her tending to her garden in the central courtyard. It warmed his heart to see that she was pruning the rose bush that Lancelot had brought her just a short time earlier.

"Well, isn't that lovely?" commented Lancelot, then he quickly pointed to the rose bush to clarify. "The roses, I meant. The bush looks like it will fit in just fine."

"It's taking root," said Elaine, choosing to ignore any misconstrued comments from Lancelot. "I do think it will flourish."

Elaine's eyes fell upon a long gash across Lancelot's chest.

"But I'm not sure you will!" she cried as she rushed to examine the wound. "My god, what happened?! Can't you leave the castle at all without losing little bits of yourself?"

"It's nothing. I've had worse," Lancelot said, and he lifted his right arm to allow his missing hand prove his point. "And I've lived to tell the tale."

"What did this to you?"

"The wildelions. We killed them this morning."

"We?"

176

"Me and Gal—"

Elaine fixed Lancelot with a death glare. Lancelot quickly corrected himself.

"Me. Just me. I don't know why I said '*we*.' I killed them myself. All alone."

"The troll. The ogre. The goblins. Now, the wildelions," Elaine said quietly before her eyes went wide. "Lancelot, you did it."

Lancelot grinned his biggest toothiest grin and said with his most modest immodesty, "Drove out all the monsters. Slayed all the beasts. Made Corbenic safe once more."

"And now you'll go?" Elaine blurted out.

Lancelot's big toothy grin vanished.

"Still can't wait to get rid of me, can you?"

"No. I'm sorry," Elaine said, blushing. "That's not what I meant. Please, believe me; I cannot thank you enough for all you've done."

"I understand," sighed Lancelot. "And I also understand that I'm not your favorite person. I know you don't want me here."

"That's true…" Elaine admitted.

"My goodness, Elaine!" cried Lancelot. "You can't even pretend to like having me around? Even after I've slain all the monsters that have made your life miserable these past thirteen years? You know, maybe it's best I just be on my way then. Would it kill you to act grateful for even a moment?"

"No, you don't understand," said Elaine. "It's true, I do want you to leave, but not for the reasons you think."

Lancelot shook his head, and with bitterness creeping into his words, he said, "It's fine. I did what I came to do. And now I'll go. You'll never have to see me again. And you won't even have to bother trying to forgive me for things that I did back when we were both young foolish children. I'll just content myself with knowing that I've made things safe here. I brought peace to these lands. For you. And for Galahad. And for… lucky thirteen."

A frown grew on Lancelot's face at the thought of Elaine living out the rest of her days happily with her son and a suitor who wasn't himself. However, Elaine didn't seem to register Lancelot's displeasure as she sank deeper into her own thoughts.

"Are we safe, though?" she asked quietly.

"Yes. And I have my own journeys to attend to. I feel like I've really pushed the bounds of my *'No Fighting'* vow," he said. "You're safe now. Maybe you and Galahad can finally find some peace."

Lancelot bowed his head and turned to leave, but Elaine called to him, and Lancelot turned back.

"Lancelot, wait!" she cried. "Do not leave me. Not yet. There's something I must tell you. It's not easy. But I owe it to you. Because, as much as I may like to pretend otherwise, you are a good man. And I am lucky to have you in my life."

Slowly, Lancelot drifted back toward Elaine, and in moments they could feel their breath mingling in the slowly chilling night air.

"Thank you, Lancelot," began Elaine. "I should've said that before and many times since. I cannot express how grateful I am to you. Life is certainly safer with you around."

"It's my pleasure, my lady," said Lancelot as he inched closer to her. His voice became soft and tender as he continued, "It is and always will be an honor to serve you."

Elaine's voice was barely above a gentle whisper as she asked, "But for how long?"

Lancelot moved nearer. They were face to face. A breath apart.

"Elaine, you need only say the word... Just ask me to stay…"

"No!" Elaine burst out, and the mood was shattered as she pulled away. "You have to leave."

"But I thought you were saying that I made things safer?" said Lancelot as his wounded pride flooded back in.

"You misunderstand me. This has nothing to do with my own wishes. It's about Galahad."

Lancelot's brow clouded with confusion. Elaine placed a soft hand on his hard face, but it looked like she was struggling with a decision.

"Lancelot, I have something I must ask of you."

"Anything."

But before she was able to speak, another voice interrupted and broke the tension between the lady and the knight.

"Ahhh! Here you are, Sir Lancelot, my brave and noble friend!"

Lancelot and Elaine spun to see King Pelles, supported by several servants, shuffling into the garden. Lancelot looked back to Elaine, but she dropped her gaze.

"You snuck in without coming to see me first!" the old man said between heavy gasps of air, wagging a playfully disapproving finger.

"That was my fault, Father," cut in Elaine. "Lancelot was on his way to see you, but I distracted him."

King Pelles simply waved away her explanation with a smile. "Nonsense, nonsense. I could never be angry on a day like today. Lancelot, you've done it!"

And the old king pulled Lancelot into a joyful hug with his ancient twisted arms.

"It was nothing, King Pelles," said Lancelot as he inclined his head ever so slightly to the king.

"And still so modest," chuckled Pelles in delight. "You are so much like I once was. I see so much of myself in you."

A strange thought occurred to Lancelot, and he gazed at the old man and he realized that he too could see himself in the old king. Lancelot saw a glimpse of his future. Exhausted, beaten, battered, but still alive. There could be worse futures to contemplate.

"Lancelot, would you join me for a moment in my throne room?"

"Certainly, King Pelles," assented Lancelot, but then he motioned back to Elaine. "However, I was having a word with your daughter. If we could just have a moment to finish."

"Of course, of course. Go right ahead," said King Pelles. "I can wait."

However, the old king didn't make any move to leave. Lancelot looked to Elaine, but she seemed unwilling to talk in her father's presence.

"Go on, my dear," Pelles prodded.

"I… It's nothing important," said Elaine, as she smiled back at her father. "I can speak to Lancelot about it later. You two should talk."

"Wonderful!" cried King Pelles as he gestured for Lancelot to follow after him. "Come with me, my boy. I have something I'm simply dying to ask you."

~ ~ ~

CHAPTER 18

Victory and Failure

It took a great concerted effort from the all gathered servants, and the night had fallen by the time King Pelles was successfully carted into the throne room, but with the help of Lancelot and the other sturdy men, the old king finally settled back upon his throne. King Pelles sank down into the well-padded chair, and took several deep breaths to calm himself as he cleared his throat so that he might be able to muster his most forceful and regal tone.

"Lancelot, as you know, it took me a long time to build this kingdom," said Pelles, once he had steadied his breathing. "There were many years of hard work to build the castle and army. I had to wage many difficult battles. But I overcame them all."

"You certainly have created something wonderful here," said Lancelot as his mind fell specifically on Elaine.

"Thank you," said Pelles, but then he heaved a great sigh and added, "But by the time I had achieved the peace here, I was no longer a young man. I married late."

"The life of a warrior sometimes gets in the way of the life of a husband or father," said Lancelot, somewhat to the king and somewhat to himself. "Sometimes, however, work simply must come first."

"Yes," King Pelles agreed. "But my greatest regret is that it never gave me time to sire a male heir, no matter how much I might've desired one." The old king paused and then he looked Lancelot in the eyes. "Fortunately, you came along."

Words suddenly deserted Lancelot as he wondered how much King Pelles might know about Galahad. However, King Pelles seemed to have other things in mind.

"I'm an old man, Lancelot, and as much as I may regret it, I no longer have the strength to hold this kingdom together."

"Nonsense; you have many long years ahead of you, my lord."

"No, I do not," said Pelles quietly. "But you do."

Lancelot's mind raced as he tried to make sense of what the king was getting at, but Pelles quickly spelled it out for him.

"King Lancelot. It has a nice ring to it, does it not?"

"You're joking," stammered Lancelot. "I could never be a king! I would never... I could never imagine myself a... *king?!*"

"Sir Lancelot, this kingdom needs you. And I need you," said King Pelles gravely, as he gazed deeply into Lancelot's eyes. *"Can I count on you?"*

The words struck deeply into Lancelot and awakened a dark and terrible memory of another day when another king had spoken the same thing.

~ ~ ~

Of course, it wasn't the first time that Lancelot had been charged with a noble duty from a king. However, King Pelles's request was the first time that Lancelot was plagued with doubts about his ability to perform the task asked of him.

Just a few years earlier, Lancelot had been in his prime when he stood alongside his fellow knights of Tintagel and listened to the words of the great King Uther Pendragon. Lancelot wore a full suit of armor over his powerfully muscled body. He bore his share of scars, but his face was still shining with hope and optimism. And he was still able to grip a sword with his unblemished right hand.

He was surrounded by several dozen of his brother knights, and each of them was also armed and ready for combat. They all bore the armor of Tintagel and they all held shields adorned with the crest of the Pendragon. Battle lay in their very near future.

But only Lancelot seemed excited about it.

Beside Lancelot stood a shorter, slighter, less impressive knight. Sir Percival was also dressed for combat, but his armor rattled ever so slightly as the frightened man quaked inside his metal suit. To be fair, Percival wasn't the only one; all of the knights seemed concerned, and one of them even seemed to have sprung a leak in his armor, as a small bit of liquid dribbled out of his boot. The reason for their fear became clear as:

The roar of a dragon reverberated through the castle.

"My noble knights, the castle is under siege," stated Uther as he addressed the assembled fighters. He too was dressed in fine armor flecked with gold and bearing the crest of a dragon wrapped with fire. However, the king maintained his confidence as he said,

"Saxon warriors attack from all sides. Vortigern seeks to take Tintagel for himself. And there's a Red Dragon in the skies."

Much of the color drained from the other knights' faces.

But Lancelot's eyes glowed with furious excitement.

"We can still win this night, my friends. I ask that each of you fight bravely. Fight true. Fight for all that is good. And tomorrow our lives will be at peace once more!" declared Uther, and the men all cheered at his words.

With a wave of his arms, Uther urged the knights forward, and with a clattering of armor, they began to march toward battle. As they headed for the door, however, Uther caught Lancelot by the arm.

"Sir Lancelot, let me speak to you for a moment."

"Yes, sir! My king!"

"I need you to lead these men," said Uther, and then he added those familiar words: *"Sir Lancelot, the kingdom needs you. And I need you. Can I count on you?"*

Lancelot grinned from ear to ear. He'd been waiting his entire life for a chance like this, and he nodded to Uther to let his king know that he could rely on Sir Lancelot.

Yet the night wasn't destined for victory.

As the rain poured down and transformed the courtyard into thick mud, Lancelot stood ready to defend the main gate and push back the invading horde of Saxons. At his side again were Percival and many more knights. They each had their swords drawn and pointed at the gate as an insistent pounding threatened to meet them at any moment.

But still only Lancelot seemed excited.

Boom.

Boom!

BOOM!

The gate cracked and scowling Saxon warriors ripped and tore their way through the wooden entrance. In moments, the villains flooded into the courtyard, and Lancelot relished the chance to cut them down. Unfortunately, despite Lancelot's enthusiasm for the coming war, his fellow knights didn't share in his courage, and in rapid succession they all abandoned their post and ran.

"I'm — I'm sorry, Lancelot... I'm sorry..." were Percival's last words as he dropped his sword and sprinted away.

Lancelot was left alone to battle the oncoming horde of Saxons.

"All right... Just me then..."

And battle them he did.

All alone, Lancelot fought against the entire army. His sword struck righteous and true. Any man who came within his reach was brought down. Dozens of Saxons fell to Lancelot's mighty blade. But even the greatest knight in the kingdom could only last so long against an invading army.

SLASH!

An enemy blade broke past the others and connected with Lancelot.

With a savage scream, Lancelot's right hand dropped from his body.

Lancelot wasn't done yet, though, and he snatched up his sword in his left hand and did his best to prevail. He fought on. But the night was relentless. The rain unceasing. The mud unforgiving. And the Saxons were never-ending. Finally, the mob rushed at Lancelot all as one, and the greatest knight in the kingdom was forced to break his promise to his king.

The mighty Sir Lancelot was overcome.

~ ~ ~

"Excuse me? Lancelot? Are you still there?"

Lancelot snapped back to the real world, and met the eyes of old King Pelles, who had leaned eagerly forward in his cushioned throne. The old man's eyes sparkled as he still eagerly anticipated Lancelot's response. However, Lancelot's face paled from the grave and unexpected request.

"Usually I'm the one who drifts off in the midst of conversation," said the king with a twinkle in his knowing eyes.

"I'm sorry, my lord…" whispered Lancelot. "It's a lot to take in. I admit I was lost in my own thoughts. I don't know what to say."

"I've been searching for a long time for someone strong enough to rule this kingdom, Lancelot. Someone able to fight off any challenges that this kingdom might face, just like I once did. Corbenic needs a new king. Corbenic needs you, Lancelot."

Lancelot's mouth fell open, but he couldn't bring himself to say the words that King Pelles so clearly wanted. The ancient king gazed at the legendary knight and willed him to agree to take over the kingdom. But Lancelot's head and shoulders sagged under the burden.

"I can't."

"I'm sorry, my boy, my hearing isn't quite what it once was," said King Pelles. "It sounded as if you said you can't."

Lancelot felt pain worse than a slash from a wildelion as he tried to explain. "My own life is a mess of destruction and pain. I can't even bring peace to myself. I don't see how I could possibly bring peace to your kingdom or your people. You honor me, my lord, but I'm not your man."

The refusal quickly settled over the king. It didn't take long before his bright eyes darkened and a slight growling seemed to accompany Pelles's every syllable as he said, "In my youth, I was known to have quite a temper when disappointed. I suggest you leave my sight before we find out if I still maintain it."

"I don't mean to disappoint you, my lord."

"FLEE!"

The old king erupted with such a fury as Lancelot had never heard before. Knowing that the only decent thing to do was to leave, Lancelot nodded to King Pelles and rushed away. As the knight left, old King Pelles sagged in his throne, slammed down a furious fist, and watched his last hope walk out the door.

~ ~ ~

CHAPTER 19

No Way Out

Lancelot hurried through the castle hallways with the intention of quickly going to his room, gathering his few belongings, and leaving Corbenic forever no matter how late in the night it might be. However, Elaine had a knack for changing his plans.

"What happened?!" she demanded as she emerged from her chambers and blocked Lancelot's path to his own room.

Lancelot struggled to know what to say. He was beginning to find dealing with Elaine to be more challenging than battling a coterie of monsters and fiends. After looking into her eyes for a moment, Lancelot searched the hallways and quickly spotted a few servants still bustling about. Deciding they were too in the open, Lancelot took Elaine's arm and led her away.

He guided her into a side room, but once again there were a few servants laying out a small table with roasted apples as a late evening snack. Lancelot was about to take Elaine to find a more secluded place, but the lady stopped him and she addressed the servants.

"Please, leave us," ordered Elaine.

The servants dutifully exited, and Elaine once more fixed Lancelot with an insistent gaze.

"Well, what has gotten into you?" she asked. "What did my father say?"

Still reeling somewhat from the shock of it all, Lancelot said, "Your father... he asked me to be king."

Elaine's lovely face was overcome with surprise, but she managed to utter, "And what did you say?"

"I said no," said Lancelot, and Elaine seemed to breathe a sigh of relief. "I can't be king. Every time I've thought I had my life together, it's come crashing down in pain and agony. I can't bring peace to a kingdom. I can't have people counting on me."

"My father must not have liked hearing that."

"I've never heard him shout before," said Lancelot with a slight shudder just from the memory. "Let's just say, I can certainly see how people once found him to be quite intimidating."

"So where will you go?"

"Back to where I came from. Elaine, I know now that you were right to ask me to go. And so I'll gather my things and be gone before morning."

"But I don't want you to leave," said Elaine.

Lancelot's head was starting to hurt trying to figure this woman out, and he said, "But... in the garden... Weren't you about to ask me to leave?"

"Yes," said Elaine, and Lancelot was just as confused as before. She continued, "But I didn't want you to go just yet."

"It is nearly impossible to keep track with you, Elaine."

"I was going to ask that you take Galahad with you."

190

This time it was Lancelot's turn to look surprised, but he could tell by the pained expression on Elaine's face that there was more to the request.

"I think... I think he would be safer with you," she said.

"There's something you're not telling me, Elaine," pressed Lancelot. "Why would you want me to take your son away from you? Why do you think Galahad is in danger?"

It took a long moment for Elaine to respond, and Lancelot could see she was blinking back tears as she finally admitted to him, "When he was born, thirteen years ago, that's when the monsters came. They've plagued this kingdom ever since. They've killed anyone that ever became close to me."

Lancelot's mind flashed back to each of his encounters with the monsters and how Galahad had always been close at hand. Several times, Lancelot had thought that there seemed to be a strange connection between the boy and the beasts, but Lancelot had pushed away the thoughts. Now, he had to ask, "So you think Galahad might be the cause of the monsters? You think he's connected to them somehow? Do you think he might be cursed?"

A single tear slid down Elaine's cheek and she said, "I don't know. He's my son, and I know he's a good boy. I don't want to believe that he might be..."

Elaine fell silent and Lancelot understood that as a mother she couldn't bring herself to say the words that her own child might be cursed, even though she might believe it in the depth of her heart.

Lancelot reached for Elaine to brush away her tears, but she pulled away from him.

"He's always had a strange relationship with the monsters. He follows them. He thinks I don't know, and I've tried to stop him from doing it, but he can't seem to help himself," said Elaine. "And then every man who's ever dared to become close to me has been met with disaster. Even you, Lancelot. As soon as I saw you again, the water boiled. Just because you still care for me."

"I don't still care for you!" lied Lancelot vigorously.

"Oh, of course, you still care for me!" said Elaine as if it was the most obvious thing in the world. Then she added fairly, "Just as, of course, I still care for you!"

Once again, Lancelot found himself struck with the thought that it was nearly impossible to figure Elaine out.

"It's as if Galahad somehow is trying to protect his mother," said Elaine softly. "It's sweet really — if it hadn't led to so many people being hurt. And I fear it's only a matter of time before he is killed too."

"Elaine, what do you think I can do about all of it?" asked Lancelot.

"Don't you see, Lancelot? You survived," said Elaine. "You survived it all. If Galahad is cursed, if he does draw dark forces to him, you may be the only one strong enough to help him. Please, Lancelot, will you help him?"

With a long heavy sigh, Lancelot nodded and said, "I know a place. It's where I've been trying to get back to. It may be able to bring him peace and healing."

"Oh, Lancelot, would you take Galahad there?" cried Elaine. "Where is it?"

"The Lakes of Avalon."

A slight laugh escaped Elaine's lips. "Come now, even you can't believe... It's not possible... The Lakes of Avalon are just a myth."

"I assure you, they are very real," said Lancelot. "It's where I came from. I seek to return. And I'll take Galahad with me."

Suddenly, the door slammed shut. That in and of itself wasn't alarming. After all, the door could've easily closed due to a draft or a clumsy servant. What was much more difficult to explain, and what caused Lancelot considerable alarm, was how the windows were closing over with oppressive stones as if the walls were swallowing the openings from their very existence. Looking around in panic, Lancelot and Elaine watched as the room sealed itself around them. Lancelot rushed to the door, but pull as he might, it wouldn't open. Elaine ran her hands along the wall where there was once a window, but it was gone. As she slid her finger across the stone, however, a small hole opened in the wall. Then another. And another. And another.

"Down!" shouted Lancelot as a flurry of razor-tipped darts began to shoot out of the holes in the wall.

Lancelot seized Elaine even as he overturned the small table in the center of the room. Lancelot held it up like a shield against the flying darts, but the barrage was unending. Dozens, if not hundreds, of the tiny killing spears flew at them, and the table quickly began to crack and splinter.

"Do you see what happens to those who care for me?!" shouted Elaine over the noise made by a hundred darts plunging themselves into the meager protection of the table.

"You're worth it, my lady."

Lancelot's eyes raked around the room, looking for any weakness that might lead to escape.

"I promise you that I'll get Galahad out of here," declared Lancelot as their shield split and looked close to giving way.

"Don't you think you're overlooking something? First, we have to get out of here ourselves."

"If the darts can get in... Then we can get out!"

With a furious roar, Lancelot charged toward the wall. He rammed himself into the stone, slamming against it and putting all his considerable weight and strength behind the charge. The many holes through which the darts flew seemed to have weakened the sturdiness of the wall, and the stone cracked and gave way under the onslaught of Lancelot's might. Again and again, Lancelot threw himself against the wall, and each time it shuddered as more and more of the stone crumbled away. Finally, after one more mighty charge, Lancelot crashed through the wall, leaving rubble in his wake.

Lancelot, with Elaine close behind, burst into the hallway and kept on running. With a backward glance toward the room that continued spitting darts, Lancelot tossed aside what was left the table that had acted as his shield, and ran toward the front gate of the castle.

"Do you see what I mean?" grumbled Elaine. "These strange kinds of things keep happening."

"But not to Galahad?" asked Lancelot. "He's immune to them?"

"No. He's been in danger from the monsters or strange occurrences almost since the moment he was born," said Elaine. "But even from a young age, he's been remarkably able to defend himself."

"He certainly is remarkable," agreed Lancelot as he mulled over the strange abilities of the young boy. Then he paused and said, "Do you hear that?"

From out the window, an undeniable roaring sound rattled the air.

"It sounds like something flying...?"

Lancelot and Elaine moved to the window and stared out into the distance. Both of their faces went slack with shock as they locked onto the disturbing sight.

A massive hand of molten fire soared through the sky.

The Hand of Fire swooped down upon a distant field and a wide expanse of wheat went up in flame. The destruction spread with astonishing speed, and the Hand of Fire shot back up into the sky to continue its reign of terror.

As any mother would, Elaine's first thought fell to:

"Galahad."

"I'll get to him," said Lancelot. "I'll make sure he's all right. And I'll take him away from here."

"Please, hurry. For his sake and the sake of anyone else who might be near."

Lancelot was about to sprint out of the castle, but then he made a decision. He decided then and there that he would stop the Hand of Fire, gather up Galahad, and then never return. With that firmly in mind, he paused for an instant, grabbed Elaine around the waist, and kissed her roughly upon the lips. After a powerful moment, Lancelot broke the embrace and gazed into his lady's eyes.

"Goodbye, Elaine."

Then the mighty knight charged out of the castle to face his destiny.

~ ~ ~

CHAPTER 20

The Fire Descends

Sprinting across the castle's drawbridge, Lancelot looked ahead and saw:

The Hand of Fire demolishing a farmhouse.

Lancelot raced down the dirt path toward the village.

The Hand of Fire set an old oak tree ablaze.

Lancelot bounded through the village, pushing his way past many gawkers who were watching the terror in the sky.

The Hand of Fire spun and dove and destroyed everything it touched.

Finally, Lancelot reached the small hut on the edge of the village, and wasted no time as he pounded on the door with his one good fist.

"Hey, hey, HEY!" came a grumpy voice from just inside the hut. Suddenly, the old man that Lancelot knew to be Galahad's guardian emerged. "My POOR DOOR!"

"Sir, my apologies, but—"

With a bitter scowl that might've just been his ordinary expression, the old man held up a finger to silence Lancelot as he began to inspect the door.

"What're you doing?" Lancelot asked impatiently.

"I'm INSPECTING my door," cried the old man. "Believe me, I'm not going to be the one to pay for it if there's any DENTS or SCRATCHES."

"Please, sir, this is urgent. Forget the door. I assure you it's fine."

"Says the big muscular OAF!"

Finally, after a frustratingly slow and detailed examination of his door, the old man turned to Lancelot and demanded, "All right. All right. What d'YOU want?"

"I'm looking for Galahad."

"Why? So you can help him with wrecking EVERY LAST THING I own?!"

"No, I—"

"WHO IS IT?!" shrieked another voice from the next room.

"Some TALL GUY. With HALF AN ARM. Wants to see GALAHAD!"

"Please, sir, we must hurry. Is Galahad here?"

"Tell him to GO AWAY!" shouted the woman as she hobbled toward the door bearing a deep frown that might've just been her normal face.

"That's what I'm TRYING to do!"

"Then DO IT!"

"You come here and you tell him if you're SO IMPATIENT!"

The grumpy woman stumped in and eyed up Lancelot.

"Who're YOU?"

"I'm Sir Lancelot; I'm looking for—"

"SIR Lancelot?! A KNIGHT, are you? What kind of a knight LOSES HIS HAND?!"

Lancelot gritted his teeth and said in a low growl, "It's really not that big of a deal."

"NOT THAT BIG OF DEAL?!" said the woman in utter disbelief.

"I think it would be a big deal if I LOST MY HAND!" chimed in her husband.

"Yeah, then he couldn't scratch his rear ALL THE TIME!"

"Then I couldn't cover both my ears WHEN YOU COME IN THE ROOM!"

"THEN YOU COULDN'T —"

"*IS GALAHAD HERE OR NOT?!*" demanded Lancelot as he finally lost his temper and matched the pitch and volume of the bickering old couple.

"Yes. I'm here."

Lancelot scanned the room and found Galahad standing respectfully aside, and it looked as if he'd been waiting there for a while, but was too polite to speak up.

"Pack some things," said Lancelot, ignoring the stares from the older couple as he let himself into the room and strode over to Galahad. "Your mother asked me to get you out of here."

"Is it bad?"

Almost in answer, screams of panic rung out in the distance. Galahad rushed to the door and looked out. His normally impassive face twisted into concern as he watched the Hand of Fire ripping through the nearby village.

"It's bad," said Lancelot.

Without a moment's pause, Galahad bolted out the door and ran directly for the Hand of Fire. Lancelot raced after the boy, calling, "Galahad! Stop! Where are you going?!"

"We've got to help those people!" yelled back Galahad without breaking stride.

"I was supposed to get you to safety, not plunge you further into it," shouted Lancelot with frustration partially from the boy's unexpected response, but also partially because Lancelot was realizing that Galahad was going to be difficult to catch up with. "Your mother is going to kill me."

The rugged knight chased after the fair-skinned young man, and together they charged toward the reign of terror ahead. The grumpy old couple stood in their doorway and watched Lancelot and Galahad shrinking into the distance as they plunged toward danger. It had been longer than either could remember since they'd been tender to each other, but with a Hand of Fire crashing through the sky, the old woman took her husband's wrinkled fingers and intertwined them with her own. Then she turned to him and said,

"How come you can't go off RUNNING TO YOUR DOOM?!"

~ ~ ~

Many years earlier, in a land far away, no one had ever heard of anything like a devastating hand of molten fire that could soar through the sky and smite anything that it touched. In the local kingdoms, no one had ever seen anything like this. In the distant countries, it was a completely unknown menace. In the far away mystical lands, a destructive Hand of Fire was unimaginable.

And someone had pointed it toward Corbenic.

Wide swaths of farmland blazed.

Villages crackled under oppressive heat.

Men, women and children barely escaped with their lives.

Lancelot and Galahad raced right for it.

"We've got to draw it away from the fields!" shouted Galahad.

Lancelot, who was still struggling to catch up to the boy, called ahead, "I'm open to ideas. This is a new one for me…"

After a moment's thought, Galahad simply skipped into the air, waved his arms, and continued running as he shouted:

"Hey there! Hey, Hand of Fire! Over here!"

"I sincerely doubt that will work," scoffed Lancelot.

The words were barely out of Lancelot's mouth, though, when the Hand of Fire turned in mid-air and careened in the direction of Galahad's insistent calls.

"Well, what do you know?" said Lancelot. "I guess sometimes the simplest answer is the best answer."

Both Lancelot and Galahad seemed pleasantly surprised until they realized:

"It's headed this way."

"What should we do now?" asked Galahad as he ground to a halt.

"You're the one with all of ideas," pointed out Lancelot.

In mere moments, the Hand of Fire had cut the distance between itself and Lancelot and Galahad. Galahad merely shrugged, turned, and ran in the opposite direction.

"I'm going to leave it up to the greatest knight in the land to tell me what to do next!" shouted Galahad as he began his attempt to outrun the oncoming flames.

Lancelot raced alongside the boy and once again was frustrated to find how difficult it was to match Galahad's pace. Even more frustrating, however, was seeing that neither of them would be able to outrun the Hand of Fire for long. With a quick backward glance over his shoulder, Lancelot saw that the fire was quickly approaching.

"We'll never be faster than it," said Lancelot between deep gulps of breath as he bolted across a field. "But if we split up, then we can draw it back and forth between us and slow it down."

The Hand of Fire grew closer and closer.

"And then what?" asked Galahad.

The Hand of Fire's heat tickled at their backs.

Lancelot gazed ahead and smiled as if it was the most obvious thing in the world. "It's fire, my boy. We've simply got to bring it to water."

He pointed ahead of them, and at first Galahad only registered Corbenic Castle itself, but he quickly caught onto Lancelot's idea:

"The castle's moat!"

"Now we've just got to keep ourselves from roasting," said Lancelot, and he looked toward the castle, which still seemed awfully far away, while the Hand of Fire was growing terribly close. "It's a good thing both my legs are still intact. Now split up!"

Lancelot and Galahad broke apart just as the Hand of Fire reached them and swiped at the ground between the knight and the boy. Lancelot felt the searing heat as he tore off to his right. Galahad raced off to the left, and for a moment the Hand of Fire seemed confused about where to go. Then it twisted and chased after Lancelot. The mighty knight strained his muscles to the utmost of their abilities. His legs pumped furiously and his body became a precision instrument of speed. His lungs and heart worked furiously to propel him along, but the Hand of Fire was inescapable. In less than a minute, the Hand of Fire's heat washed along Lancelot's back. Tiny beads of sweat collected along every bare inch of Lancelot's flesh. The fire was about to overcome him when:

"Hey! Over here! Come and get me!"

Galahad bellowed and waved his arms in the distance, and to Lancelot's immense relief, the Hand of Fire adjusted its course to chase after the boy, who continued sprinting toward the castle. Lancelot paused for just a moment to refill his lungs and he watched the Hand of Fire pursuing Galahad. Once again, it was clear that the Hand of Fire would catch up in no time, but it was also clear that Galahad was giving it a good challenge. There was no doubt about it: the boy could run. Pushing his own legs to their limits, Lancelot beat his own path toward the castle and thought with an equal mixture of admiration and bitterness:

I could run that fast, if I wanted to...

The Hand of Fire had nearly overtaken Galahad when:

"Try and catch me, you cowardly fingers of flame!"

The Hand of Fire darted away from Galahad and chased after Lancelot.

Lancelot sprinted with all his might, but the Hand of Fire quickly caught up.

"Pardon?! Did you forget about me?"

The Hand of Fire turned and pursued Galahad once again.

"What's the matter?! Knew you couldn't catch the greatest knight in the land?!"

And the fire resumed its chase of Lancelot.

Back and forth and back and forth the two of them taunted the Hand of Fire, and they kept it from falling upon either of them. All the while they led it closer and closer to Corbenic Castle. However, and despite the fact that he'd never admit it out loud, Lancelot was tiring, and he suspected Galahad was too. Any wrong move meant death beneath the merciless Hand of Fire. As they got closer to the castle, Lancelot saw a crowd of panicked people emerging and congregating on the drawbridge.

King Pelles shuffled out of the castle, or more precisely, he was dragged along by two guards. At the king's side, Elaine took in the strange scene and her eyes went wide with confusion and fear as she registered:

"Lancelot?!"

Then she caught sight of her son and screamed:

"Galahad!"

In a panic, Elaine pushed through the crowd, crossed the drawbridge and quickly reached the bank on the other side.

"Elaine! Get out of the way!" shouted Lancelot. "Get everyone to safety!"

It was too late, though, and Elaine's moment of motherly intuition had grabbed the attention of the Hand of Fire. The monstrous molten hand urged itself onward and zoomed past Lancelot and Galahad as it careened toward Elaine. Both Lancelot and Galahad added a final burst of speed to try and overcome the Hand of Fire, but it was no use. They were too tired, the Hand of Fire had a straighter path, and it was pointed directly for the lady.

"Elaine!"

"Mother!"

Galahad's shout of concern rang clearly through the air and everyone assembled couldn't help but hear it.

Everyone including King Pelles.

Lancelot and Galahad strained with everything they had to catch to the Hand of Fire. Lancelot's lungs ached from the effort. Galahad's heart pounded against his chest. Both of their legs screamed with exertion. It was no use, though: they couldn't possibly make it in time.

The Hand of Fire was nearly upon Elaine.

Almost......

Almost...

Almost.

Elaine turned and dove into the moat.

And the Hand of Fire crashed after her, splashing into the water with a roaring sizzle.

Unable to stop their momentum, both Lancelot and Galahad also tumbled into the water of the moat, only moments behind Elaine and the Hand of Fire. A great deal of roiling and sputtering ensued, but Elaine emerged first, quickly followed by Lancelot and Galahad. The Hand of Fire, fortunately, did not resurface. The three of them clambered onto the shore, each dripping wet and gasping for breath. Lancelot especially was bent over double and desperately trying to refill his lungs with air.

"Are you all right?" Galahad asked his mother, and Lancelot was disturbed to see that Galahad didn't seem nearly as out of breath as he was.

"Are you all right?!" cried Elaine to Galahad at nearly the exact same time as she pulled her son tightly into her arms.

"Isn't anyone going to ask me if I'm all right?" said Lancelot.

"No," said Elaine.

"Are you?" asked Galahad with a bit more politeness.

"Yes. Thank you. I'm fine," said Lancelot, finally able to draw a full breath again. "In fact, I'd say everything turned out perfectly well."

"TREACHERY!"

Lancelot, Elaine, and Galahad all spun to see King Pelles marching furiously toward them, and his anger seemed to balance him far more than any cane or servant ever could. The normally feeble old king barely wobbled as he strode toward his daughter and the two men in her life.

"Well, maybe things didn't turn out perfectly well…" said Lancelot.

King Pelles stormed at them. Two guards tried to steady him under the arms, but there was no need and he waved them away. The king moved more forcefully than anyone had seen in years, and the rage in his eyes seemed to be the clear explanation for it.

"Who is this boy?!" demanded the king. "Why did he call you 'Mother'? What in heaven's name is going on?!"

Elaine looked crestfallen as she grimaced and said, "Father, say hello to your grandson…"

"Hello, Grandfather," said Galahad with his usual sincerity and politeness.

But King Pelles's face turned furiously red as he roared, "GUARDS! Seize him!"

Several guards moved forward to grab Galahad, but Elaine thrust herself into their path.

"No, Father, this is between you and I," she said. Then she turned to Lancelot and demanded, "Get Galahad out of here."

Before Lancelot could move, however, Pelles sputtered, "You mean *he's* the father?!"

"No, I'm not!" shouted Lancelot.

But at the very same moment, Elaine declared, "Yes, he is!"

Lancelot spun and gaped at Elaine.

"What?! You said he wasn't mine!"

"I lied," said Elaine truthfully.

"MORE TREACHERY!" cried the king as his face turned an even brighter shade of red. Pelles's age was finally starting to catch up to him, and his chest rose and fell in great heaving gasps as he bellowed, "More guards! More seizing!"

Suddenly, many more guards flooded out of the castle. King Pelles pointed them toward Lancelot.

"Seize him!" the king ordered.

"Father, listen to me," pleaded Elaine. "Lancelot isn't responsible for this."

"I promise you I had no idea," said Lancelot.

The guards continued following orders, though, and roughly grabbed Lancelot's arms. In the back of his mind, Lancelot knew that he could probably take on the entire contingent of guards and win. There were only about a dozen of them, and it couldn't be forgotten that he was a fairly renowned monster slayer. However, he also knew that he had been caught, and he chose not to put up a fight as the guards harshly pinned his arms to his sides.

"Arrest them," said Pelles as he pointed to Galahad as well. "Arrest both of them."

As the guards moved in to grab Galahad, Lancelot finally felt compelled to put up a fight. He wrenched his arms free and shoved the guards away from Galahad.

"You take your hands off that boy!"

"Is this bad?" asked Galahad, as innocently as ever, and refusing to fight back.

"Father, leave him alone," demanded Elaine, and her fury flared like a mother bear protecting her cub. "He is just a boy. He had nothing to do with this!"

"He is the treachery itself!" said Pelles. "Take him to the dungeon!"

One of the guards shoved Elaine aside as three more took hold of Galahad. A moment ago, Lancelot had been prepared to accept his fate, but no longer. Lancelot clenched his one good fist and tensed his legs as he decided that he was going to show the entire contingent of guards what the full fury of the greatest knight in the world looked like. Yet his decision was a moment too late as a guard snuck up behind him, and with a vicious swing of a club, Lancelot was cracked over the head. As Lancelot stumbled and fell to his knees, he saw Galahad was surrounded by several more guards, and Elaine was being bound up by her father.

Unable to help them, darkness clouded into Lancelot's vision and he fell unconscious.

~ ~ ~

CHAPTER 21

Dark Places and Terrible Choices

An hour later, Lancelot's head throbbed as he gingerly forced himself to sit up in the dungeon. His vision blurred a bit, but Lancelot quickly saw Galahad shaking the iron bars and immediately realizing that it was no use. Lancelot groaned as he took in the heavy manacles and stone walls. Galahad spun as Lancelot sat up, and the boy rushed to his side. Doing his best to maintain an air of bravery and composure, Lancelot waved Galahad away even as the dungeon seemed to spin ominously around him.

"Thank you for fighting for my mother and I," said Galahad. "It was very kind of you."

"My pleasure," groaned Lancelot.

"How's your head? That seemed like quite the blow they gave you," said Galahad, but then he attempted his own casual air as he added, "However, you are one of the mightiest knights in history. I thought maybe you didn't mind it as much as most people would."

Feeling appreciative for Galahad's positive spin, Lancelot nodded and said, "Yes. For a man like me, it was nothing whatsoever to worry about."

But since Lancelot nearly collapsed as he rose to his feet, he figured that his boast might not be entirely believable. Galahad was kind enough not to question it. Although his legs felt leaden and his head still ached terribly, Lancelot moved around the tiny cell and tested the windows and bars for any weaknesses. There were none. After a few short moments, Lancelot slumped back down against the wall in momentary defeat.

"Is this bad?" asked Galahad.

Lancelot shrugged and said, "I've been through worse…"

~ ~ ~

Of course, Lancelot had been through worse.

In fact, the dungeon in Corbenic was far from his lowest point. That honor lay with the day a few years earlier when Lancelot had lost his arm. It had almost been Lancelot's greatest victory as he nearly managed to slay an entire army of Saxons. However, the difference between ultimate victory and devastating failure is oftentimes determined by a finger length.

After his terrible battle, Lancelot was short that finger and several others.

As the rain streaked down and flooded the courtyard of Tintagel Castle, Lancelot had lain in a heap amongst the bodies of the many warriors that he had successfully slain. His weakened mass sunk slightly into the mud, and his breath became so shallow that the women who were tasked with clearing the courtyard after the battle didn't even notice him. Lancelot was piled onto a straining wooden cart with all of the corpses. He was wheeled outside of the castle's walls and dumped into a shallow ditch. He knew that in a short time gravediggers would come to fill in the pit and he would be lost beneath a wave of mud.

211

But the old woman, Morgana, came first.

Despite her unsteady legs and ancient crooked back, Morgana descended into the pit of bodies. The old woman carefully sifted through them and sought any sign of life as she prodded for softly beating hearts or faint breath. When she found Lancelot, Morgana could scarcely believe her luck.

Lancelot drifted in and out of consciousness as Morgana brought him back to her meager hut. It must've taken her an immense effort, but she dragged him back to her home. She laid him upon the poorly cobbled table, and her rough, twisted fingers poked and jabbed at Lancelot's many wounds. She staunched the bleeding where she could, she cleaned the filth from the most vulnerable places, and she tied off Lancelot's right arm where it had been severed above the hand.

When he finally came out of his haze, Lancelot writhed in anguish on the rough hewn table, but Morgana simply pushed him back. Even her withered strength was enough to overcome Lancelot in his pitiful condition, and he was forced to recline at her touch.

"Lie still," the old woman croaked. "I shall take care of you, my dear."

In the corner of his eye, Lancelot saw a burst of orange light emanating from the cauldron in the hearth.

"Can't... breathe..." muttered Lancelot. "Can't... stay awake..."

"But stay awake you must, my dear," said Morgana, as she bustled about and continued treating his wounds. "You cannot rest. Never rest. Rest will be your death."

Fighting with every ounce of resolve he had left to stay awake, Lancelot caught glimpses of Morgana at work. He saw bubbling potions. Strange colors. Floating fumes. He wasn't sure how much time passed. It could've been minutes. It could've been hours. Or it could have been the eternity that lies between life and death. Eventually, Lancelot became aware that Morgana was holding a hand-carved cup to his lips. Reflexively, Lancelot opened his mouth and sought to drink, but the old woman pulled the cup away.

"I cannot give this to you, my dear, unless you ask."

Lancelot could barely form the words, but he whispered, "Why...? What... what is it...?"

"It has the power to restore you, my dear. It can heal your wounds. It will restore your strength. It will set you back on the path to becoming what you once were."

Lancelot opened his lips once more to ask for the potion, but Morgana quickly silenced him.

"But..." she said as she held the cup tantalizingly close to Lancelot's mouth, "it will come with a price."

"Tell me..." said Lancelot.

"It will bind you to me," said Morgana. "One day, I will ask for your service. For good or for ill, you must agree to my wishes. You will belong to me, my dear."

With that, Morgana pressed the cup to Lancelot's lips. He could feel the steam rising into his nostrils. A drop splashed against his skin and he felt blessed relief washing over that single spot. He wanted more. Lancelot's eyes met Morgana's and he nodded. Lancelot opened his mouth and whispered:

"Give it to me… I'm asking you… I'll do whatever you wish…"

In an instant, the liquid flooded down his throat, and Lancelot was filled with fire the likes of which he had never felt before. It was as if his insides were melting, twisting, and reforming. He screamed in agony, but was unable to make a sound. Finally, he erupted with the most pained shriek of his life, and he collapsed onto the table.

Lying still and barely conscious, Lancelot muttered, "Pain… Loss… Destruction… it's all I'm good for anyway…"

And reveling in his desperate decision, Lancelot drifted into unconsciousness. He barely heard the old woman's words.

"You can sleep now, my dear," she whispered. "Morgana will take good care of you. She will keep you safe. For you now belong to the Queen of the Feys…"

~ ~ ~

After his bitterest failure in years, Lancelot now sat beside Galahad in the dungeons of Corbenic Castle. His head still ringing painfully, Lancelot breathed deeply and his eyes took in his own battered, mangled body. There was barely an inch of him that didn't have some sort of scar or another. His joints ached and his insides hurt. With a jolt of regret, Lancelot's mind raced through the many battles and wars that he had come through. He remembered all the men and beasts he had vanquished. He recalled all the pain and destruction he had wrought.

Then he looked to the unblemished young man who sat beside him. His son. Lancelot had journeyed from kingdom to kingdom and undertaken all sorts of quests. He had struck down villains and avenged those who had been wronged. Yet now Lancelot saw that the person he may have wronged the most was the son he hadn't even known he had. The son that Elaine felt would be better off without him. The son he had left behind.

"I'm sorry, Galahad."

But Galahad simply shrugged in his calm, good-natured way as he asked, "For what?"

And the innocent look on the boy's face showed that he really seemed to have no idea what Lancelot might want to apologize for.

"I should have been here for you," said Lancelot.

"You didn't even know about me."

"Your mother could have found me if she wanted to," argued Lancelot. "But she thought you were better off without me. And she was right."

"You've done a lot of good out in the world, Father."

"Don't call me that. I don't deserve it."

"You've served kings and lords all over the land. You helped take back Tintagel."

But Lancelot shook his head as he spoke. "Arthur would've found a way to do that with or without me."

"He wouldn't have been able to get the White Dragon without you," pointed out Galahad, and then it suddenly occurred to him. "Say, we could use that right now! Whatever happened to it?"

"Don't ask…" was Lancelot's terse reply.

Galahad fell silent, as he politely assented to not press the point.

"I may have done good for other people. But I've caused just as much pain for others. For myself most of all. And I'm afraid for you." Lancelot shifted to look Galahad in the eyes as he vowed, "But I will get us out of here, Galahad. I have been a poor, unworthy father to you so far, and you've had a harder life than you should because of it. I vow to fix that. And, I swear, I'll help you find peace."

But Lancelot's vow was lost to a soft chuckling from the shadows of the dungeon.

"Oh, I think not, my young friends," said an old weary voice.

Lancelot and Galahad turned to see old King Pelles creeping toward them out of the shadows as he was supported by two guards, one under each arm.

"Grandfather!" called Galahad and he started to rise.

But the old king shouted, "Not another word from you!" and Galahad dutifully bowed his head and fell silent.

"King Pelles, let us go," pleaded Lancelot. "I promise to take the boy and leave this kingdom. I swear to you, you will never hear from us again."

"And then what?" asked Pelles as he stifled a small cough. "Then the two of you will go to your Lakes of Avalon?"

Confusion flashed across Lancelot face as he asked, "How do you know about that?"

"I was told of your conversation with my daughter. Nothing is said in this castle that I do not know about. Nothing happens within these walls that I do not control."

Recognition dawned in Lancelot's eyes.

"You made the darts fly."

Pelles nodded and his eyes twinkled as he said, "Go on."

"Go on?" said Lancelot with confusion. "You mean there's more?"

Lancelot's mind flashed through his experiences in the castle, but there hadn't been any other strange events. The boiling pool of water had occurred out in the countryside. Suddenly, it all clicked and Lancelot cried out in surprise:

"You summoned the troll! The ogre! The goblins! The wildelions! All of it!"

King Pelles wheezed with self-satisfaction as he admitted, "Of course I did. What kind of a king would I be if I didn't ensure my kingdom's safety?"

"But you failed," said Lancelot. "You've made the lands far less safe. How many of your people have died due to your foolish actions?"

"I'm disappointed in you, Lancelot, and here I thought you might've been worthy," King Pelles said with a reproving wag of his finger. "You see, a kingdom is only as strong as its king, and I've been looking for a new one for a long time. However, I couldn't simply hand over my kingdom to anyone. I worked too hard to build it. To bring it under my will. So I had to make sure that whoever took over for me was strong enough to hold these lands together."

"You've been filling your own kingdom with beasts for thirteen years to test potential heirs?"

"Yes, ever since my daughter brought that first fool, Sir Bromell, around. He was weak. And easily crushed. So were each of her other suitors. I couldn't have possibly entrusted any of them with this beautiful kingdom I had built."

"So you had no idea about Galahad?" asked Lancelot. "None of this was about him? He's not connected to the monsters as his mother feared?"

King Pelles shook his head bitterly.

"As much as it pains me to admit it, I did not know about the boy," the old king said. "Although it now makes sense why she became so suddenly intent on quickly finding herself a suitor. You see, I know everything that happens within this castle, but my daughter was clever enough to keep him hidden outside of my walls. I suppose I should've known. She's never had any lack of interest from the stronger sex."

"But you killed them all."

King Pelles nodded, and there wasn't a hint of remorse in his face as he said, "I told you, I had to test them. But none of her many suitors were strong enough."

"Until me."

Only now did a grimace appear on the king's face as he said, "And what a disappointment you've turned out to be."

Lancelot moved toward the bars of his cell as he implored the king, "But Galahad won't be. He's a remarkable boy. Once you get to know him, you'll see. I know you'll be proud of him. I can help you train him. He can be the heir you've been looking for."

Lancelot looked over to Galahad, who still remained silent, listening in the corner. However, at Lancelot's kind words, the boy's face brightened as if to say, *"That's very nice of you to say!"*

King Pelles didn't share the look of kindness.

"Ah, but I no longer need an heir," said the old king.

Once again, confusion furrowed across Lancelot's brow. Fortunately, King Pelles explained, "Now that I know about your Lakes of Avalon, your Fountain of Youth, I can restore the true king: Myself. I can rule my kingdom once more and forever. I really can't thank you enough for your miraculous gift, Sir Lancelot."

Lancelot gripped the bars and he all but shouted, "No! You can't go to the Lakes of Avalon. You'll defile them."

King Pelles's eyes twinkled with excitement as he replied, "I will claim them. I will conquer them and bring them under my rule. And then I will emerge young, strong and powerful once more."

"I'll never tell you where they are," spat Lancelot.

But King Pelles just chuckled again as he said, "How little do you think of me? Do you really think I won't find them?"

Lancelot glared angrily at the king, but the king paid him no heed as he turned to go.

"You've truly been a gift to have here, Lancelot. I must admit, I feel younger and more hopeful already," said the king. "But now I'm done with you. And you'll die in the morning."

Chuckling to himself happily and in fact seeming to move with more energy and lightness than Lancelot had ever seen, the old king shuffled out of the dungeon, barely needing any assistance from his guards. Once he had gone, Lancelot turned to Galahad, who was still waiting patiently in the corner.

"You could've spoken up for yourself!" shouted Lancelot.

"He told me not to say another word," said Galahad in his most innocent tone. "I was taught to respect my elders. Is that bad?"

~ ~ ~

CHAPTER 22

The Conditions for Escape

Lancelot had been pounding on the iron bars for hours.

They seemed just as solid as ever.

Nonetheless, Galahad stood quietly aside and let Lancelot try. The young man figured that Lancelot might know something that he didn't. After all, who was Galahad to question a mighty knight like Lancelot?

Yet after about the hundredth attempt to knock the door down with his shoulder, Galahad couldn't help but ask, "Is this one of the lessons of being a knight? To never give up? Even when it's clearly impossible?"

Grinding his teeth and rubbing his bruised shoulder, Lancelot said, "I've broken through worse than this."

With that, Lancelot charged the gate again, but quickly rebounded with a yelp of pain and frustration. Finally seeming to have had enough, Lancelot collapsed to the ground.

Trying to be as polite as possible, Galahad asked, "How long did it take when you broke through the doors that were worse than this?"

Lancelot didn't answer; he just roared with anger and pounded against the gate with his fist. Galahad figured that was part of his father's strategy too. Or if it wasn't, Galahad figured that his father didn't want to answer any more questions about it.

"Don't worry, Father," said Galahad meekly. "I'm sure it'll all work out."

"You're a good boy, Galahad," said Lancelot. "But you must learn to face reality. Things don't always work out for the best. I've tried to be idealistic throughout my life. I've led grand crusades and tried to align myself for good. And do you know where it's gotten me?"

"Locked in a dungeon?" suggested Galahad.

"Locked in a dungeon," agreed Lancelot. Then he added bitterly, "Leaving nothing but pain, destruction and war in my wake."

"I believe we'll find a way out of here very soon," insisted Galahad with his eternal optimism.

Lancelot didn't seem to share the hope, however, as he bellowed, "And how exactly do you think that might happen?!"

At that very instant, the door to the dungeon burst open.

Lancelot stared in disbelief. Then he looked to Galahad to see if the boy could explain a dungeon door suddenly swinging open. Galahad shrugged. After a moment, Elaine hurried in.

"Elaine!" cried Lancelot. "How did you get here?"

"I am the princess of this castle," said Elaine as she rushed over to the cell door. "I can do whatever I wish."

"So you brought the keys?!" said Lancelot.

"Well, maybe not everything that I wish," she admitted, but then she dug into her pockets as she added, "But I did bring this!"

With a grand gesture, Elaine produced a small jagged piece of metal. She thrust it forward with pride. Lancelot didn't seem so impressed.

"And just what do you expect to do with that?" asked the knight.

"I intend to pick the lock with it," replied the lady haughtily.

Elaine plunged the jagged metal into the door's lock. With a look of utter determination, she wiggled it expertly inside of the internal mechanism.

Nothing happened.

"I've never actually done this before," Elaine admitted.

"Don't look at me," said Lancelot. "Subtlety has never exactly been my strong suit."

"Can I try?" offered Galahad.

Galahad took the piece of metal from his mother. He slipped his hand through the bars and slid the metal into the lock. He had fiddled with it for no more than a few moments when the door clicked and neatly swung open.

"You could've picked the lock this whole time?!" said Lancelot with his mouth slightly agape. "I could've gotten us something to work with!"

"I didn't know..." said Galahad. "I've never done it before in my life."

"Unbelievable," muttered Lancelot, and then he and Galahad rushed out of the cell and exchanged quick embraces with Elaine. "I've got to get back to the Lakes of Avalon. Before your father arrives. Maybe we can mount a defense."

"I will try to reason with my father," said Elaine, "but it won't be easy. I haven't seen him this worked up in years. He even skipped all three of his naps this afternoon."

"I'll go with Lancelot," said Galahad, stepping up next to his father.

This clearly was not what Elaine wanted to hear, and an immediate fire blazed behind her eyes as she said, "No! You must stay here. I can hide you again."

"Mother, I don't want to hide anymore!" shouted Galahad and his sudden forcefulness surprised all three of them. Quickly resuming his normal politeness, Galahad bowed his head slightly to his mother and said, "I'm sorry. I hope I didn't upset you. But, please, you must understand that Lancelot needs help. And I would like to help him."

After a long moment, Elaine nodded. Then she faced Lancelot directly and the fire behind her eyes locked upon the mighty knight. Lancelot wilted ever so slightly beneath her gaze.

"Let us get a few things straight, Sir Lancelot," she said. "I am trusting you with my son."

"He's my son too," pointed out Lancelot.

"Don't try to be cute with me," said Elaine and her voice seemed more threatening than any voice Lancelot had ever heard in all his dealings with villains and tyrants. "You've known him since sunrise. I have raised him for thirteen years. So I have my rules. No drinking. No debauchery. And keep him away from the kind of women that you yourself are drawn to."

Once again, Lancelot felt compelled to point out, "But you're the kind of woman I'm drawn to."

"And no fighting!" stated Elaine, ignoring Lancelot's last statement.

Lancelot sighed as he responded, "I don't know if I can make that promise anymore. Fighting may be inevitable. But I swear to you, with everything that I am, I will keep him safe."

~ ~ ~

Night had fallen and the moon was simply a sliver in the sky. It provided the perfect cover as Lancelot and Galahad crept out of the castle and approached the stables. The great knight and his son untied two horses and led them out.

"You do know how to ride, right?" Lancelot asked the boy once they had properly secured the saddles.

Galahad shrugged and said, "I've never ridden a horse before in my—"

"In your life," Lancelot said, completing Galahad's thought. "Somehow I expect you'll pick it up just fine."

Sure enough, Galahad easily swung himself into the saddle and settled in. Lancelot smirked with pride and then mounted his own horse. With a kick of their heels, they urged the horses forward and rode off into the night.

The scarred knight and his youthful charge had barely shrunk into the distance when King Pelles's best tracker slipped out of his hiding place. Everything had worked perfectly so far. He had dismissed the guards stationed at the dungeon to give Princess Elaine easy access. Shortly thereafter, the knight had come to the stables and stolen a horse just as was expected. The tracker's sharp eyes carefully followed the trail of Lancelot and Galahad, but the tracker's eyes were nothing compared to the falcon that perched upon his gloved right hand. The Falconer lifted the hood from his bird's eyes and immediately urged the falcon to rise. With a few flaps of its powerful wings, the falcon soared into the sky and began its careful pursuit of the foolish knight and the naive boy.

~ ~ ~

CHAPTER 23

Nimue Is Right Again

The falcon flew tirelessly in pursuit of its unwitting prey down below.

Yet while the bird was able to continue on unflinchingly, the long journey took a toll on Lancelot. When Lancelot first journeyed from Avalon to Corbenic, he had gone at a more or less leisurely pace. He had travelled by land and sea. He had spent nearly two weeks in the crossing, and even that would've been considered an ambitious undertaking. This time, however, he and Galahad went the long way so as to stay on their horses and forgo the need to secure a ship. Even despite the fact that they were going a longer distance, they were still doing it in less time. Lancelot and Galahad maintained a brisk, challenging pace the entire way. They left in the night, then the night turned to day, the day faded back into night, and day rose again. On and on it went like this with the knight and the young man pressing onward with utter determination. At first, Lancelot waited for Galahad to ask for a break, but the boy never did. Galahad, who still claimed to have never ridden a horse, kept his eyes ever forward and expertly rode his steed over hill and field. The young man never seemed to get tired.

But the journey was becoming agonizing to Lancelot.

Finally, after several days of riding, with barely a pause to water and rest the horses, Lancelot attempted his most casual tone as he said, "You know, Galahad, we've been riding for days. Do you need a proper rest?"

"No," said Galahad simply, but then he quickly added, "Should I?"

Lancelot stared at the boy in disbelief but rallied; after all, he was the mightiest knight in the world, and he wasn't going to be shown up by a boy.

"No, of course you shouldn't!" said Lancelot. "I don't need one either. I just wanted to check on you; make sure that you're not too tired to continue."

"Oh, thank you for asking, but I'm just fine."

"Me too," said Lancelot as he tried to shift off of his aching, cramped thigh. "Me too…"

They rode on.

Another day and night passed.

"Need a break now?" asked Lancelot, trying to sound to relaxed even though both of his feet had gone numb.

"Not yet," said Galahad pleasantly. "But we can stop if you need to."

"No need on my account…"

They continued their journey.

The sun rose and fell.

"Galahad, my boy, perhaps I should give you a rest," said Lancelot generously, as his back quaked with painful spasms.

"Oh, that's so kind of you, Father," said Galahad. Lancelot's heart leapt and he started to pull up on his reins, but then Galahad continued, "But there's really no need to stop for me. I'm perfectly fine. I wouldn't want to delay you."

Feeling like he might burst into tears, Lancelot forced a good-natured laugh. "Well done, boy, well done. If you can continue on... Then. So. Can. I."

Gritting his teeth with determination, the mighty knight and his indomitable son pushed on. Lancelot contented himself with the knowledge that Avalon was getting closer and closer and closer. He'd make it. He would make it. No doubt about it. If the boy could, he could. He'd be damned if he was going to show even a hint of weakness.

High above, throughout the long days and nights, the falcon circled and followed.

It took them just over a week to reach Avalon, traversing through marshlands and cutting through thick fogs. Finally, they arrived at the serene grotto, and the horses slowed to a trot amongst the luscious groves of fruit trees.

Galahad lightly bounded off of his horse.

Lancelot collapsed to the ground.

"Oh? Are we here already?" Galahad asked as he skipped around, and Lancelot saw the boy slightly shaking out his legs. "I thought you said it was a long journey..."

Respectfully pretending that he didn't see his father lying sprawled out on the ground, Galahad quietly took in his new beautiful surroundings. The boy plucked a pear from a tree and drew in a deep sniff of appreciation. He gazed off at the shimmering waters that stood a short distance away. He kicked off his boots and skipped barefoot in the lush grass.

Lancelot painfully rolled onto his back and just lay there.

After a few moments, the plump figure of Nimue appeared. She stumped toward them with her stubby hands on her broad hips, and she looked down on Lancelot, groaning and writhing in the grass, as she asked:

"So? How'd things work out for you?"

~ ~ ~

A short time later, Lancelot and Nimue strode side by side through the fruit groves. He hungrily snatched peaches and apples off of the branches and sunk his teeth into the delicate fruits. Juices dribbled freely down Lancelot's face, when Galahad suddenly popped out of the thick branches of one of the trees. Effortlessly, the boy swung and leapt amongst the trees with the ease and agility of a monkey.

"This place is amazing!"

Then with a quick movement, Galahad jerked himself back upward and disappeared into the heavy canopy of leaves.

"Interesting boy," remarked Nimue.

"He doesn't get out much," said Lancelot. "He hasn't had the happiest upbringing."

"*Wheeee!*"

Just that moment, Galahad swung upside down on a tree branch by only his toes as he erupted with an unrestrained whoop of glee.

Nimue couldn't help but smile as she watched the joy on the young man's face, and she said, "If he's had as hard of a life as you say, then I'd be glad to help him. You, on the other hand, I'm not so sure about."

After his short rest and with some food back in his belly, reality set back in for Lancelot as he stated, "The Lakes of Avalon are in danger. We've got to set up protections. We can't let King Pelles get his hands on this sanctuary."

Nimue shook her head. "He'll never find his way here."

"He was very capable in his day. I wouldn't put anything past him," warned Lancelot.

"It's magically protected," said Nimue with a wave of her hand that caused a burst of wind and a shadow from the clouds. "I think you know how these places work, Lancelot. It can only be found by people who've already been here."

"Then he'll find someone who's already been here."

"Do you think there have been tours of people perusing this place over the past few years?" laughed Nimue. "This is a mystical place. I can count the visitors from the last decade on one hand. I don't let just anyone in here."

Suddenly, the screeching of a bird overhead cut through the serenity of the grotto. Lancelot and Nimue looked up at the same instant and watched as a falcon spun in the air and soared off into the distance. Nimue sighed.

"I really shouldn't have let you come here..."

~ ~ ~

Off on his own, Galahad jogged up to the edge of the shimmering pond. The sun shone warmly overhead and created a perfect mirror on the water's calm surface. Galahad leaned over and gazed at the water and saw a face looking back at him. Galahad gasped and pulled away. Shaking slightly, Galahad recomposed himself and warily approached the edge of the water again. Slowly, he looked back at the surface and saw a young man with thick brown curls and soft dimples in his cheeks. The young man looked directly back at Galahad, their eyes locked upon one another. Galahad extended his hand, and the young man did the same. Their fingertips came within inches of touching when:

"Whoa, whoa, whoa there, sonny, I wouldn't do that."

Galahad pulled away and spun to see Nimue waddling toward him. For a moment, Galahad thought that she would reprimand him, but there was nothing but kindness on her full features.

"Those waters are tempting, there's no doubt about it," she said warmly. "And boy oh boy, do they feel nice to dip your toes into after a long day. But only when you're ready."

"Who was the boy in the water?" asked Galahad.

Nimue fixed him a long questioning glance. "Are you putting me on?"

"No," said Galahad honestly. "Who was he?"

Even though he was only thirteen and she was ageless, Nimue was so short that she had to reach up slightly to take hold of Galahad's shoulders. With soft hands, she turned him back to the surface of the water, where the young man looked out once more.

"That's you," she said.

"Me?" he gasped.

"Not many mirrors where you've been holed up, huh?" asked Nimue.

"The old man I lived with didn't want there to be any sharp objects near at hand for his wife to get ahold of," explained Galahad.

He gazed down at the water again and became entranced by his own reflection. He waved his hand and his reflection waved right back. Once again, he reached for the surface, but Nimue pulled him back.

"So many people get caught up on what they look like on the outside. It's what's inside that they should really be focusing on."

"I've never... I didn't even know I looked like that."

"Do you finally understand why the little ladies take such an interest in you?"

Galahad shook his head and with complete honesty said, "No. Why?"

Nimue chuckled as she said, "I'm sure they don't hate that innocence either. You're a good boy, Galahad. You'll be a good man." Then she placed a reassuring hand on his shoulder as she continued seriously, "I wish I could tell you that you'll have a good life. But I see a lot of pain and struggle ahead for you."

To Nimue's surprise, Galahad simply shrugged. "I'll bet you say that to everyone."

"What?! No, I don't!" sputtered Nimue.

"You said it to my father. You're saying it to me."

"But I don't say it to everyone! Not everyone!"

"It's perfectly understandable," pointed out Galahad. "You're the steward of a mystical lake that brings peace and healing. It stands to reason that most of the people who are drawn here would be in need of, you know, peace and healing."

"Huh... I never thought of it like that..." Nimue said as it hit her that Galahad was exactly right. After a pause, she said, "But still, boy, you're a special case. You've got a big destiny ahead of you. Bigger than any of us. And that kind of thing never comes easy."

Once again, Galahad just shrugged. "I figure it's a choice. You can find peace anywhere. And you can find struggles and pain anywhere too. Even here."

Nimue chuckled again. "Pretty wise, boy. Maybe I should just leave you in charge here and I'll take off for a nice long vacation."

Both Galahad and Nimue laughed, and there was considerable lightness in both of their hearts. However, Lancelot had a knack for ruining that kind of levity. Coming from the nearby grove of trees, the grizzled knight stepped up and joined them, and his tone wasn't anywhere near as airy as Galahad and Nimue as he said, "I don't think any of us can leave anytime soon. There's a lot of work to do if we're going to defend this place."

Nimue turned to Lancelot and her tone was equally serious as she said, "Do you really think you can do this? Do you think you can save this place? If I'm understanding you, a lot of bad things are on their way."

Galahad chimed in before Lancelot had a chance to speak for himself and said, "He's been through worse."

~ ~ ~

CHAPTER 24

Taming the White Dragon

A long time ago, in a land far away, the White Dragon burrowed itself deep into its underground cave, sank beneath the waters of an underground lake, and went into an underground sleep. As was the custom with dragons, the beast settled in for a nap that could very well last centuries. The freezing chill of the waters soothed the fire that raged within its belly and the silence of the cave sequestered it from the troubles of the outside world. The dragon slept. Years turned into decades which rounded the corner toward a century.

Then a troublesome, one-armed knight came along.

Lancelot had been through more than his share of trials to get to this cave. At that point in his life, he was far from the bright-eyed, idealistic knight that he had been as a young man. He had served King Uther Pendragon, and lost his arm in the service. He had been dragged back from the point of death by the healer, Morgana. He had dueled with the mighty Sir Gawain, fallen victim to the crafty Lady Guinevere, and struck an alliance with the young King Arthur. It was Arthur who had sent Lancelot on this most daring mission to bring back a dragon to aid them in battle. The kingdom of Tintagel had been conquered by the mad King Vortigern, and

Arthur wanted to reclaim his throne. The problem was that Vortigern had a dragon at his disposal, and Arthur needed one too.

It was Lancelot's job to get it.

Armed with the ancient book "The Art of Dragoneering," which he had liberated from the devious wizard Merlin's personal collection, Lancelot had raced across the countryside in search of this particular dragon. It had been the source of many rumors and legends over the years, and King Uther Pendragon himself had manipulated those legends to make it seem like this dragon was his own royal pet. In actuality, this dragon had a fierce reputation for devouring even the bravest of knights and for massacring entire armies that dared to stand in its way. Everyone had been relieved when it disappeared without a trace. However, an old historian had decided to compile a comprehensive guide to the lost locations of every dragon still in existence. That compilation had guided Lancelot into the depths of this cave, and he flipped through the pages as he sought the incantation that would awaken the ancient monster.

Lancelot moved past the opening chapters that were filled with rules for how best to handle a dragon. He had read those through on his journey, and doubted that any of them would be terribly useful. Instead, Lancelot found the archaic inscription that could summon the beast. Lancelot was pleased to see that the author had even phonetically transcribed the dead language for any interested reader. Lancelot sighed a breath of relief: the hardest part of these lost tongues was getting the vowels right. It took a half-dozen tries, but Lancelot finally got his throat to produce the correct guttural sounds, and the underground lake began to roil and break.

As the White Dragon rose from the depths of the water and roared with a fury that cracked the stone overhead while it breathed a lungful of furious flames, Lancelot's mind flickered to the book's first rule:

RULE #1: "Don't make a dragon angry."

Is this book kidding? thought Lancelot as he watched the massive beast clambering onto the rocky shore and shaking its great head with what was unmistakably a furious rage.

Lancelot hadn't a moment to dwell upon the foolishness of the book, however, as the White Dragon charged at him with its fangs bared. The dragon was nearly fifty feet long so as it snapped its neck around and whipped its long tail, it seemed to be everywhere all at once. Lancelot tossed aside the torch that had been so essential for the trip into the cave. It didn't matter anymore as constant bursts of flame from the dragon's mouth illuminated the cave far better than any meager torch ever could. Lancelot just had to make sure that he could stay one step ahead of those flames himself.

"Listen to me!" shouted Lancelot as he dodged a slash from the dragon's front talon. "Would you just give me a second to explain myself?!"

The dragon didn't seem to heed Lancelot as it lunged forward and tried to swallow him whole. Nonetheless, Lancelot tried to remain calm as he remembered the book's fifth rule:

RULE #5: "Dragons can understand the language of man, and can be surprisingly reasonable if given the chance."

As Lancelot crouched behind a boulder to shield himself from another flood of flames, he began to doubt that the rule was actually true. He had no choice but to trust it, though. Lancelot had to believe that the fearsome creature could understand him and would be willing to listen to reason.

Or he'd be eaten.

"Look, I really don't want to fight you," said Lancelot, dodging the dragon's powerful barbed tail as it cracked against the ceiling and sent a shower of stalactites down toward Lancelot.

Another rule flashed through Lancelot's mind:

RULE #17: "A dragon's most unpredictable feature is its tail, which can whip and snap with astonishing force seemingly independent of the rest of the dragon's body."

Narrowly avoiding another belch of fire, Lancelot cast his mind toward the book and tried to recall the many various rules. There had to be something that would be helpful. He could only keep up this fight for so long, and the dragon showed no signs of tiring.

RULE #25: "Dragons can live for centuries, but hate being asked their age."

Not too useful.

RULE #46: "Most dragons enjoy the bawdy poetry of Aristophanes."

Good to know. But Lancelot doubted he could recite a sonnet at the moment.

RULE #91: "It's wise to skip breakfast before meeting a dragon."

As Lancelot narrowly ducked another vicious swipe by the dragon's razor-sharp tail, he felt fairly certain that it didn't matter whether or not he had had toast that morning. To shield himself from another blast of fire, Lancelot dove into the dark waters of the underground pond. As he swam, he saw the dragon's menacing yellow eyes searching the surface and waiting for Lancelot to emerge, and it finally hit him.

RULE #101: "The dragon's most vulnerable point is its eye."

Knowing that it was his only chance, Lancelot burst out of the water and dove forward to avoid being ripped in two by the dragon's slashing claw. Lancelot sprinted toward the cave wall, and then kicked off of the stone to propel himself high up toward the monster's head. By some miracle that he had no intention of questioning, Lancelot missed the snapping jaws and landed on the beast's snout. He seized hold of the horn directly in the center of its nose, and Lancelot looked directly into the dragon's yellow eyes.

"Could we possibly call a truce for a moment? I have something I'd like to discuss with you," shouted Lancelot as he desperately clung on for dear life amidst the dragon's furious attempts to dislodge him. "I don't want to kill you. I want to help you!"

The beast flailed even more violently at Lancelot's entreaty.

"All right, all right! I want you to help me!"

The dragon calmed a bit at this sentiment, but it still seemed very intent upon getting Lancelot between its teeth.

"Would you calm down so we can talk?!"

The dragon showed no signs of calming.

"I admit, I'm not much of a fight for you!" said Lancelot as he missed by mere inches a snort of a fire from the dragon's nostril. "But I know another dragon that is!"

The dragon finally fell still.

Much to Lancelot's relief, it narrowed its yellow eyes ever so slightly, and for the first time, Lancelot felt confident that it could understand his words. The beast seemed to consider his proposal for a long moment, and then it growled in such a way that Lancelot was fairly certain it was saying:

"I'm interested."

~ ~ ~

CHAPTER 25
From the Bottom of the Lake

The next several days at the Lakes of Avalon passed in a flurry of planning and labor. Lancelot knew that King Pelles and his army could arrive in a little over a week depending upon the swiftness of the Falconer delivering his message, and King Pelles's ability to mobilize his men. It didn't leave much time. With that in mind, Lancelot set about the difficult task of preparing a peaceful sanctuary for the cruel realities of battle. Grudgingly, Nimue agreed to help set up defenses, and she assisted in choosing acceptable places to set up snares and traps.

Galahad proved to be invaluable.

The young man worked tirelessly day and night as he dug ditches, built traps, and trained amongst the safety of the trees. Lancelot watched Galahad bounding about with enthusiasm, and the mighty knight felt his stomach tighten. Lancelot had been through wars. He had battled to the death with powerful foes. He'd faced enemies that he had little reason to believe that he could defeat. And he bore the scars and gray hairs of his effort. A lifetime of violence and destruction left Lancelot no longer a whole man. As he followed the eagerness of Galahad who was still young, bright-eyed and unblemished, Lancelot knew what he had to do.

242

One warm afternoon, after having spent the day finalizing several traps, Lancelot found Galahad training amongst the trees in the fruit grove. Lancelot marvelled as Galahad nimbly leapt through the air, snagged ahold of a branch with little more than a finger, then spun himself and bounded off toward another branch. Galahad made it seem so effortless, so graceful, so pure. Lancelot, with his feet firmly on the ground, stood beneath the thick branches of the trees and cleared his throat.

"Galahad," he called. "Come down here."

With breath-taking speed and precision, Galahad pounced down from the branch he had been perching upon. The young man was like a panther, handsome and mighty. Yet the moment he landed in front of Lancelot, Galahad looked up with his wide friendly eyes and Lancelot was quickly reminded that he was just a boy.

"I've been practicing to use my momentum against any attackers," said Galahad with unhidden pride. "Anyone who comes through here will certainly be bigger and heavier than me. So I'll have to be quicker, and come down hard on them. They won't know what hit them."

One side of Lancelot's mouth threatened to flicker with a smile, but the knight fought back the impulse. He had come here with a serious purpose, and he intended to follow through.

"I'm ordering you to leave here, Galahad," said Lancelot.

The light that had flickered in Galahad's face only moments earlier faded and he said, "What? You can't be serious. I want to fight alongside you. I want to defend this place."

"And I refuse to let you."

"But, Father, I just want to help."

Lancelot winced at the words, but he redoubled his intensity. "And I'm telling you, I don't want your help. You may think I'm your father, and that may be true in the strictest sense of the word. But I don't know you. And I want you gone."

Galahad, whose face was normally so bright and carefree, now looked like he was blinking back tears as he asked, "Do you really think you'll have much of a chance without me?"

"I'm not sure I have much of a chance with you," said Lancelot gravely. "And I'll have less of a chance to succeed if I have to keep my eye on some foolish, inexperienced boy."

"But you let me help with the wildelions! And didn't I save you with the goblins?"

"Galahad, you have to go."

"No! I'm not leaving you! I want to stand with you!"

Galahad's outburst left Lancelot shaking inside, but Lancelot stood straight, he broadened his chest and shoulders, and he spoke with a calm measured voice. "Galahad, you and I have sparred several times now. But I have never really fought you. Believe this when I tell you, I will fight you if you ignore my command. I will bring my full and considerable strength down on you. And I will compel you to leave."

Galahad stared in disbelief.

Lancelot's furious gaze intensified as he said, "I don't want you."

Finally seeing that this was a battle he couldn't win, Galahad's face fell and he asked, "Where can I go? I can't return to Corbenic."

"Go to Camelot. From what I understand, the castle there is nearly finished," said Lancelot, and it pained him to add, "You'll be much better off under Arthur's care. He and Lady Guinevere will look after you. Take the horses and tell them I sent you. They'll take you in if they know it's a favor to me. You may be able to find some peace there."

"But I want to help you find some peace here, Father," came Galahad's small words.

Lancelot darkened and he sighed painfully as he said, "Peace isn't something I excel at."

And with that, Lancelot turned his back on his son and left the boy behind.

~ ~ ~

Several hours later, Galahad departed from Avalon. He rode one of the horses and led the other so that the animals might be safe from the looming battle. Their saddle bags had been filled with fruit and supplies, and Lancelot had drawn up a map for Galahad to follow to the new shining kingdom of Camelot.

Once the boy had shrunk into the distance, Lancelot approached the edge of the shimmering lake. He gazed at the serene waters and desired nothing more than to dive in head first. He didn't know if he would emerge. He didn't know if he would be healed or if he would be torn apart. He only knew that he didn't want to feel like this anymore—alone, friendless, with nothing but more war and fighting on the horizon until he inevitably met the darkness that comes for all men.

Suddenly a breeze danced across the water, causing tiny ripples on the surface, and Nimue stumped up next to Lancelot with a ruffled bundle under one arm. Her free hand was outstretched, and as she waved it, Lancelot felt cool winds snaking around him and ruffling his hair. In spite of himself, he smiled.

"Warming up for the fight?" he asked.

"Oh yes," said Nimue with mock seriousness. "We'll make those soldiers quake beneath my awesome powers of helping fruit trees to grow."

With a snap of her fingers, the lightest sprinkle of raindrops fell.

"We'll crush them with refreshment," observed Lancelot.

Nimue sighed as she stood beside Lancelot, "Just you and me against the world. Right, big guy?"

Lancelot's mind flashed to the image of Galahad leaving Avalon and he said, "I had to send him away. If anything happened to him, I could never have forgiven myself."

"So you finally learned to worry about someone other than yourself?"

"Oh, I wasn't worried about Galahad," joked Lancelot. "I was worried about what his mother would do to me if she found out I led him into battle."

Nimue laughed as she placed a reassuring hand on Lancelot's shoulder and said, "You did the right thing. I suppose even a big bonehead like you has to do something right every so often."

"Not just any bonehead. The greatest bonehead in all the land," said Lancelot. "Surely I can overcome one little army on my own."

"I'm glad to hear you're starting to feel like your old self again. We're going to need him," said Nimue as she began to unravel the bundle under her arm. "Let's see if we can bring back that old swagger."

Nimue pulled back the cloth and revealed Lancelot's old sword arm. He took it from her and felt the blade. He ran his fingers over the notched steel. Then he began fastening the leather straps upon his mangled forearm. As if no time had passed, Lancelot felt the weapon become an extension of his own body and he waved it instinctively as if he was flexing his own fingers.

Lancelot grunted with satisfaction and said, "Wonderful. Excellent, in fact! I can't wait for King Pelles and his men to feel my wrath!"

Nimue sighed.

"Seriously?! *'Wonderful,' 'Excellent,' 'Simply Savagely Smashing!'* Who're you talking to? I'm your spiritual guide, big guy. I know I haven't exactly done the best job of bringing your soul to peace, but you can still be vulnerable with me. So tell me how you're really feeling, before I rip off your other arm."

Lancelot's shoulders slumped and he allowed his head to drop as he admitted, "I'm nervous. I'm going up against tremendous odds. There was a time in my life when I wouldn't have batted an eye at this. But, you know, the last time I took on an army all by myself..." He gestured to his wounded right arm. "...it didn't end so well."

"That's true. But what are the chances something like that would happen twice in one lifetime?"

Lancelot just glared at her with a look that clearly said, *You're not helping.*

With a soft smile, Nimue looked deeply into Lancelot's eyes and said, "For what it's worth, I know you can do it."

"How can you still believe in me? You trusted me, and I've brought this upon you. I feel horrible."

"Well, good; you should. You've managed to put an ancient sanctuary of peace in peril."

If possible, Lancelot's head sunk even lower.

"But if there's a bright side here, it's that some people do their best work when they're in misery," said Nimue in her usual blunt way. "Some people thrive on challenges and torture. And you're one of those people."

"I'm still waiting to hear about the bright side."

"And here it is: You have a noble calling, big guy. Because of the war and battles and strife that you've gone through, other people will have a chance to live in peace."

"I was hoping to have peace for myself."

"I was hoping for that too," said Nimue, shaking her head slightly. "But it's not in the stars for everyone. Some people are destined to always be fighting. But it can have its benefits."

Then with startling abruptness and surprising agility, Nimue dove into the lake. For a large squat woman, Nimue managed to disappear beneath the surface without roiling the waters all that much. After several moments, she burst back to the surface, but she was now far farther away from the bank. She also seemed far less graceful.

Spitting out a mouthful of water and sputtering, she called back to shore, "Just a second! I just need to look again! I know it's down here somewhere!"

Once more, Nimue dove underwater. Again she popped up, looking disappointed.

"I swear, I just saw it…"

She disappeared again.

She resurfaced again.

"Geez, for a mystical lake, it's surprisingly murky down there…"

Yet another time, she went down into the depths. This time she stayed under far longer, and Lancelot began to wonder if it was possible that she had drowned. He quickly dismissed this idea since he was still fairly certain that she was part-mermaid, and even half-mermaids didn't accidentally swallow lungfuls of water. However, the moments lengthened and Lancelot began to seriously question whether or not he should go in after her. Finally, Nimue burst out of the waters. As she did, Lancelot's eyes went wide with astonishment.

Clutched in Nimue's hand was a dazzling sword the likes of which Lancelot had never seen before. The blade itself seemed to shine of its own accord and the steel was bright and unblemished. The handle gleamed and sparkled with jewels and precious stones. Lancelot couldn't tear his eyes off of it. The weapon seemed imbued with an otherworldly beauty, and Lancelot instinctively knew that it was a thing to be treated with the utmost respect and awe. However, as Nimue clambered out of the water, she dragged the sword behind her with a distinct lack of reverence. She pounded on one side of her head to dislodge some water from her ears, and then thrust the beautiful sword out to Lancelot.

"Here," she said. "The spoils of war."

Extending his left hand, Lancelot took the sword, and he immediately felt a rush of warmth spread throughout his entire body. His stomach eased, his heart calmed, and even his mind cleared. Aches that had lingered in his knees and back lessened. His breath deepened. His eyesight focused and sharpened. Lancelot had encountered many things in his varied journeys, but nothing like this sword. He gave it a few smooth swings and marveled at the balance. It was light, but strong and true. He'd never felt anything like this.

"I thought one day you might be the man to master this sword," said Nimue as she watched Lancelot brandishing the weapon with expert skill. "But, I'm sorry to say, it's clear that sword will never truly belong to you."

Lancelot looked at her with a gaze that bordered on heartbreak.

"Now, don't give me that sad sack look! It can still aid you in this fight!" continued Nimue. "It'll just never serve you in the way that it truly should."

Lancelot sighed and knew that she was right. Feeling the sword's power radiating through him, Lancelot could sense that something was missing. Like a beautiful garment that didn't fit quite right, Lancelot knew that this sword wasn't made for him. Nonetheless, he forced a grin and decided that he would enjoy the blade as best he could for the time that he had it.

"Well, I've never been one for fancy things anyway," said Lancelot, trying to make light of the situation. "But I must say, this sword is a beauty! Does it have a name?"

"Excalibur," Nimue said.

Lancelot gave a low whistle of approval. "Say what you will about the ancient mystical sword-makers... they sure knew how to name things."

~ ~ ~

CHAPTER 26

The Battle for Avalon

The long trip to Avalon had been hard on old King Pelles. His royal carriage wobbled and jostled and creaked over the uneven terrain. His frail old body bounced and lurched and rattled over rocks, hills, and nasty tree roots. Nonetheless, he demanded that the pace never slacken. At Pelles's command, the Falconer led the way with his keen-eyed bird soaring high above them. The king urged the horses onward, he ordered his men to never break their march, and he himself kept his gaze ever fixed upon the coming horizon. His carriage stood open at the front, and his seat was set high so that he could easily look over the heads of the horses and the driver, and watch for the appearance of the mystical healing pools of Avalon.

In point of fact, he already felt younger than he had in years.

It had been so long since he'd been able to stay awake through an entire day. He couldn't remember the last time his joints didn't ache from the chill of the night. With his goal of Avalon firmly in mind, he salivated at the chance to peel back the ravages of age from his weary bones and regain his former glory.

Elaine acted as a desperate voice of reason. "Father, I beg you, stop this march! It is not too late. No good can come from this."

Pelles had chained his daughter up in the carriage beside him. Originally, his plan had been to leave her behind, but he quickly thought better of it. Elaine had proven herself quite adept at deception what with her ability to hide a son for the past thirteen years. Even now, as the carriage rattled along day after day, barely an hour had passed that Elaine hadn't tried to wriggle free from her bonds, or pick the locks about her wrists, or bribe some weak-minded soldier into releasing her. Pelles would've been proud of his daughter if she wasn't so intent on using her guile against him.

"Silence, my dear," croaked Pelles. "You've caused enough trouble. But you'll see soon enough, once I've regained my strength, the greatness I can once again achieve will be well worth it. I'll make you understand. And I will crush all those who oppose me."

Elaine looked at her father as if she had never seen him before. "What has become of you? What happened to the kind-hearted man who sought to take care of farmers and commoners?"

"I never sought to care for them," said Pelles with a derisive laugh. "I sought to rule them. They were sheep and I was the dog that herded them together."

"They loved you."

"I care not for their love. I wanted them to fear my teeth. It was the struggle that I loved. The battle. The war. I craved the thrill of conquering others. And I can't wait to have that strength again."

In the distance, a grove of trees took form, and a glittering lake came into view.

"This is it, my lord!" shouted the Falconer from the head of the marching soldiers.

Pelles shifted forward in his seat and his eyes locked upon his prize. His heart beat faster, his breath quickened, he licked his lips eagerly and waved his hand to signal the march to continue. The shimmering waters of Avalon grew closer. Only the length of a field separated Pelles from his goal when they heard:

"HALT!"

The march of Pelles's soldiers froze and even the king's carriage lurched to a stop as they all looked ahead and saw a man standing on the other end of the field. Lancelot strode toward them, dressed for battle. He wore light armor, and he bore a blade strapped upon his wounded right arm. In Lancelot's left hand, he wielded a sword so dazzling that many of the soldiers had to shield their eyes just to glimpse it. Lancelot was one man ready to stand against an army, and he made them all pause in awe.

"This is your last chance, King Pelles," roared Lancelot from across the field. "Leave this place of peace. Or face my wrath."

King Pelles bellowed back with as much force as his aged voice could muster. "Ah, the mighty Lancelot! Stand aside, boy! Or be ground into the mud."

"I won't let you take this sanctuary, King Pelles."

"You have no choice. Even the great Lancelot can't hope to overcome one hundred to one odds!"

King Pelles waved his hand and gestured to his small army of men. Lancelot may have been a great warrior, perhaps the greatest single warrior in a hundred years, but Pelles had built an entire fighting force. He had ruthlessly drilled military techniques into them. He had commissioned fine weapons and shields for each man. He had prepared them to overcome any challenge, and a lone knight standing in their way seemed laughable.

Across the field, Lancelot shook his head, and once again cursed himself for not realizing that if Pelles had this force at his command, he could've easily slain any of the monsters that plagued his kingdom. Lancelot chided himself bitterly for not recognizing long ago that something was amiss with the whole situation in Corbenic.

King Pelles raised his hand to give the order for his men to charge, but he looked to Lancelot one last time and called, "Move aside, Lancelot."

"Never!"

"You are a brave man," said King Pelles with the merest hint of admiration, then he continued mercilessly, "And I regret having to destroy you."

King Pelles was about to drop his hand but Lancelot, looking undeterred, called back.

"You still don't understand where you are, Pelles! This place isn't going to give up without a fight!"

Almost upon Lancelot's word, thick black clouds raced in and blocked out the sun. The skies darkened. The low rumble of thunder rattled in the ears of every man gathered. Fog crept in along the ground, and light cold rain seeped down from the clouds above. Trying to maintain their confidence, many of the soldiers gripped their swords and were disturbed to find frost already beginning to stick upon their blades. The soldiers doggedly kept their faces stern and determined, but as their breath came out thick and their teeth chattered from the unexpected chill, the gathered men couldn't deny that their spirits were dampening along with the unnatural weather.

"I say that this is your last chance, King Pelles," called Lancelot as he seemed to continue urging on the storm. "Turn your men back. Or die!"

The soldiers shivered uncomfortably, but the king seemed unfazed as he sucked in a long rattling breath and shouted:

"CHARGE!"

King Pelles was pleased to see that his men only hesitated for a moment before they drew their weapons and pounded across the field toward Lancelot. The softening earth caused several of them to slip and stumble, but they quickly regained their footing and sprinted on toward the fight.

"Divide your forces!" bellowed King Pelles. "Flank him from both sides! Come at him from the trees, and the hills, and the fields!"

The line of soldiers split three ways, and several dozen men broke toward the grove of trees. Many more raced in the direction of the foothills. The largest force, however, continued charging directly at the lone figure of Lancelot.

"Father, stop this!" cried Elaine as she strained helplessly against her chains. "Don't kill him, please!"

"He has chosen his fate," said Pelles, watching the gap shrink between Lancelot and his soldiers. "If the greatest knight in the land must perish for me to rise again, then so be it. His death will herald my rebirth."

Their armor clanging, the soldiers closed in on Lancelot.

Lancelot readied his weapons and waited for them to come.

Closer. Closer. Closer…

CRASH!

With a roar of delight, Lancelot clashed into the oncoming army. His two blades sparkled and flashed through the air, cutting through anyone who came into reach. Lancelot became a whirling dervish of blades. Slashing, blocking, twisting, striking. Excalibur filled him with warmth and strength even as the freezing rain stiffened and slowed the opposing soldiers. His sword arm bounced amongst the dozens of blades struggling to reach him, and Excalibur cut through suits of armor as if they were made of nothing but paper. As the battle raged, Lancelot actually laughed as he barked at his opponents:

"It's been far too long since I fought an army all by myself!"

~ ~ ~

The Falconer, with his bird perched upon his gloved forearm, led a contingent of a few dozen soldiers into the fruit groves. The fog hung thick amongst the heavy branches and contributed to the eerie scene. The trees creaked and groaned as their leaves became

LANCELOT OF THE LAKE

weighed down by the icy rain and the bitter winds. Yet the Falconer urged the men forward.

"This way, men," hissed the Falconer. "We'll loop around Lancelot from behind. He'll never be able to stop us all!"

The soldiers marched steadily through the groves when:

WHAM!

The fog was split, and a blur streaked out of the tree branches. It collided with two of the soldiers with such force that the men collapsed into a heap upon the ground. With the same speed and precision, the blur darted back into the leaves. The Falconer and his soldiers paused with alarm.

"What was that?!" cried one of the men.

"I've heard stories of spirits that live amongst the trees," whispered another.

"You fools," spat the Falconer. "There's no such thing as vengeful spirits or angry ghosts!"

He barely had the words out, however, when:

CRACK!

BAM!

SPLAT!

Time and time again, the blur reappeared with startling speed and ferocity. The fog parted, the leaves rustled, and soldiers fell.

Another blur.

Another crack.

Another man down.

"Stand strong, you cowards!" shouted the Falconer.

Blur.

Crack.

Crumple.

"Show yourself!" screamed the Falconer as he waved his arm. The falcon rose from its master's glove and began to swoop around the trees in pursuit of the attacking spirit.

Amongst the tree branches, Galahad waited for his next opening.

He relished the panic that he had been able to cause in the soldiers. He knew that Lancelot would be furious to find that he had stayed, but Galahad also knew that his father needed him. It would have been rude to leave. And he had been raised to never be rude if he could help it. Even more than that, he could already tell that he might be the difference between victory and defeat.

As the soldiers turned in confusion, Galahad suddenly leapt forward again. He hooked onto a tree branch, built his momentum, swung and released. His fists thrust forward with blinding speed and Galahad plunged them into a nerve cluster along the neck of the one of the soldiers. The man stiffened and fell unconscious immediately. Then, with the same speed and dexterity, Galahad bounded back into the safety of the fog and trees as he waited for his next opportunity.

"What are you?!" shrieked the Falconer.

In response, Galahad dove again.

Blur! Crack! Crash!

Galahad didn't say a word, but as he felled two more soldiers, he answered the Falconer's cry with his thoughts: *I'm like nothing you've ever seen before.*

~ ~ ~

Several more of the soldiers trudged through the foothills and hoped to come at Lancelot from the side. However, as they marched they found themselves slowing nearly to a halt. They looked down and saw that the earth there had been torn and dug and overturned many times. Beneath the falling rain, the earth thickened into mud and clung to the boots of the men who tried to slog through it. Their feet slopped. Their ankles soaked. Some of them even sank down as far as their knees in the soft earth.

"It's a trap!" cried one of the mired men.

Suddenly thick lumps of hail rained down upon them, pelting the soldiers with painful shards of ice. The soldiers held up their arms and tried to protect themselves from the onslaught, but it was no use. The hail soared through their outstretched arms and beat them over the heads. The sudden icy cold temperatures froze the wet earth and gripped the soldiers helplessly in place. Beaten and flailing, the men roared in frustration. It was at that moment that Nimue finally emerged from her hiding spot amongst the hills and rocks.

"How do you like my garden, boys?" she said with a wry smile. Then she looked over the men stuck in the icy mud and said, "But it seems like it's getting filled with all sorts of weeds and other foul stuff... I wonder if I should just let it all frost over so I can start again?"

Then with a wave of her hand, Nimue sent a bitterly cold howl whipping down upon the terrified soldiers.

~ ~ ~

In the field, Lancelot valiantly battled dozens of men at once. He swung, blocked, and spun with astonishing accuracy and skill. Excalibur struck straight and true, shattering the shields of oncoming soldiers. Lancelot's sword arm rang against the blades of his challengers. As the minutes passed, many of the men lost their courage, dropped their weapons, and ran in the opposite direction.

As unbelievable as it might've seemed, Lancelot was winning.

Perched in his carriage several hundred yards away, King Pelles watched the fight with mounting dread. He had conceived of the training for his soldiers. He had perfected it over a lifetime of study and precision. Now, he watched as it proved futile against a single mighty warrior. Beyond that, the Falconer and his followers seemed lost among the foggy fruit groves. And another group of men was mired amongst the hills. Just hours ago, King Pelles flushed with excitement at what seemed to be his inevitable rejuvenation. Now, that prize looked to be slipping through the king's fingers.

He couldn't let it happen.

Carefully but unsteadily, King Pelles rose from his seat and clambered toward the horses at the head of his carriage. Still locked up behind him, Elaine shook her chains as she reached for her father.

"Call your men back!" said Elaine. "Father, don't force your the soldiers to die at Lancelot's hand. Don't force Lancelot to strike them down. You must see that you can't win."

"Of course, I can still win," muttered King Pelles as he settled himself onto the back of one of the horses and began untying it from the others.

"Father, stop!"

"My only mistake was trusting others to do my work for me…"

Freed from the carriage and the other horses, King Pelles struck his chosen steed and it leapt forward. The horse galloped across the field, and King Pelles clung to the saddle with all the strength he could muster. His eyes locked on the lake in the distance and he willed himself toward it. King Pelles was a man who overcame any challenge set before him, and he was determined to overcome this one too.

~ ~ ~

Upon the battlefield, the soldiers fell all around Lancelot. To the best of his ability, Lancelot aimed his blows at the soldiers' shields and simply tried to repel them. If possible, he struck his attackers over the head with the hilt of Excalibur so that he might incapacitate them but not kill them. Lancelot knew that they were just men following orders, and he tried not to make them pay the ultimate price if he could. Nonetheless, the field was splattered with blood and gravely wounded men lay sprawled in all directions.

262

"Is this all you've got, Pelles?!" shouted Lancelot as he brought down three more men with a single blow of Excalibur. "Is this all you brought for the mighty Sir Lancelot?!"

Suddenly, Elaine's screams rang out on the air, and Lancelot looked to the carriage where she sat alone, pulling painfully at the chains around her wrists, and shouted:

"Lancelot! You've got to stop him! He's headed for the lake!"

Scanning the field, Lancelot's eyes fell upon the lone horse charging through the battle. Old King Pelles lay flat upon the horse's back and seemed on the verge of tumbling off. However, the old man's strength held firm as he grew closer and closer to the edge of the lake.

With a roar of determination, Lancelot swung his two blades and dispelled every soldier that clambered to challenge him. An opening emerged amongst the crowd of men, and Lancelot charged out of their midst. His legs pumped furiously as he chased after King Pelles's horse. It was man against beast, though, and Lancelot had no hope of overtaking it.

King Pelles pulled the horse up along the bank of the lake. Lancelot sprinted with every ounce of energy he had. King Pelles staggered to the edge of the water. Lancelot reached for the old man, but he was still too far away.

"King Pelles! Don't!" roared Lancelot.

But with a twisted smile, the old king extended his arms, and flopped backward into the lake. A few bubbles erupted along the surface as King Pelles disappeared beneath the water. Lancelot finally reached the edge of the lake and frantically searched for the king beneath the softly lapping waves. Within moments, Nimue arrived at Lancelot's side, and she seemed equally anxious as she gazed into the water.

"It's always nice to have you and your friends visit, Lancelot!" Nimue said through gritted teeth.

"Is there any chance he could simply drown?" Lancelot asked, trying to maintain a glimmer of desperate hope.

As if in answer, the water began to roil and churn. The edges of the lake splashed with violent waves and the normally clear surface turned dark and ominous. And then the king broke through. Dripping wet, with water cascading off his shoulders and arms, King Pelles rose from the water, and the figure he struck was unlike anything Lancelot or Nimue had ever seen before. He was decades younger, tall, handsome, and rippling with strength. His eyes burned furiously as he strode out of the lake.

"Ah! It feels so good to be young again!" King Pelles bellowed, his voice shaking with resonance.

Nimue rushed up to Pelles and pleaded, "It's not too late. We can still save you. You can still find your peace. But you have to listen to me!"

"Too late?!" Pelles laughed as he grabbed Nimue by the throat and, with unnatural strength, lifted her up into the air. "Why should I listen to you?! Peace is for the weak!"

And almost lazily, Pelles tossed the woman aside. She flew several feet through the air and crumbled down in a heap.

Rearing back to strike with Excalibur, Lancelot rushed at Pelles, but with brutal speed, the newly resurrected king struck Lancelot with a monstrous uppercut. King Pelles's fist collided under Lancelot's jaw and there was a sickening crack. Lancelot sailed backward and flipped end over end before crashing painfully to the ground. As he reeled from the blow, Lancelot reflected that he'd recently been hit by a beast made of solid rock and it hadn't hurt as much as the king's fist.

The remaining soldiers rushed toward the lake and assembled in front of King Pelles. He laughed savagely, though, as he commanded them, "I have no need of your help with this puny fool. Go to the fruit groves. Assist the Falconer. Kill anyone who stands in your path."

As the soldiers rushed away at their king's command, Pelles glared down at Lancelot, who was still struggling to his feet, and Pelles growled with anger, "I'll handle this one myself."

~ ~ ~

Perched high up in the branches of the trees, Galahad watched as dozens of soldiers flooded into the fruit groves. Only moments earlier, he had been sure that he could take on the handful of men who still were clambering amongst the trees, but as more and more soldiers charged in, Galahad's hopes faded. He was completely outnumbered, surrounded by fully grown, well-trained soldiers. And they seemed determined to hunt him down and kill him.

"Make this easy on yourself, you freak," spat the Falconer. "Come on out and we'll make it quick!"

However, Galahad didn't rise to the taunts. As always, he maintained his calm demeanor, because he knew he was safe up in the trees. He could take refuge here, and the soldiers down below would have quite the job of even finding his exact location. Galahad took comfort in the safety of his position. Until he looked over his shoulder:

And found the falcon perched in a branch beside him.

Galahad raised a finger to his lips in a desperate attempt to silence the bird, but it was no use. The falcon shrieked, and its cries made every man on the ground turn and look up into the trees.

"It's just the boy!" cried the Falconer in astonishment. Then as the falcon glided down to reunite with its master, the Falconer grinned and shouted, "Get him!"

With their overwhelming numbers, the soldiers converged on Galahad's tree, and the normally optimistic boy was overcome with dread.

~ ~ ~

Many years earlier, in a land far from Avalon, a young boy wasn't satisfied by his life as a farmer. Pelles yearned to do more than just bring in the crops year after year until he grew old and died. He believed he was meant for something more. With that thought lodged firmly in his mind, Pelles united the local farms. But still he wanted more. He built himself a castle and forced the people to call him king. But still he wanted more. He raised an army and took himself a queen. But still he wanted more.

He devastated rival kings and lords.

He commanded monsters and beasts.

But still he wanted more.

As murderous strength and boundless vigor surged through his veins, King Pelles felt he was finally back on the path to his true destiny. Soon, he would return triumphantly to Corbenic. Then his reign could continue for another hundred years. And another hundred after that. And another hundred after that. With the Lakes of Avalon under his control, Pelles's rule could continue for all eternity. First, all he had to do was conquer the greatest knight in the land. It was almost too easy.

Lancelot couldn't do anything about it. He gathered himself up and fought man to man against King Pelles, and it wasn't even close. Almost unbelievably, King Pelles was head and shoulders better than Lancelot. The king was impossibly fast. His strength was immense. His reflexes and skills were unparalleled. It was all Lancelot could do to just stay one step ahead of him.

"I can't thank you enough, Lancelot," laughed Pelles as he seized Lancelot and ripped the blade off of Lancelot's maimed right arm, snapping the leather straps that held it in place as if they were no more than dried straw. "It's so good to be my old self again."

"I'm going to stop you..." Lancelot groaned, even though he was currently pinned down by Pelles's incredible strength. "If it's the last thing I do, I'm going to save this place."

"Ah, but that's not what you do, my friend," said Pelles as he grabbed Lancelot by the front of his armor and savagely hit him over and over again. "You're not a savior. Even when you try to help people, you only bring them more pain. You bring destruction, death and war to everything you do."

King Pelles struck Lancelot again, and the usually unbeatable knight careened backward and slammed into a rock. Darkness edged around Lancelot's vision, the breath squeezed out of his lungs, the coppery tang of blood flooded his mouth. Worst of all, as Lancelot gasped, he realized:

Excalibur had slipped from his left hand.

"My, my, my, Lancelot, do your gifts to me never cease?" said the king as strode toward the exquisite, jewel-encrusted sword.

In a panic, Lancelot scrambled to retrieve Excalibur, but he wasn't nearly fast enough. With another vicious kick, King Pelles sent Lancelot sputtering to the ground.

And the mad king claimed Excalibur as his own.

Even through swollen eyes and a bleeding muddy face, Lancelot could see the power surging through King Pelles. The muscles in Pelles's neck, arms and chest swelled, nearly doubling in size. His eyes bulged in their sockets, and they reddened around the edges as if Pelles's own blood was surging and burning within him.

"My god, the power!" roared the king. "It's remarkable! Absolutely astonishing! With this sword, there is nothing I cannot accomplish! I will bring all the kingdoms under my will! All who dare oppose me will fall! And I shall start with you!"

King Pelles swung the mighty sword at Lancelot, and Lancelot was just barely able to escape the blow. Again and again and again King Pelles advanced, and the blade only missed Lancelot by the space of a breath. It took everything Lancelot had in him simply not to perish. He didn't know what to do. He was completely outmatched. He had no idea how to fight this beast of a king.

"Please, Pelles, you must stop this destruction," pleaded Lancelot as he narrowly avoided another killing stroke.

"Don't you realize, Lancelot, that DESTRUCTION CAN BE A GIFT?! A way to impose your STRENGTH UPON OTHERS?" shouted Pelles, his voice shaking with unrestrained fury as he slashed at Lancelot again.

Lancelot rolled away from another attack as he insisted, "I want to bring peace."

"Peace is AN ILLUSION!" laughed Pelles, and every word he spoke grew into a furious, high-pitched bellow. "CREATED BY THOSE WITH THE POWER TO RULE! TO BEND OTHERS TO THEIR WILL!"

But as King Pelles bore down on Lancelot, the king became more and more crazed and wild. His eyes turned completely red and bloodshot. Thick veins bulged and snaked along nearly every inch of his skin. His mouth clenched and grinded with rage. Finally, Lancelot was seeing a glimmer of hope. It was becoming clear that King Pelles couldn't possibly keep this up. Lancelot simply needed to stay out of Excalibur's path long enough for King Pelles to burn himself out. That was easier said than done, however. King Pelles kept up his attack, and his devilish strength and monstrous speed was relentless. Lancelot dove, crawled, and dodged. King Pelles slashed, thrust, and advanced.

And King Pelles won.

Shaking with strength, King Pelles caught Lancelot by the leg. The king pinned the helpless knight to the ground beneath his boot. With savage glee, King Pelles raised Excalibur high into the air, preparing his final terrible blow.

"NOTHING! CAN! STOP! MEEEE!!!"

Yet before the king could bring down the sword, something seemed to explode inside of him. His face contorted with pain and he clutched at his chest, twisting in agony and roaring with anguish. King Pelles collapsed to the soft earth and gasped frantically, but he didn't seem able to refill his choking lungs.

"Nothing… can… stop… me…"

The king whimpered, then fell still.

"Only yourself," said Lancelot as he looked down on the twisted body of the once great man.

A few moments later, Nimue hobbled up to Lancelot's side and poked Pelles's lifeless body with her toes. "I tried to warn him. The waters can heal the body, but if the spirit isn't prepared…"

She drew a short finger along her neck and made a cutting noise. Then with her stubby, slightly webbed foot, Nimue kicked Excalibur out of King Pelles's twisted claw-like hand.

"He couldn't handle the power," said Lancelot. "And I suppose holding Excalibur put him over the top…" Suddenly, Lancelot spun and glared at Nimue as he demanded, "Did you know that was going to happen?! Is that why you gave me Excalibur? So that he would take it, and destroy himself with it?"

Nimue shrugged.

"What if I hadn't been able to stay ahead of him for long enough?!"

She shrugged again.

"You could've gotten me killed, you know?!"

"Yeah... It was a risk. I took it."

"I could've beaten him on my own..." said Lancelot sulkily.

"Cheer up, big guy," said Nimue, patting him on the shoulder. "You'll have plenty more chances to prove your greatness."

At that moment, the shouting from the nearby groves snapped both Lancelot and Nimue back to attention as they heard:

"Get the boy!"

Without another second of hesitation, Lancelot snatched up Excalibur and raced off to help his son.

~ ~ ~

CHAPTER 27

Elaine's Greatest Challenge

Lancelot charged toward the fruit groves, and quickly found himself overtaking several of Pelles's soldiers who were also rushing in that direction. Scanning ahead, Lancelot saw with a flush of panic that Galahad stood thoroughly surrounded. There must've been at least forty men crowded around the boy, and many more were on their way. Yet Galahad seemed to be keeping calm. With his astonishing presence of mind, Galahad appraised the situation. He looked for avenues of escape, he weighed the few options that were still available. Nothing looked good. Nonetheless, Lancelot barreled forward. He cast men aside as he split the crowd of soldiers and took his place by Galahad's side.

"I thought I told you to leave Avalon," said Lancelot.

Galahad shrugged. "I figured you'd end up dead without me."

"Fair enough. Well, what do you think now, my boy?" asked Lancelot, as his eyes cast around the circle of soldiers and estimated there were at least sixty of them. "Do you think we can take them all?"

Galahad examined Lancelot's battered body, and then said with his usual blunt honesty, "No."

"We're going to need to work on your boasting," said Lancelot.

272

The soldiers, led by the Falconer, closed in tighter. Lancelot and Galahad stood back to back, and Lancelot saw that Galahad had raised his fists and was prepared to fight. Lancelot gripped hold of Excalibur and felt its warmth surging through him, helping to numb the many aches and wounds he'd received from his battle with the king. He wasn't sure if they could prevail, but Lancelot was absolutely certain they could go down in a blaze of glory. Lancelot raised Excalibur, and he was about to bring all the strength he could muster upon the gathered soldiers, when:

"I COMMAND YOU TO STOP!"

Lancelot, Galahad, the Falconer and every last soldier froze in confusion. They all searched for the source of the decree, but no one stepped forward to claim it. Everyone looked at one another, trying to ascertain if it was their fellow who had given the order. But there were only shrugs and confused glances. Then one by one, they locked eyes on the woman striding into their midst, parting the crowd, and glaring at all of them with the fury of a firestorm.

Elaine had arrived.

"All of you will drop your weapons," she said, her eyes blazing with intensity. "NOW!"

Several of the men immediately did as they were told. Many more at least lowered their swords, although they didn't abandon them completely. Even Galahad dropped his meager dagger, but Lancelot quickly motioned for the boy to retrieve it.

It was the Falconer who maintained his resolve and sneered at Elaine. "And why should we listen to you?"

Elaine strode up to the Falconer, and looked him dead in the eye, nose to nose. When she spoke, it was with deadly seriousness. "My father is dead. And that makes me your queen."

All those assembled seemed to be holding their breath, and there was complete silence as Elaine addressed them with unflinching resolve.

"Who would like to see if I have inherited my father's cruelty?"

The seconds lengthened. No one moved. Not a soul wanted to be the first to test the will of the awe-inspiring lady that stood before them.

No, not just a lady:

Their queen.

In rapid succession, the soldiers began to drop their swords, one after another after another after another. Weapons and shields fell to the ground and were cast aside. Even the Falconer abandoned his bow and quiver. Then, one by one, the soldiers fell to one knee and bowed their heads to their new leader.

Elaine moved among them.

"The fight is over," she stated in a tone that left no possible room for argument. Then she addressed the Falconer. "Gather your men and prepare for the return to Corbenic. There's going to be a lot of changes."

With a nod of his head, the Falconer rose and motioned for the rest of the soldiers to follow. They reformed ranks and marched out of the fruit groves.

Once the dozens of soldiers had departed, Elaine spun and shot a look at Lancelot and Galahad. Only then did her mask of fury fade, and her eyes went wide with excitement as she squealed, "Can you believe I just did that?!"

~ ~ ~

After the soldiers had marched into the distance on their way back to Corbenic, Lancelot found Nimue by the lake's edge. She extended her slightly webbed fingers and waved her hand over the water, causing it to ripple gently and form tiny whirlpools.

"It's different, that's for sure," said Nimue. "But different isn't always bad. The power may never be quite as strong again, but I can work with it."

"I'll do whatever I can to help you rebuild what's been lost," offered Lancelot.

An unbidden laugh burst from Nimue's lips and she all but shouted, "Oh no, you won't! Lancelot, I'm not letting you stay anywhere near here anymore. You've broken pretty much every rule I've ever laid down for you."

"I didn't break any rules! I wasn't fighting! I was..."

Nimue raised an eyebrow at Lancelot, challenging him to come up with a good excuse. Lancelot sighed as his head dropped in defeat.

"...fighting," conceded Lancelot. "I was fighting."

"If it's any consolation," said Nimue, "you're a damned good fighter. I mean, I could still give you a beating, so don't get any ideas. But I have to admit, you're good at what you do."

Lancelot forced a smile and said softly, "When I was in the fight, the rest of the world went away. I wasn't tortured by the things I've done in the past. I wasn't worried about what may lay ahead. I just was. Simply was." Then sadness washed over him as he spoke his terrible truth: "And it only came to me through battle."

"Sir Lancelot, the artist of war," Nimue dubbed him as she gestured with her hand like a king tapping a knight with his sword.

"I had really hoped that I might find some peace," said Lancelot.

"Doesn't seem to be in the fates for you, big guy. But like I've said before, there's a bright side. And it's a big shiny sparkly bright side. You have the chance to bring peace to a whole lot of other people," said Nimue. "Starting with this."

Nimue slipped Excalibur back into Lancelot's hand, and he immediately felt his mood lifting. The sword's warmth swam through him and lightened his heart.

"The man who can truly wield the full power of this sword is rising now," said Nimue. "It's your destiny to deliver it to him. I have a feeling he's going to need your help."

"Who is it?" asked Lancelot, although he was fairly sure he already knew.

"You may have taken your share of hits over the head recently, but even you can figure this one out," chided Nimue. "You know who that sword's meant for."

"Arthur?"

Nimue nodded.

Lancelot gazed down at the breath-taking sword in his hand and once again he marveled at the power that it radiated. He stroked his fingers across the jewels encrusted into the hilt. He watched the light emanating from it. He also felt the weight of it.

"Eh... I'm left-handed now," shrugged Lancelot as he dispensed with any disappointment he might've felt. "The balance of this sword is all wrong for me anyway."

~ ~ ~

A short while later, Lancelot found Elaine and Galahad amongst the fruit trees. Elaine scrubbed at Galahad's cheek with the sleeve of her gown, trying to remove some of the filth from the recent battle. She was a mother cleaning up her son after playing in the mud. Some things never changed. However, upon catching a few words of Elaine and Galahad's discussion, Lancelot hung back and tried to give them space as they argued.

"Do not say that about yourself, Galahad," insisted Elaine, completely unaware of Lancelot's close proximity. "You are not strange. You are not unusual."

"Yes, I am," Galahad disagreed in his most polite tone.

"You have simply been raised under terrible circumstances," said Elaine. "It's not your fault that you've been hidden your whole life. That you haven't known your father. That anyone who dared to care for you found themselves in mortal peril."

"I know, it's not my fault, Mother, but it is why I'm different. And it's why I can never truly fit in here," said Galahad without a hint of bitterness.

"You are not different," said Elaine, and her voice shook with motherly love.

"Yes, I am," said Galahad a bit more firmly, and then he observed, "But who isn't?"

Elaine blinked back a tear as she stroked the soft curls across her son's forehead. "My sweet boy, now that I am queen, you won't have anything to fear anymore. You can finally have a proper home. We can give you the life you've always deserved."

"I'm... I'm sorry, Mother," Galahad said softly, and for the first time, he was avoiding his mother's eyes. "But I don't wish to return to Corbenic."

Of all the frightening things that they had happened that day, those simple words seemed to cut the most deeply at Elaine, and she barely managed to utter, "What are you saying, Galahad?"

"I want to leave. I want to find a place that holds new promise, and doesn't fear and misunderstand me. I want to find a place where I belong."

"But, my love, you can finally live free."

"Exactly, Mother. That's what I want more than anything. To go out into the world, and live freely. Corbenic holds nothing for me anymore." With that, Galahad inclined his head toward the tree where Lancelot had stood respectfully at a distance. "I'd like to go with my father."

Hastily wiping away tears, Elaine looked at Lancelot and said with her motherly protectiveness returning, "Well, he wants to go with his father. Does his father want him?"

"Of course, he can come with me! I would be honored to have him with me," said Lancelot, and he was pleased that it came without a moment's hesitation. "How bad of a father do you think I am?!"

Elaine spun toward Lancelot, and as he found a menacing finger being thrust into his face, he understood the fear that the soldiers had felt under the intensity of Elaine's fury. She spoke slow and measured so as to make sure that Lancelot understood her. "My son is the most valued treasure in my life. I am entrusting you with this treasure. And if you ever treat it with anything less than the utmost care, then I will remind you that I now have an army at my command."

Lancelot tried to laugh, but the Elaine didn't look like she was joking. Instead, Lancelot nodded seriously and suddenly had a hard time swallowing.

"You can go with him, Galahad," said Elaine, turning back to her son and wrapping him in a tight hug. After a long moment that seemed to take all her strength, Elaine released Galahad and said, "Go gather your things. I need to talk to your father before you depart."

Galahad's eyes widened with excitement and his entire body seemed to glow as he hurried away to start preparing for his departure. Tears welled in Elaine's eyes as she watched Galahad rushing to make himself ready. Lancelot stepped up beside her and put a comforting arm around her shoulder.

"Don't worry, Elaine, I'll keep him out of harm's way."

"Oh please," coughed Elaine through a soft sob. "He's more likely to keep you safe than the other way around."

Lancelot and Elaine turned to face each other, and a moment deeper than intimacy passed between them. They were a father and a mother charting a confusing course for their child. Lancelot seemed certain; Elaine didn't. Trying to lighten the mood, Lancelot tugged on one of the wispy curls fighting its way out of Elaine's pulled-back hair and smiled at her.

"Once we've delivered Excalibur to King Arthur in Camelot—" then he added with a smirk and shrug, "and had a few adventures, Galahad and I will return. Maybe then he'll be prepared to be a prince. Maybe then he'll be able to appreciate the future he can build here. And maybe then you and I can too."

Gently, Lancelot lifted Elaine's chin and leaned in to kiss her, but she placed a soft hand on his chest and pushed him away.

"Don't," she said quietly. "Lancelot, there is no future for you and I. There is no reason for us to be together. You don't love me."

"What?! I never said—"

"Oh, of course, you do not love me," she said, hiding a slight catch in her voice as she added, "Just as, of course, I do not love you."

Unable to tell if she was lying, Lancelot simply brushed a single tear from Elaine's cheek.

"Are you sure you'll be all right?" he asked. "You'll be stifled in Corbenic. The queen of a castle that's never felt like your home. You won't have the freedom you've always sought."

"It's still the wild," said Elaine. "Just a smaller wild." Then she added with a wry smile, "And it will be good to be the queen."

Within a few hours, Lancelot and Galahad sat upon their well-stocked horses. Elaine showered Galahad with farewell kisses and then they were off. Side by side, the grizzled knight and his bright-eyed son headed toward the sunset and slowly shrank into the distance.

"We have a long journey ahead of us, Father, and I hope it's not rude to ask, but there's one thing I still must know…" said Galahad as they trotted off toward their destinies. "What did happen with the White Dragon?"

Lancelot sighed. "All right, all right, I'll tell you…"

~ ~ ~

EPILOGUE
The Fate of the Dragon

Of course, it wasn't the first time that Lancelot had ridden off victoriously.

And it certainly wasn't the most memorable.

It hadn't been all that long ago that Lancelot had flown on the back of the mythic White Dragon toward danger and glory. Together they had stormed Tintagel Castle. Together they had battled and slain the devilish Red Dragon. Together they had vanquished the Saxon hordes and freed the castle so that King Arthur could take his rightful place upon the throne.

Then together they had soared into the distance and left it all behind.

The majestic dragon covered impossible distances with a few flaps of its mighty wings. It traversed the entire length of the country in a few hours before finally landing at the edge of a small pond to quench its thirst. Lancelot slid off of the beast's back and gave it an affectionate pat upon its long neck as it dipped its head into the pool. The knight's heart swelled as he felt a deep affinity for the noble monster, and in his very soul, Lancelot knew that he was connected to the dragon in a way that was beyond words.

The dragon didn't quite share the sentiment.

After an indifferent snort, the dragon spread its expansive wings, rose into the air, and in a matter of moments had vanished into the distance. All alone, Lancelot watched his noble companion disappear amongst the clouds without so much as a backward glance in his direction.

He sighed.

"I really must come up with a better story than this…"

~ ~ ~

THE END

~ ~ ~

For more of
THE LEGENDS OF KING ARTHUR
look for these installments:

Book 1 - THE FIRST ROUND TABLE

Book 2 - GAWAIN AND THE GREEN KNIGHT

Book 3 - LANCELOT OF THE LAKE

Book 4 - THE MIGHT OF EXCALIBUR

Book 5 - TRISTAM AND ISEULT

Book 6 - GALAHAD AND THE GRAIL

Book 7 - THE FALL OF CAMELOT

~ ~ ~

AUTHOR'S BIO

Ben Gillman is an L.A.-based novelist and screenwriter. He's been a fan of Arthurian legend ever since *First Knight* (starring Sean Connery as King Arthur) became the first movie he ever saw twice in the theatres. In college he studied English Literature and immersed himself in Arthurian legends as told by Sir Thomas Malory and T.H. White. Now he's the writer of dozens of action-adventure novels and films, as well as many comedic sketches and plays. He lives with his wife, Vered, in Southern California.

Made in the USA
Columbia, SC
04 April 2019